VLIDUS-V

White Rocket Books by Van Allen Plexico

Harper & Salsa
Vegas Heist
Miami Heist
Monaco Heist (w/Alan J Porter) (forthcoming)

Sentinels:
The Grand Design Trilogy
  When Strikes the Warlord
  A Distant Star
  Apocalypse Rising
The Rivals Trilogy
  The Shiva Advent
  Worldmind
  Stellarax
The Earth – Kur-Bai War Trilogy
  Metalgod
  The Dark Crusade
  Vendetta
Alternate Visions *

The Shattering:
Lucian: Dark God's Homecoming
Baranak: Storming the Gates
Karilyne: Heart Cold as Ice
Hawk: Hand of the Machine
Legion I: Lords of Fire
Legion II: Sons of Terra
Legion III: Kings of Oblivion
Cold Lightning

Other Fiction:
Validus-V
Alpha/Omega (Revised & Expanded) (forthcoming)
MultiPlex (Collection)
Gideon Cain: Demon Hunter (Revised & Expanded) *
Blackthorn: Thunder on Mars *

Comics Commentary:
Assembled! Five Decades of Earth's Mightiest *
Assembled! 2 *
Super-Comics Trivia *

*Editor

VALIDUS-V

A NOVEL OF GIANT ROBOTS
AND GIANT MONSTERS

VAN ALLEN PLEXICO

WHITE ROCKET BOOKS

For Doug Moench and Herb Trimpe,
who showed us all the way.

VALIDUS-V

Cover design by Jeffery Hayes of Plasmafire Graphics.
Map and robot schematics by Van Allen Plexico for White Rocket Books

A White Rocket Book
www.whiterocketbooks.com

ISBN-13: 9798841938194

First printing: August 2022

0 9 8 7 6 5 4 3 2 1

DRAMATIS PERSONAE

HUMANS

David Okada, teenager; sixteen-year-old brother of John Okada.

John Okada, former US Air Force pilot; pilot of Validus-V.

Wen Zhao, former pilot, Chinese air force; pilot of Torander-X.

Bashir Sajjadi, pilot of Z-Zatala.

Sergei Morozov, pilot of King Karzaled.

Sir Anthony Graven, professor; discoverer of Rapa Hoi.

Dr. Ian Visser, assistant to Professor Graven.

Elaine Odashu, David and John's aunt, Honolulu.

Clint and Curt Donner, students at Kaimuki High School, Honolulu.

Mark Murphy, friend of David Okada.

Lisa Poole, EPA scientist assigned to Johnston Atoll.

Doug Hollis, photographer, Johnston Atoll.

ROBOTS

Validus-V, Blue and silver with orange trim.

Torander-X, Green and orange with white trim.

Z-Zatala, Purple and black.

King Karzaled, Dark red with gold trim.

MONSTERS

Tyranicus, green and gray with gold-flecked eyes; lizard-like.

Gamaron, yellow and black; giant caterpillar/centipede with claws.

Mordirah, black; giant bat.

Arzen, brown/tan; Yeti-like, savage, giant humanoid.

LOCATIONS

Rapa Hoi, an island in the South Pacific, located 230 miles southeast of Rapa Iti. The island was undiscovered until the 1950s. It is shaped like the letter "C," with mountains surrounding a broad natural harbor lagoon on three sides. The highest peak, Mt. Jaru, is due west of the harbor. Primary Ahlwhen base location.

Rapa Lau, an island 200 miles due south of Hawaii, between Hawaii and Kiribati. This Island was already known at the time of the discovery of Rapa Hoi, but was believed to be too small and seemingly insignificant to merit much attention. Secondary Ahlwhen base location.

Johnston Atoll, a partially man-made island 750 miles southwest of Hawaii, controlled by the United States and used for military testing and chemical weapons storage.

VALIDUS-V

JOHN OKADA

LASER SWORD
ELECTRO WHIP
MISSILES
FLYING FIST
PULSE BOMB CANNON IN CHEST
ARM SHIELD
LEFT ARM BECOMES PARTICLE BEAM CANNON

HEAD BECOMES AIRCRAFT:
"DELTA-V"

TORANDER-X

PULSE CANNON IN LEFT
INDEX FINGER

MISSILES

FORCE FIELD

WEN ZHAO

ENTIRE ROBOT TRANSFORMS
INTO SUPER-FAST AIRCRAFT:
"REDNATOR-OH"
--WITH PARTICLE BEAM GUN

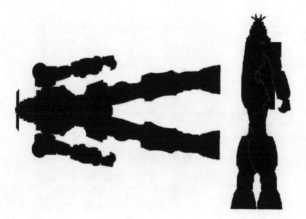

Z-ZATALA

BASHIR SAJJADI

ENERGY SWORD

SCREAMER MISSILES

INDESTRUCTIBLE METAL SWORDS

KING KARZALED

SERGEI MOROZOV

- PLASMA TORCH
- TURBO CANNON – IN CHEST
- ENERGY AXE – STORES IN BACK
- MISSILES

JAPAN

HAWAIIAN ISLANDS

HONOLULU

JOHNSTON ATOLL

RAPA LAU

PACIFIC OCEAN

AUSTRALIA

RAPA HOI

NEW ZEALAND

FALL 1978

PROLOGUE

The young couple crouched behind an outcropping of coral and watched in fascination and horror as ants sprayed acid on their victims and then fell upon them, devouring.

The tropical sun had just met the horizon, coloring the western Pacific sky a blazing orange. Long shadows crept across the tiny island's surface. The breeze picked up, carrying with it the scent of chemicals and heavy metals that were the island's dark legacy.

"Crazy," Doug Hollis breathed, looking on in astonishment as the insects attacked a pair of terns with their devastating biological weapon, blinding them and preventing them from flying away. Absently he scratched at his three days' growth of black beard before remembering to bring his camera up to take a couple of pictures of the tableau before them.

"Crazy *ants*," Lisa Poole corrected, running her hand through her short, sun-bleached hair. "The only form of life crazy enough to want to live here."

"Aside from us," Doug noted. He continued to watch, aghast, as the ants attacked the birds a short distance away.

"Well, I won't be here much longer," Lisa said. "The EPA only offered a one-month contract, and—as far as I'm concerned—that's more than enough time to get my fill of Johnston Atoll." She looked away from the birds, already jaded with the sight, and out to sea. "And I've done three weeks already," she added. "Come next Saturday, I'm on my way back to Honolulu."

"Lucky you," Doug said, his wary eyes never having moved from the crazy ants. "I'm on a two-month stint, and I've barely been here three days so far."

Lisa snorted a laugh. Then, "Sorry," she said. "That seems a little long to be stuck here."

"I thought so, too. But the Air Force wants everything you EPA people do here well-documented, so here I am. And they're adding in bonus pay, so..." He shrugged and grinned.

"I should hope so," she said to him. "You'll probably need that money for all the medical treatments after you grow your third arm or third eyeball."

Doug started to laugh, then realized she wasn't laughing. Frowning, he looked at her, finally forgetting about the ants for a moment. "What do you mean?"

Lisa looked back at him. "You mean the Air Force didn't tell you?"

"Tell me what?"

She shook her head. "So typical," she said. Then she pointed in the other direction, beyond the old military buildings they'd taken over as their main shelter during their stay on the island. "Why do you suppose nobody is allowed to go more than a hundred feet past our camp?" She gestured at the row of flapping red banners standing in a line there. "What do you suppose all those warning flags are for?"

Hollis looked doubtful. He scratched at his beard again. "Um. I guess I figured there might be some old, unexploded mines or something at that end of the island. Something left over from the War."

She laughed humorlessly. "Oh, there's stuff here from *lots* of wars," she told him. "Everything from the Spanish-American War to Vietnam." She nodded her head in the direction of the far end of the atoll. "There's chemical and biological stuff down that way. Agent Orange is just the beginning. Thousands of drums full of it. What they didn't drop on the Viet Cong, they stashed here." She shook her head. "But it was the Cold War that did the most damage here. The nuclear stuff."

Doug's eyes widened. "Nuclear stuff?" he said slowly.

"How did nobody tell you this before you came here?" Lisa wondered aloud. "Yeah. The Air Force used to test-launch missiles here. Believe it or not, a few of them carried full nuclear warheads." She rubbed her forehead and groaned. "And they aborted a couple of them—blew them up, right on the launch pad. Didn't cause an actual nuclear explosion, of course, but sure did spray chunks of plutonium everywhere." Again she pointed some distance beyond the old stone buildings where all the scientists and others lived. "Right down there."

Hollis swallowed drily. "Down there?"

"Yep. Now half the island is contaminated." She grinned. "So we avoid that half."

Hollis opened and closed his mouth a couple of times, but couldn't manage to say anything.

"Honestly, human beings have no business on this island at all," Lisa went on. "This place is Hell on Earth. It's no place for normal plants or animals, much less for people." She turned back and pointed at the mound of acid-spitting crazy ants. "I mean— what if those things decide they're not hungry for terns anymore? What if they want something different for dinner tonight? Something that lives here in this camp, and walks around on two legs?"

Hollis was pale now, and looked as if he might faint at any moment.

"I mean, I'm all for conservation of nature, yeah," Lisa said, "but in this case I'm willing to make an exception. I think we'd be better off dropping a nuke on this island and erasing it from the surface of the Earth. And from everyone's memories."

"It… sounds like they tried that already," Hollis muttered.

"And they left it unfit for anything but the crazy ants. Not for anything normal. Not for people. Just…" She shrugged and stared down at the salty, sandy ground. "Just for monsters, I guess."

"Monster Island," Hollis said softly, nodding.

Lisa looked up at him. "Monster Island. Yeah," she said. "I like that." She raised her arms and turned in a slow circle, grinning, as she indicated their one-square-mile home. "Welcome to Monster Island."

Whether Hollis had anything clever to say back to her, neither of them would ever learn. For, as it happened, the true residents of Monster Island chose that moment to appear.

A dark shape scuttled past; Lisa saw it out of the corner of her eye.

"Was–was that an *ant?*" she said. Her former bravado vanished; her face was now a pale mask of surprise and fear. "A really, really *big* ant?"

Hollis looked at her. "An ant?" He studied the ground around them. "I don't see any. I think we're safe here."

"Not–not down there," Lisa stammered. She grasped Hollis's shirt and shook him. She pointed. "Up here!"

Doug Hollis looked up and for a moment wasn't sure exactly what he was seeing. There was an ant, sure—right in front of them. So close, in fact, that it gave the illusion of being huge.

Then his sense of scale and proportion reasserted itself, and he realized it wasn't an illusion. The ant he was seeing wasn't a normal-sized one, a few inches from his face. It was dozens of yards from them–and it was gigantic.

"It–it can't be," Lisa gasped.

Together they ran, as fast as they could over the broken, uneven ground, heading for the buildings where their team had made camp. They hadn't gone far when the nightmare worsened. An unearthly screech sounded from ahead of them, followed a moment later by a deafening roar. The two young people skidded to a halt and looked around, frantic. A tremor shook the ground, nearly enough to hurl them from their feet. Again the screech, and then a different sort of roar.

A shape flew overhead, pitch black, momentarily blotting out the sun.

The ocean off to their right bulged and rose up, disgorging a massive, horrific form—the shape of a thing not seen on Earth in ages.

The two stared in abject awe and terror at the sight they beheld.

They were the first human beings to learn exactly why Johnston Atoll had been, and now was again, truly an island of monsters.

Johnston Atoll was a place where monstrous things had happened, and monstrous forces had been unleashed. And now, after untold millennia, the real monsters were back.

The monsters had returned to Johnston Atoll.

The monsters had returned to Monster Island.

CHAPTER 1

The robots were trying to kill them.

David Okada dug his fingers into the armrests as the giant, man-shaped figures ahead of them lashed out with violent attacks once again. The cabin rocked violently; it felt like he was riding a malfunctioning roller coaster.

"John," he shouted at his older brother, who was strapped into the command seat just ahead of him. "What's happening? What are they *doing?*"

His older brother didn't take the time to offer a comprehensive explanation. He merely called back over his shoulder, "I don't know—just hold on!"

So David held on—held on for dear life—and tried to make sense of what he was seeing.

David wore a snug-fitting helmet of dark blue and light gray, with a featureless, glossy black visor for a faceplate. The visor seemed to be interacting with the curved display in front of him to create a three-dimensional holographic visual that David could look at and into. The panoramic image hovered there—though whether it was being generated in front of him or beamed directly into his eyes or his brain, he wasn't sure and couldn't exactly tell.

In the holographic image he could see the endless blue of the Pacific Ocean all around, except for directly ahead. That portion of his field of view was filled with the beautiful, lush greenery covering the island of Rapa Hoi. And popping into and out of the image as they darted about were three massive yet shockingly quick and nimble machines, each of them configured in the rough shape of human beings.

Human beings more than three hundred feet tall.

David Okada could no more wrap his mind around that fact—giant mechanized men attacking them—than he could around the idea that he and his brother currently occupied the "head" portion of a fourth giant robot.

"Back off," John shouted. Clearly he intended the words for the gargantuan figures in front of them and not his little brother in the back seat. "What's the matter with you people?"

A man's voice sounded over the earphone speakers in David's helmet. "We know of your treason, John," it said in a South Asian accent. "You need to stand down."

David blanched at that. He felt the blood drain out of his face. Treason? *John?* How could such a thing be possible? John was the paragon of everything good—everything David was supposed to aspire to being. His mother had beaten him over the head with that for his entire life; at least, when she was around: John was the good son, the great example to follow.

Treason? It made no sense.

After a pause, one additional word boomed out. This one came not over the helmet speakers but through the air, vibrating across the divide between them and the other three robots. It resonated like the voice of some angry and misplaced god. And what it said was: *"Surrender!"*

"Surrender?" David could see his brother shaking his head, as much in confusion as in refusal. "But I am not in conflict with—"

"Land your Titan and shut it down," came another voice, this one female, with what David recognized as probably a Chinese accent.

"Then get out and raise your hands," ordered a third voice, this one sounding harsh, male, and Eastern European.

The three robots all hovered in view now, arrayed across the holographic display. David gawked at them in wonder. He assumed the three voices had come from the three of them—from the pilots that sat inside their heads, just as he and his brother currently sat inside this one. He studied them closely, even as he marveled at their very existence.

While different in shape and structure, each of the gigantic robots featured smooth limbs with oversized forearms and lower legs, along with heavily armored torsos and stylized heads. Sections of each robot looked to have been constructed of smooth metal, multifaceted crystal, or some strange combination of both. Each sported white and light gray as its base colors. Beyond that, each featured a different primary and secondary color scheme.

The robot on the left was the smallest of the three, though not by much. It was mainly green across the chest and forearms, with bright orange trim running along the edges of its surfaces. Its crystalline eyes glowed a fierce yellow. In place of its right fist, a massive cylinder protruded, spinning with a whine, aimed at them like the barrel of some impossibly huge cannon. Floating above it on the holographic display was the name TORANDER-X.

The robot on the right was only slightly larger; not much taller but thicker in places. Its featured color was purple, trimmed in black. It possessed a lean shape overall, sleek and angular. Its crystal sections appeared rounded rather than angular. For something so incredibly large—at least three hundred feet tall, David guessed—it moved very quickly. Its eyes glowed pale green. The label floating above it said Z-ZATALA.

Of the three, the robot in the center scared David the most. Its main coloring was dark red across its torso and extremities, with shining gold trim here and there. At least thirty feet taller than the other two, and downright bulky in places, it appeared massive and mighty indeed. It possessed the least crystal of the three; this one was built mainly of metal. Its head was a massive cylinder, and two more huge cylinders David assumed were some type of cannons rotated up onto its shoulders as he watched, aiming directly ahead. Its eyes glowed indigo as it spoke. It was labeled KING KARZALED.

"Down," the booming voice from the crimson robot cried. "Surrender yourself now, or face the consequences of your treasonous actions!"

"What are they talking about?" David asked his older brother, his voice plaintive. "What did you do?"

"I don't know!" John snapped back at him. "Now—keep quiet while I try to understand what's happening!"

David sat back, his heart racing, and closed his mouth with great effort. He had so many questions.

Just a few hours earlier, his biggest concerns in life were how to ask Tracey Lynn to the dance and how to explain to his aunt why he'd earned a B on his Chemistry midterm. As a sixteen-year-old sophomore honor student at Kaimuki High School on Oahu in Hawaii—and hopeful valedictorian of the Class of 1980, just two years away—he wasn't supposed to ever earn a B on a big test. But he'd been geeking out with his buddies, speculating over what the next Star Wars movie might be like, instead of studying, and the exam had snuck up on him.

So there he'd been, walking home from school, his thoughts mostly focused on a long time ago in a galaxy far, far away. As he'd started to cross the broad, grassy park that lay about halfway along his daily route, a strange aircraft had swooped down and landed just ahead of him. Silver and blue, curvy and compact and shiny, he'd first thought it was some kind of experimental plane from one of the military bases nearby. But then a voice he recognized had boomed out over a hidden loudspeaker: "Hey, little brother—come aboard!" And a doorway had slid open in the side facing him.

"John?" he called out, not quite knowing what was happening or how to react to it.

"Yes! It's me," the voice replied. "Come on in and check this all out!"

David hesitated at first. But it was John, and he trusted John above all others in his life. Plus, his curiosity demanded he see what this was all about. Within moments he'd stepped inside the futuristic vehicle. The door slid closed behind him, startling him, but then his brother leaned around from his pilot's seat in the forward compartment and waved to him. He wore a blue and gray helmet, the visor pushed up to reveal his face. Seeing John always reminded David of how everyone said he was the spitting image of his dashing older brother, though John kept his dark hair trimmed tight and neat, while David had longer, floppier hair. For his part, David didn't think they resembled one another all that much. It just made him feel like a poor, pale reflection of his heroic sibling.

"Come grab a seat," John said, flashing a smile. "I've got a lot to tell you!"

David just stared at him. "What *is* all this?"

John's expression had darkened somewhat, and instead of answering, he posed his own question to his younger brother. "You're okay, aren't you? Nobody's been messing with you?"

"What?" David barely heard him; he was too busy looking around at the sleek interior of the vehicle. When the words registered, he turned back to John. "People mess with me all the time," he said, scrunching up his face. "Especially the Donners."

John waved this away dismissively. "I don't mean the usual bullies," he said. "I mean anyone else. Anyone…kind of out-of-the-ordinary."

David stared back at him. "What are you talking about, John?"

John studied his brother's face a moment longer, then snorted. "Nothing. Nothing. I'll tell you everything later," he promised, brightening again. "But first–welcome aboard the Delta-V!" He grinned. "Now–put on your protective flight suit and helmet, and grab a seat and enjoy!"

David quickly changed from his t-shirt, shorts and sneakers into a light gray jumpsuit that matched his brother's outfit. At first, he thought the jumpsuit was too big for him, but it seemed to automatically adjust itself to fit him perfectly. Once that was done, he dropped into the second cushioned seat, directly behind his brother, and pulled on the snug-fitting helmet. An instant later, John had the craft back up in the sky, zipping along smoothly.

The front of the Delta-V aircraft featured a broad window, but with the helmet on and the visor down, the view appeared very different to David. It was enhanced dramatically, expanding into three dimensions and filled with constantly-streaming notations and targeting icons. The total effect was almost overwhelming, and David gasped out loud.

"Yeah," John said in response. "It takes a while to get used to the data flow. It's something else."

"A little bit, yeah," David said. And because he just couldn't wait, he asked, "John—what is a 'Delta-V'? When did the Air Force get jets like this?"

John laughed out loud at that. "Oh, little brother—the Delta-V isn't anything the US military ever built," he said. "Or any other American—or human—company."

"Not...*human?*" David said, his face scrunching up in puzzlement. "What do you mean?"

"Like I said, there's lots to tell," John replied. "You'll see some of it for yourself, pretty soon. I left V-V back on Rapa Lau. It's easier to sneak this aircraft into Hawaiian airspace than his big old self."

Now David was lost again. "Vee Vee? What's that?"

John grinned back at him. "Oh, just you wait and see!" he said.

And David had waited—very impatiently—and he had indeed seen.

The little aircraft crossed the hundreds of miles between Oahu and Rapa Lau in mere minutes. "How fast must we be going?" David wondered—and very soon it was swooping down on the small, tropical island in the middle of a vast field of blue waves.

"There he is," John said, pointing.

David squinted into the distance, trying to understand what he was seeing. Somehow the scale appeared all wrong.

There, just up from the beach, stood a man. A man wearing some kind of metallic armor, all blue and silver, all over his body.

But it couldn't be a man. The size was just... *wrong.*

And it was missing its head.

The trees around and behind it were way too small. The beach in front of it seemed terribly out of scale. And, as they swooped down to the level where its face should be, they seemed to still be a few hundred feet above the ground.

It wasn't a man, David understood then. It was a robot.

A *giant* robot.

The Delta-V craft pulled back a bit, and now David could see a circular opening—a socket of some sort–where the robot's neck would normally be. So–where was the head?

As he watched in amazement, John hovered their aircraft right above that opening. The aircraft dropped a short distance and settled firmly into place. David could sense more than see or hear their vehicle locking onto the body.

The vehicle they were in–it *was* the robot's head!

"This is V-V," John said. "His full name is Validus-V. And he's mine."

"He's *yours?*" David asked, awe filling his voice. "What the heck *is* he?"

"I'll explain everything," John replied, "on the way."

"On the way to where?"

"To Rapa Hoi. That's our main base."

"Okay..." David nodded slowly, not really understanding. "So–you're not with the Air Force, then?"

"Not anymore," John answered. "I got a better offer. And, I think, a more important offer."

"More important than the Air Force?" David's eyes widened at the thought. He'd been so proud that his older brother was serving their country. "Oh man–when Mom finds out, she's gonna go bananas!"

John frowned. "Yeah... Maybe we better keep this a secret between us, at least for now," he said. "I think this is even more important, but I'm not sure she would understand."

David nodded, looking around inside the aircraft-that-was-now-a-robot-head. "So–how long will it take us to get to that base?"

"Rapa Hoi? Not long. Validus can really go when I want him to."

"Okay," David said. "Because Aunt Elaine will be looking for me to get home soon."

"Don't worry," John said with a smile. "I'll have you back in no time." Then he grew more serious. "I meant it, though–you need to tell me if anybody's been messing with you. Or following you, or just watching you."

David felt himself growing a bit more concerned. "No more than usual," he said. "John–what's going on?"

His older brother didn't speak at all for a long moment. Then, haltingly, he said, "I–we–have enemies now, David. And they're bad. They're bad enough that I was willing to leave the Air Force and join up with the team I'm with now, in order to protect the world from them."

David looked back at him, eyes widening. "Oh. Huh. I figured you did it so you could fly a giant robot like this."

John's glacial expression cracked, and he snorted a laugh. "Well, let's be honest. That part didn't hurt!"

David laughed.

"But I'm serious," John said a second later. "My team and I have enemies. Bad ones. And I'm worried they could try to get to me through you. So you're going to have to be extra-careful in the days ahead."

David took this in. "...Okay," he said slowly. "For how long?"

"Until we get them taken care of," John said. "Until we beat them, and remove them as a threat to the whole world."

David didn't know what to say to this. He had so many questions, but his brother was well and truly freaking him out.

They flew the rest of the way to Rapa Hoi mostly in silence. And then, when they'd arrived, they'd received an extremely rude reception from the other robots.

"Surrender now!" boomed the big red robot again.

A volley of missiles erupted from its chest, flying directly at Validus-V.

CHAPTER 2

An explosion in the here-and-now nearly hurled David out of his seat, shocking him out of his recent memories and back to the present. Back to the larger island of Rapa Hoi, where John had taken them—only to find themselves attacked by John's own teammates.

David's forward view shook and then lurched into motion as their robot dodged more incoming attacks. He could see the big red enemy firing its shoulder-mounted weapons, bolts of searing orange plasma streaking just past them to the left. Then his eyes moved to John, or what he could see of him, around the back of the forward pilot's seat. His brother was moving his hands across various controls like a concert pianist working the keyboard. But there was more to it than that. His brother's body language indicated some deeper level of interaction and control happening. It was as if the robot were reading his mind, anticipating his desired movements even as he made them.

How long has he been doing this? David wondered. He'd thought his brother was off at college. How long had it taken him to gain such mastery over such an incredible machine?

"Professor Graven," David could hear John calling over the headset. "Are you there? Can you tell me why the others are doing this?"

Nothing. No reply. David wondered who Professor Graven might be.

Another explosion, the flames from it visible across the lower half of the holographic display. Their robot—what was its name? Oh yeah: *Validus-V*. Ol' Validus was taking some hits. David cringed at the thought of the damage it might be suffering. And he marveled at the scale of the firepower being unleashed here. It was mind-blowing, and it would have been such fun to look at, if so much of it wasn't currently aimed in his direction.

John must have ordered Validus-V to retreat. The three enemies still filled their forward view, hovering in midair above the island, but the distance between them increased as Validus backed away. Then the others surged forward. After a moment the screen focused on the purple and black robot. It moved faster than the others and now drew up close to them.

"Uh oh," John commented.

The enemy robot held out its fist, gripping a silver cylinder. On a normal sized person, the item would have appeared to be the equivalent size of a flashlight.

It was not a flashlight.

Out from the cylinder extended a long, shimmering bar made entirely of light or energy. Orange in color, it halted when it had reached the relative length of a sword blade. David had to remind himself it must be over a hundred feet long. Despite its mammoth size, however, he knew exactly what it was; he'd only recently seen Star Wars, of course.

"Holy crap," David whispered. "A lightsaber."

The purple robot brought its arm back and swung the energy sword in an overhand move, bringing the blade down, aiming directly for Validus-V. John reacted instantly, combining hand movements on the controls with body language that somehow resulted in their robot's left arm coming up and blocking the deadly stroke. David could see Validus's arm now somehow held a diamond-shaped shield that had not been there before.

Sparks showered out as the orange blade slashed again and again at them, only to be parried at every turn by the shield. Whatever substance the shield was made of, it had to be remarkably strong to turn away such a weapon.

From his limited perspective, David watched the battle unfold and, despite the danger it posed to himself and to his brother, he was captivated. He had to know more. He had to know what John was doing—and how he was doing it.

After several more blows, John backed them away again. Clearly he did not want to go on the attack—not against what must have been his former allies.

What David wanted was to get out of there. He wanted to go back to the park on Oahu. He wanted above all to never have stepped aboard his brother's weird plane that turned out to be the flying head of a giant robot. He still had no idea what John had gotten himself into, but he definitely wished he hadn't dragged David in with him.

John apparently wanted out of there, as well. Even as the other two robots came up behind the first one and prepared to attack, John swung Validus around, pointing him away from his adversaries, and kicked in the afterburners.

The room around them—David kept reminding himself it was the interior of a gigantic head—rattled as the robot's rockets kicked in. The vibrations shook him hard, even through his ultra-cushioned seat. Idly he wondered just how fast they must be going.

Alarms wailed. The holographic view broadened and swung around to reveal a trio of missiles streaking after them, launched from the big red robot. John must have seen them too; he veered sharply to the right, then to the left, all the while decreasing altitude until Validus streaked just above the waves, a rooster tail spraying up behind them. The first missile struck the water and exploded, sending up a massive column of foam that quickly disappeared in their wake. The second missile met a similar fate.

The third missile either had been better-aimed, was better-guided, or just got luckier. It countered all of John's moves and caught up to them, exploding in the vicinity of Validus's left hip.

Validus-V spun about, control gone, tumbling head over heels. Fighting the controls hard, John managed to put the head back in front and the feet back in the rear, but by then they were too low, too close to the water. Within a couple of seconds the robot's shoulders impacted and dug into the ocean's surface, flipping the robot again, smashing it repeatedly into the water, which at their velocity felt more like bouncing along a concrete parking lot. David lurched in his seat, the seatbelts restraining him by the hardest, keeping him from ricocheting repeatedly off the walls even as Validus bounced off the Pacific Ocean.

At last their momentum died away and the big blue robot lay there, floating atop the waves. In its command compartment, David shook his head, trying to regain his senses. He knew he had blacked out for at least a second or two.

He heard John's voice, faint and weak, more over his headset than from his spoken voice, even though John sat only a short distance ahead of him. He was saying something, words that David could barely make out.

"Obey… him. Obey… his… commands."

A groan then. David heard it with his own ears as much as over the helmet. His brother did not sound good. When David called to him, he received an incoherent reply.

Obey him? Obey *who?* Who was John wanting him to obey? Surely not the pilots of the other robots. He'd done all he could to keep them away from those people and their machines.

Then another massive shock rattled the room. David shifted his attention from his brother's plight and his musings about his words to the holographic view still floating before him. He blanched.

The big red robot had caught up to them. It loomed over the downed form of Validus-V, its twin shoulder cannons smoking. Now it drew back one massive fist, brought it forward and down, and struck Validus with an earth-shattering blow. David found himself clinging to the seatbelts and crash webbing around him as even more alarms kicked in, causing a deafening cacophony in the confined space. What looked like damage reports were lighting up in red on the display. There was no text—at least, not in English—but a three-dimensional schematic of the robot appeared in the holographic view and damage was clearly visible.

That was when he noticed that his brother was hanging limply out of the right side of his own crash webbing. His head was slumped down and forward, blood trickling onto the rubbery gray floor.

"John!"

The webbing held his brother differently from how it held him. David understood after a couple of seconds that John's seatbelts must have come loose, at least in one or two key points. After that, he must have struck his head on something when the missile detonated and they'd gone down.

Again the big red robot struck, not wasting its ammunition now, simply pummeling Validus with fists the size of fire trucks—or bigger.

Alarms continued to wail. Red lights flashed across the banks of computer displays and controls that lined both sides of the interior of the head.

David shouted for John to wake up, but received no response whatsoever. Outside, the big red robot raised its fist to deliver yet another crushing blow.

"Sergei," came a deep, resonant, and very British voice over the speakers in David's helmet, "Diagnostics show John is unconscious, if not outright comatose. You have done enough damage to our valuable equipment. You should be able to retrieve Validus with no trouble now. Please return him to base—as intact as possible."

David didn't know how to react to those words. On the one hand, maybe that meant the attacks would cease. After all, hadn't that voice just said they wanted the robot returned intact? But, on the other hand, he wasn't sure how thrilled he should be about returning to base, when the people and giant robots of that base had just brutally assaulted them.

"Understood," the gruff voice replied after a moment's delay.

David watched in the display as the big red Titan's hands reached down, grasped Validus-V under the shoulders and lifted him up. Then it leaned backward and activated its boot rockets, propelling itself towards the island and pulling Validus along with it.

The journey didn't take long. Within a few minutes they were back on Rapa Hoi, and the big red robot dropped Validus unceremoniously onto the sands just above the beach.

"John, if you can hear me, come out now," came the British voice over the helmet. "Come out or we will have to force our way in."

David could see the big red robot leaning down over Validus's head—the space he currently occupied. A massive crimson hand came up and it seemed it pointed directly at him. "I thought you said he was in a coma, professor. I'll just cut him out."

"John!" David shouted at his brother's limp form ahead of him. "John—wake up!"

Nothing—no movement, no response at all.

The pilot of the big red robot didn't seem to care all that much about the orders he had been given. He appeared intent on dealing out more damage.

"I will use my plasma cutter," he said. And with that, a blinding light flared from the fingertip of the red robot's index finger, and it descended towards him.

"No," the British man snapped. "Stop. We can get John out of there without causing extensive damage to Validus-V."

The plasma flame hesitated in midair. "And how do you propose we do that? If he is unconscious, or worse?"

"I will examine him and see. Perhaps I can override the locking mechanism on the head."

"Bah," the other said. "This all takes too long. I will cut him out."

The blazingly bright plasma cutter resumed its descent toward Validus's head. David could feel himself sweating from imagined heat.

"John! *John!*"

Still no response from his brother.

The plasma torch touched the side of Validus's head. Alarms shrieked and lights switched to red all over the boards.

David had no idea what to do. In a panic he switched from shouting his brother's name to shouting the Titan's name.

"Validus! I don't know if you can hear me, but you've got to do something! Now!"

It almost felt to David as if the damage were being done to his own body, as well as to that of the robot. His left temple was burning. He cried out in pain and instinctively brought his left arm up to block the phantom attack.

Instantly Validus raised his left arm, knocking the hand of the red robot away.

The pain in David's head diminished.

He blinked, startled. What had just happened?

Was it some auto-defense programming? That had to be it, right? Validus must possess a set of basic moves for when the pilot was disabled.

But the move it had made—he'd seen it, there on the holographic display—it had been exactly the move he had made.

Coincidence? Maybe. *Maybe.*

The pilot of the red robot was not happy about being brushed away. "There's some fight left in you after all, is there?" the gruff, Eastern European voice hissed. "We can remedy that."

On the holographic display, it appeared so vivid—as if the red robot were a bully in an alleyway of Honolulu, ambushing David and trying to beat him up. The gigantic red fist drew back, cocked, and started down, aimed right at Validus's head section, where it lay there on the beach. Terrified, David raised his left arm again, as if to somehow deflect the fist.

A diamond-shaped shield had unfolded from Validus's forearm. It took the brunt of the blow and deflected it away. Caught by surprise, the red robot stumbled forward, going down on its hands and knees.

David had no idea how he was doing it, but somehow Validus appeared to be mimicking his actions. He concentrated on getting up off the beach, and the big robot did just that, then turning around to face their adversary.

The red robot had by then recovered as well, and was advancing on him.

"So. You are awake, John," the Russian voice said. "Well. You know you cannot contend with King Karzaled. Do not make me beat you and your Titan into submission."

"John is still unconscious," the British voice asserted. "All our diagnostic systems show that clearly."

"Then how did Validus do what he has done, Professor?" came the voice of the pilot, its tone angry.

"I—I don't know," the British voice replied. "Validus should not have been able to—*wait.*"

A pause, as the red robot stood there, not moving but looming dangerously, a massive coiled spring waiting to go into action. A short distance further back, the green one and the purple one towered like statues, unmoving, deferring to it.

"We are picking up a second set of mental patterns coming from Valdius's command deck," the professor said.

"A second set? That makes no sense," the Russian barked. "Unless—"

"Yes," the professor said. "I am overriding the cockpit cameras now. Stand by."

David frowned at this. Cockpit cameras? He looked around, spotting a couple of small circles on the walls that must have been the surveillance devices.

"There he is," the professor announced. "Another pilot. Records show it is John's younger brother, David Okada."

"The younger brother? What is he doing there?" asked the Russian. "No one else was supposed to be there!"

"I don't know, Sergei," the British voice replied. "But he's received no training and can't possibly understand how to operate even the most rudimentary systems of a Titan, even if he happened to be compatible and were accepted by it. He cannot possibly pose much of a threat to you, if any at all."

The one called Sergei offered a few words, likely obscene, in Russian, then said in English, "You, aboard Validus-V. David Okada. We know you are in there. Your brother has committed numerous crimes and acts of treason. He is under arrest. Cease any resistance and come out." The big crimson hands flexed menacingly. "Or else I will rip open the head of your robot and pour you out."

Crimes? Treason? David didn't believe any of it. But he definitely believed the Russian's warning.

"John," he called out. "You need to wake up and do something!"

Nothing happened.

"John! *Wake up!*"

Nothing.

He changed tack. "Validus!" he called. "We're in danger! You have to *do* something!"

For a moment, nothing at all happened. Then the words PULSE BOMB flashed in David's head. Later he would think back on the moment and realize he hadn't actually seen those words, or even heard them uttered. He'd simply understood, somehow, that he was about to activate such a weapon, if he only said the words.

"Pulse bomb?" he whispered aloud.

A panel at the center of Validus's chest popped open. There came an explosion that nearly blinded David and sent the red robot stumbling backwards, across the beach, and collapsing into the water. Off to the right, the other two robots lurched back and shielded their faces with their arms.

This so took David by surprise that he wasn't prepared to take any other action at that moment. Wasting the opportunity, he just stared, shocked by what had happened. Consequently, Validus simply stood there as well. On the display schematic showing Validus's body, a red light flashed in the region of the left side of the robot's chest. The right side showed a green light.

A wordless roar of anger came over the audio system. Water pouring from its armored form, the red robot started to emerge from the Pacific. Its body language very clearly indicated a deep and profound outrage at what had just happened.

"You little punk," the Russian growled. "How could you have known to do that? What did John tell you? Who else has he shared our secrets with? He was a bigger traitor than we knew!"

The red robot launched itself up into the air, rockets in its boots blazing, then lowered itself down almost gently until its feet nearly touched the ocean's surface. It surged forward, its spiked red hands reaching out to grasp Validus.

Again acting on instinct, David swung his right fist out, at the image now filling the holographic display.

Validus swung a big blue fist around and punched the red robot in the face.

The Russian screamed in fury as his robot flipped backwards and, almost moving in slow motion because of its massive size, came down hard onto the ocean waves again.

David was pretty sure now: he had somehow done that. He had caused Validus to move.

"Obey him," David had said. He hadn't been speaking to David. He'd been speaking to Validus-V. He'd been telling his robot to do what David commanded. And it had done so, at least a couple of times so far.

If he could make his brother's robot fire a pulse bomb and throw a punch, what else might he be able to do?

The other two robots had gone down on a knee, apparently still dazed from the pulse. As the purple one tried to rise, David turned toward them and spoke the words "Pulse Bomb" again, this time louder and with more confidence.

BOOM. Both robots went sprawling back into the tropical forest, crushing dozens of palm trees under their mass.

Lights and indicators moved across the display. The chest region of Validus, on the schematic of the robot's body, now showed both sides of the chest flashing red. Nothing was in English, but somehow David understood this to mean he'd either used up that particular type of ammunition or at least could not fire that weapon again for some time.

On the display, the big red robot was attempting to get up again. David punched forward with Validus's right fist with all of his might.

Contact. The red robot's head bucked back, its body arched backwards, and it crashed back down into the water.

Now, David knew. Now was his only opportunity to escape. Maybe the only chance he would get. His big weapon was at least temporarily disabled, and the other pilots would likely be more cautious with him, now that they'd seen him actually controlling the robot.

"Go!" he shouted, his words intended for the big robot within whose head he currently dwelt.

He wanted to know more—to understand how and why the robot was obeying him, in however a rudimentary a fashion. But that was a mystery for later. For now, he had to get away.

He had no idea what pose to strike, what button to push, to make the robot fly again. So instead he tried concentrating on what he wanted—*rocket-powered flight, at supersonic speeds!*—and simultaneously called out, "Fly! Get us out of here, or we're finished!"

Validus-V turned around, crouched down, and leapt into the air. Rockets in the robot's feet kicked in and it powered into the air, then zoomed away. It left the red robot and its companions behind, traveling at a speed David could scarcely believe.

David sat back in his seat, sweat running down the sides of his face, and he allowed himself to breathe for the first time in what seemed like forever.

He'd gotten away. He'd escaped three gigantic, terrifying robots, and the apparently crazy people in control of them.

But a question hovered there, at the center of his thoughts; a question for which he currently had no answers:

Now what?

CHAPTER 3

*M*eanwhile:
    An unnamed island some forty miles north of Rapa Lau. A beautiful, sun-drenched day in the South Pacific. Birds calling; fish jumping. Not a human to be seen in any direction; only the blue of the sky and the blue of the water.

And then the waters about a half a mile away from the shoreline began to bubble and churn. They splashed; they danced. They parted. Something broke the surface, moving with slow but deliberate pace.

Up out of the ocean came a shape, but it was no shape normally seen within the oceans of planet Earth. It was big–and bigger with each step it took, deep beneath the waves. It was green and gray. And it featured two big, gold-flecked eyes that looked this way and that, scanning ahead of itself for any foes.

Across the beach it trod, dripping seawater, leaving massive footprints behind–though prints that would soon enough be erased by the tides. Into the trees it trudged, knocking over surprisingly few in its passage, as if it wanted to leave as little of a trace of itself behind as was possible. Over a low ridge it climbed, before settling down there, turning around, and gazing back down in the direction it had come.

From this place of concealment, the big green and gray shape lay still and watched–watched with its sparkly golden eyes.

Occasionally a big, red tongue would dart out, as if tasting the day, before disappearing again within a mouth that could easily swallow a school bus.

It lay there, and it watched.

And it waited.

Aboard Validus-V:

John still wasn't responding, though an occasional moaning or muttering did come from the seat just ahead. David was growing very worried about him. But the first thing he had to do was get them away; get them both to safety. Then he could check on his brother.

As he piloted Validus-V over the ocean, David could still hear the others over the audio system in his helmet.

"How is the child doing this?" the Russian was demanding. "It's not possible!"

"Never mind that for now," the British voice—Professor Graven?—said. "I want that robot back here immediately."

"I will go and get him," the Russian said.

"No," Graven replied. "You have demonstrated you cannot be trusted to simply secure a Titan with no actual pilot."

"How dare you speak to me that way?" The Russian cursed vehemently.

"Wen," Graven continued, ignoring him. "Are you alright?"

"Yes, Professor," came the female voice with the Chinese accent that he'd heard earlier. "Damage from the Pulse Bomb was superficial only. Torander-X is ready."

"Excellent," Graven said. "Then you will pursue Validus. You have the speed. You can catch up to him before he gets very far away. I trust you will not fail me, the way Sergei has."

"I obey," the woman replied, even as the Russian continued to rail and curse in his native language in the background.

Speed, David thought. *They're sending a fast one after me.*

"Give me everything you've got, Validus," he said aloud. "We have to get away from here. We have to get some help for John." He hesitated, then, "And for us."

The holographic screen was showing the other three robots; apparently Validus was still receiving their video feed. David was therefore able to watch in amazement as the green and orange robot launched itself into the air, somehow transforming its shape as it moved. By the time it was fully into the air and traveling more like a rocket than a big humanoid, its shape had become that of an exotic aircraft. A very *large* exotic aircraft. The legs had become twin rocket engines, making up nearly half its mass. They roared to life.

"Transformation complete," the woman reported. "We have assumed the shape of Rednator-Oh."

"Very well. Report back when you have caught up to the target."

Now more orange than green, the pursuing robot screamed through the sky in Validus's wake.

"The little brother is controlling it somehow," the woman noted, wonder evident in her voice. "Can it be so? And—where does he think he's going?"

"No matter," Graven said. "Go and bring me back Validus-V."

"What if he continues to resist?"

"Then do whatever you have to do. I would prefer all four of our Titans fully functioning and under our control. If necessary, though, we can certainly make do with only three. But I will not tolerate a rogue Titan, loose in the wild–especially not one controlled by a child."

Hearing this, a fresh wave of fear washed over David. Mentally he called out to the big blue robot in which he rode, urging it onward, faster and faster—as fast as it could possibly go.

In the rear view of the holo display, the orange and green shape of Rednator-Oh slowly grew in size as it closed the distance between them.

CHAPTER 4

*H*onolulu, hours earlier:
   David Okada knew he was being watched.

Backpack slung over his shoulder, he jogged down the steps of Grover Cleveland High School and hung a quick left onto the sidewalk. The other kids flowed around and beside him, chattering away, none of them paying him the slightest bit of attention. He was used to that, and also very happy about it. He liked being as anonymous as possible.

Somebody, though, was watching him. He could feel it. Not his schoolmates, not the teachers… but *somebody*. Eyes were boring into him—eyes from somewhere—sending goosebumps across his skin.

"David," came a voice from behind him, and he started, then looked back over his shoulder. He was relieved to see it was one of his friends, a heavy-set, red headed kid named Mark Murphy. "I'm still coming over today, right?"

"Sure," David said, continuing to move along with the tide. He wanted to add, "I've got those two issues of *Avengers* we've been trying to find." But he didn't dare blurt that out. The Donner brothers might be within earshot, and they lived to beat up David and his friends whenever they or their favorite hobbies were brought to the brothers' attention. They liked to call it, "Having a Donner Party."

So, instead, he said, "Aunt Elaine will be home at four. She said she'll make an extra helping of fish sticks for you."

"Yes! Count me in," Mark replied with a grin. They had discovered very soon in Aunt Elaine's stay that the one thing she cooked—if you could call it that—that actually tasted halfway decent was fish sticks. Not the greatest accomplishment, since all she did was take them out of the box and heat them up. Especially considering they lived on an island in the middle of the ocean, surrounded by fresh seafood. Of course, the boxed mac and cheese she whipped up along with them didn't hurt. His mom always complained that Aunt Elaine cooked too much stuff with chemicals in it, as if that was going to mutate him into some kind of monster. But David always retorted that if his mom had to eat the food Aunt Elaine cooked from scratch, she'd definitely want more chemicals added to it.

"See ya then," Mark called as he rounded a turn and disappeared from view.

David continued along the sidewalk, the crowd around him thinning out. He still felt like someone was watching him, even though the list of potential suspects was growing thin.

His aunt had been staying at their apartment for two weeks now, ever since his mom had left on her latest business trip to Japan. She wasn't due back for another week, which meant seven more days of awkwardness. Elaine was a nice enough person; a little younger than his mom, so somewhere in her mid-thirties. But she did things different from what David was used to. Like, for instance, come to Hawaii and make fish sticks.

His mind filled with such thoughts, David came to the end of the block and turned right, planning to stop off at the arcade halfway between the school and his apartment building. He had two quarters burning a hole in his jeans pocket, and there was just enough time to get in a couple of games of Space Invaders.

He came up on two palm trees that leaned partway out into the path, obscuring his view of the sidewalk ahead. He veered around them—and directly into the clutches of the Donner brothers.

Merely looking at the Donners, one would never guess they were brothers. Clint Donner was tall and lean, wiry and spiky-haired, with thick glasses. Curt Donner was shorter, stockier, and sported a buzz cut. No, visually they didn't have much in common. But personality-wise, that was a different story.

"Well, well," said Curt Donner as David bounced off him and stumbled back a couple of steps. "If it isn't the comic book kid."

David spun around to run, but the other Donner—the skinny one—had moved silently up behind him.

"Where ya goin', goober?" Clint Donner demanded.

Curt shoved David hard from behind. The backpack absorbed most of the impact, but it caused David to crash into Clint. Angrily, Clint shoved David away. "Watch it, punk," he snapped, cruelty dripping from every syllable.

David ended up stuck there between them, a human ping pong ball, looking from one of them to the other and back, starting to panic.

"Where ya goin'?" Curt asked, apparently unaware his brother had already broached that topic. It didn't matter; they both already knew the answer. It was where David went after school almost every day.

"To the arcade," David reluctantly admitted.

"Is that so?" Clint looked to his brother. "Young David here is on his way to the arcade." He said it like a scientist narrating a nature film.

"The arcade, eh?" Curt eyed his brother for a moment, then turned back to David. "That must mean you have some quarters on you. So you can play the games."

"We like games too," Clint said. "We'd like to play, too, if we only had some quarters."

David saw where this was going and he frowned. "Have you guys thought of maybe getting after-school jobs so you could earn some—"

"Have you thought about us whipping your butt and taking the quarters you have?" Curt interrupted. "Because right now that's the plan I'm leaning toward."

"Yeah, I like that plan," Clint agreed. "I mean, it has two things about it I like. The free quarters and the butt-whipping."

David didn't care for the direction this encounter was heading. They're going to beat me up and take my quarters no matter what, he knew for certain. And they'll probably throw in a few extra licks once they discover I only have two.

But with this realization came a certain amount of freedom. There was no more need to try to be halfway-respectful or deferential to them. They were going to beat him up, maybe badly, and there was nothing he could do to change that. But his understanding of that fact somehow altered the overall equation for him. They'd removed his other options and left him with only the violent defending of himself. *They've backed me into a corner, and I have nowhere else to go.* And that wasn't super-smart of them.

Curt was balling up his fists and scowling at David. Clint was stretching.

If I'm going down, David told himself then, *I might as well go down fighting.*

Finished with their elaborate pre-fight rituals, the Donners turned as one to face their intended target—their victim—of the day.

David relaxed himself as best he could, took a couple of deep breaths, and prepared to fight for his life.

Clint advanced first, popping his right fist into his left palm, over and over. He drew back, stepped forward and uncorked a haymaker in David's general direction—

—There was a strange sound, like a buzzing, in the air—

—and David watched as Clint folded up in mid-swing like a cheap metal chair and collapsed to the concrete sidewalk.

For a long moment, nobody moved. Including Clint.

The heavy-set Donner only gawked at his brother at first. Then he rushed to his side and knelt down, patting him on the shoulder, trying to rouse him, to no avail.

"Clint! What's wrong?"

Curt was frowning, and his look only deepened as he seemed to suddenly remember David was there. He looked up and demanded, "What did you *do* to him?"

"What? Nothing! He was about to hit me!"

"And you—what? *Shot* him? What did you *do?*"

"I didn't do *anything!*"

Curt growled in the back of his throat and returned his attention to his now-seemingly-unconscious brother.

David's eyes flicked up from the two of them on the ground to movement across the street and a bit farther down. He didn't register what he was seeing at first; it only came to him later, when he had a moment to breathe, and to reflect on the events he'd just been a part of. And what he saw was a pair of figures dressed very peculiarly for the Hawaiian climate, in long black cloaks and boots, with dark, wide-brimmed hats pulled down over their faces. As David's gaze fell upon them briefly, they turned and moved away, quickly disappearing into the shadows. After another couple of seconds he scarcely remembered seeing them at all.

Any lingering thoughts were washed away by another tirade of profane threats and protestations from Curt Donner. His brother was still out, and he was growing more agitated by the moment.

"He's barely breathing," Curt was saying, his voice completely different now; higher and whiny. "I think he needs to go to the hospital. I think something's bad wrong with him."

For his part, David had long believed there was something bad wrong with *both* the Donner brothers. They were, after all, rumored to have sent a number of kids to the hospital. This, however, didn't seem like the time to point that out. Instead he offered to go and call for help. Curt's reaction to the suggestion was simply to wave David along his way and return all of his attention to his stricken sibling.

Some thirty minutes later, David looked on as Clint Donner was placed on a gurney and loaded into the back of an ambulance. Before its back door was closed and it pulled away from the curb, Curt Donner seemed to suddenly remember David was there, for the first time since the incident had happened. He fixed David with a long, lingering glare that seemed to say very clearly and in no uncertain terms, "I hold you responsible for this, and will exact my revenge at a later date."

David Okada was left standing there all alone on the sidewalk, his eyes still wide and his hands splayed out wide in an unconscious gesture that said, "I have no idea what just happened."

When the ambulance had traveled three blocks down, turned and disappeared around a corner, David started moving again at last. But he was no longer headed for the arcade. The two quarters, both of them still safe in his pocket, weren't burning a hole in it anymore. They were, for the most part, completely forgotten—much like the two shadowy figures he'd only partially noticed during all the commotion.

No, he was headed for home now. Straight home. After everything that had just happened, Aunt Elaine's fish sticks and mac and cheese didn't sound so bad anymore.

Eyes from the shadows continued to watch him as he walked away.

CHAPTER 5

The eyes sparkled golden in the bright sunshine of the South Pacific.

They were large eyes–very, *very* large eyes–but they were mostly concealed behind a ridge topped by thick brush and palm trees. They sparkled, and they watched, and they waited, there on an unnamed island to the north of Rapa Lau. Nothing moved, and the massive breathing sounds that had been coming from behind that ridge slowly subsided to a soft rumble that blended in with the pounding of the surf on the beach surrounding the atoll.

For about half an hour, the only movement was the gentle sway of the palms and the crashing of the waves.

And then something moved. Something large, in fact. It broke the surface of the ocean as it strode confidently, perhaps arrogantly, up onto the beach. It had six legs, was purple and brown, was covered with scales, and looked very little like anything else ever seen on Earth. When it had fully emerged from the water, it was revealed to be more than a hundred feet long and about half as tall. Its tiny head contained three blood-red eyes that darted here and there as the bizarre creature crept across the beach and began to move inland.

It did not make it far.

With no advance warning whatsoever, twin orange beams of raw energy speared out from somewhere atop the ridgeline and caught the purple creature in the side.

The six-legged beast screeched in pain and anger. It stumbled back, its hindmost leg dipping in the Pacific, as its head thrashed this way and that, searching for the architect of its pain.

Those gold-speckled eyes remained hidden, and they remained focused intently on the creature. Again came the shimmering blasts of energy, and this time they took the purple beast off its feet and sent it rolling sideways down the beach and into the water. As it splashed about, seeking to regain its footing, pale pink liquid spilled from its wounds and pooled around it.

Before it could recover in any way, a quick yet massive movement signaled that its attacker had decided to reveal himself. And reveal himself he did.

A gigantic lizard-like form, some three hundred feet tall, crashed through the brush, swatting palm trees aside as it came. Its roar vibrated off every surface; its footsteps quaked the ground. It resembled in some ways a massive, time-lost Tyrannosaurus Rex, though that comparison was not entirely apt. Its hide was green with areas of gray here and there, including its belly. And its eyes sparkled with golden flecks of light–and with no small amount of intelligence.

The purple creature saw clearly what was attacking it, and all traces of arrogance evaporated instantly. It made as if to back into the ocean–but the big lizard was having none of it. The green and gray monster surged forward, charging on its two massive hind legs, its two smaller front limbs reaching out like hands to grasp its foe.

The six-legged purple monster reared up on its rearmost legs, attempting to make itself look as big and imposing as possible. But such an effort was doomed to failure against the enemy that stalked it now.

The lizard loomed like a giant over the smaller beast, and now its foreclaws managed to grasp ahold of the spiky purple hide. The attacker raised its quarry up high off the ground and then brought it down hard, and the sound of cracking exoskeleton filled the air. Before the smaller creature could attempt to recover, the lizard unleashed another blast of orange energy from its golden eyes. At such close range, the beams had a devastating effect. They punched twin holes ten feet wide through the creature's carapace and beyond. With a final wail, the purple monster ceased to struggle.

The lizard roared its victory. It grasped its fallen enemy in its claws and raised the creature high up over its head, then brought it down hard, smashing the exoskeleton to pieces. Pink ichor sprayed all about, to drip from the trees not knocked over already by the giant lizard.

The creature known as Tyranicus roared one last time, as if to warn any other beasts lurking in the vicinity that this was its territory, and its kill. Then, slowly and deliberately, it began to drag its beaten foe away in the direction of the hills.

CHAPTER 6

Now, aboard Validus-V:
David Okada again found himself faced with a seriously injured person. This time, however, it was his brother. And this time, there was no ambulance to call; no hospital within thousands of miles. And the aircraft form of his pursuer, Rednator-Oh, relentlessly closed in.

"John would know what to do," David whispered to himself. "I've got to do something to help him."

Validus-V streaked a hundred meters above the surface of the Pacific, engines in the boot sections roaring. In the head section— the robot's command deck—David finally managed to unlatch his seat belts and extricate himself from the crash webbing. It had taken a number of overrides to the robot's safety protocols. Fortunately, he was finding the interface with Validus increasingly intuitive. In some cases, he merely had to think what he wanted; in others, he had to press a button or speak a command out loud before he got the results he wanted. In a very short amount of time, however, he was making progress.

Free of the seat at last, he took one more look at the holographic image of the orange and green robot pursuing them. Then he moved around to the front of the command deck. Now he could see his older brother, and the condition he was in. It wasn't good.

John Okada lay slumped to his right, held entirely by the crash webbing. His seat belts had all separated from their moorings. His left arm dangled down while his right was twisted behind him. His head slumped forward into the netting and blood was dripping from his nose.

Quickly but carefully, David began to extract his brother from the webbing and then lower him back into his seat. He looked over the seat belts but they appeared beyond repair, at least for the moment.

"Validus," he called out to the room around him, hoping the robot's—computer? Mind? Soul? He wasn't quite sure what he was trying to speak to, only that it might be there and might be listening—would hear him. "I think John is badly hurt. What can we do?"

For a long moment nothing happened. Then a panel to David's right separated from the wall and slid out, like a large drawer opening. Small twinkling lights blinked along its outer surface, while a softer, warmer light shone from within; soft but almost painful in the dimness of the command deck. Another light, green and brighter than the others, flashed on and off inside the newly revealed compartment. It flashed four times and stopped.

David left John safely in the cushioned seat and crossed the short distance to the now-open drawer. He looked inside. The lining was cushioned with gray material, and there was even a thicker section at one end in the form of a pillow. To David's eyes, it appeared to be a coffin, built into the side of the room.

"He's not *dead*," David called out, more confident now that somehow the big robot was hearing him. "We need to get him to a hospital." Even as he spoke the words, David knew such a thing would be very difficult. They were thousands of miles from Hawaii and even further from most any other place likely to have sophisticated health care options available. The fact that another giant robot was hot on their tail only made matters worse.

As if in response to David's words, the green light inside the drawer flashed four times again, now more urgently.

Slowly a different idea came to David. Maybe it wasn't a coffin. Maybe it was some sort of… high-tech hospital bed?

He looked back at John, knowing that there was nothing he could do for his brother. Certainly nothing he could do here, in this robot's head, while being attacked. The coffin-drawer seemed like as good an option as there might be.

Reluctantly at first, David grasped his brother under his arms and began to pull him out of the crash webbing. The task was hard enough because John was a good bit bigger and heavier than David. On top of that, first John's left knee and then his right foot got hung up in the mesh, requiring David to stop, release his shoulders, and untangle the other body part. Finally, after minutes of work, he pulled his brother free and lowered him as gently as possible to the rubbery gray floor. It only took about a minute to slide him over to the wall, but then he realized he would never be able to lift the dead weight of a larger person up and into the drawer—and certainly not without causing him some other kinds of physical harm in the process. He stood there, frustrated, not sure of what to do.

And then, with a soft hum, the drawer slowly lowered itself. At the same time, its outer panel tilted down, until the whole contraption sat flush with the floor.

David easily pushed John into the drawer and onto his back on the gray cushions, making sure his head rested on the pillow. With that, the front panel tilted up and the entire drawer raised itself into its previous position, then recessed into the wall.

Just like that, John was gone.

"Gone—but only for now," David said out loud.

His words might have been intended for himself, but Validus seemed to answer anyway: A light on the wall next to the drawer flashed green, four times.

Will this cure him? David wondered. *Is he dying? How will I know if he dies while he's in there?*

All the questions running through his mind only made him feel worse.

But remember, he told himself, *if I hadn't been here aboard Validus-V, able to take over when he was injured, he'd be dead now, or in the clutches of the bad guys.*

Clutches? Jeez, David, he chided himself. *You're starting to talk, or at least think, like a comic book character.*

He was always too hard on himself. He knew that. He also knew it was probably because his mother was so demanding—and had brought him up to be demanding of himself. Having a super-successful older brother only contributed to that. He was always expected to live up to the accomplishments of John, a task that usually felt impossible.

John Okada had graduated with top honors from the University of Hawaii, then moved seamlessly into a career as an officer in the Air Force. He had piloted a variety of aircraft for them, including prototype models, exhibiting tremendous skills. There had been talk of him being on the fast track to the absolute upper echelons of that service. Then one day about a year earlier, he'd come home just long enough to utter some mysterious statements about a top-secret assignment that would take him "off the grid" for a while. He'd told his parents he'd said all he was allowed to say, but to trust that he would be fine, and that he would speak to them again as soon as he was able.

And with that, John had vanished.

Now David thought he understood at least a little of what had become of his brother.

He had no idea where these giant robots had come from, but clearly John had been recruited to pilot one. Without question that explained why he'd been so excited about his new and secret job opportunity.

But something, somewhere, somehow, had gone terribly wrong. The others had turned on him, called him a traitor. It had to be a mistake—or worse.

David shook his head. He needed to learn the whole story, and learn it as quickly as possible. It didn't seem that Validus was going to fill him in on anything, so he would have to either revive his brother or find some other way of learning about these robots and the people piloting them.

The thought came to him then: *Aunt Elaine. How long have I been gone? She was expecting me to come home after school. She'll be furious. She might even call my mom in Tokyo, and then I'll really be in trouble.*

"Validus," he said aloud, looking all around the enclosed space, "can I make a telephone call? Is that something you're able to do?"

He laughed at that last part of his own question. The big robot could fly at supersonic speeds, fire missiles from its belly, and apparently halfway read his mind. But a telephone call might be too much for it?

As if in response, a light flared from the area of his co-pilot's seat. He walked over and looked down at the wide, glass-like panel that curved in front of the seat. A rectangle about six inches tall and four inches wide, filled with lines and numbers, had lit up on its previously dark surface. He sat down and studied it.

It was a grid of numbers, laid out in four horizontal rows and three vertical ones. Was this the telephone, somehow? Reaching out tentatively, he tapped the first digit of his home number. It lit up momentarily. "Ah!" The idea came to him quickly. "Instead of dialing the numbers, you touch them."

Quickly he tapped out the rest of the digits for his parents' home phone, then waited. But there was no dial tone, no ringing, nothing.

He inquired out loud about this issue, but this time received no response at all—other than the number grid turning red and then fading from view.

Was something wrong with it? Maybe they were too far out of range of Hawaii's telephone network. Or maybe Validus's communications system had been damaged during the earlier fight. He really had no idea.

Alarms sounded then, and the lights in the room shifted red.

The main holographic display split in half. The left side showed a camera angle, presumably from the point of view of Validus's eyes. He could see an object in the distance, flying through the air, approaching rapidly.

The right side showed what must have been a view from orbital satellites, broken down into basic colors and shapes, each shape labeled with a name or description. A blue star pulsed at his location over the ocean.

A short distance away, but approaching fast, was a green and orange dot. It was labeled TORANDER-X, and its pilot was listed as one WEN ZHAO.

"She's not coming to apologize," David said to himself.

Time to get ready.

Standing to one side, David looked over the holographic display, currently showing a satellite view of the entire area. He saw that Validus was heading directly toward a small island. On the display, it was labeled RAPA LAU, and marked with a shimmering golden star. Rapa Hoi was marked the same way. He frowned, wondering at the significance. He supposed he might find out before long; it looked as if they would arrive there very soon.

Before he could return to his seat—the same rear seat he'd occupied before, because of the damage to the seat belts in the front one—a violent explosion sent him stumbling to his knees. For the first time he found himself grateful the floor was covered in a layer of rubbery material that absorbed the shock of his impact.

He understood immediately what was happening. The pursuer had caught up to him. He was under attack.

CHAPTER 7

Aboard the command deck of Torander-X, currently operating in the form of Rednator-Oh, Wen Zhao leaned forward in her seat, her eyes flickering across the images filling her holographic display. Slight but muscular, the former pilot in the Taiwanese Air Force stood only a bit above five feet tall. Her hair was black and cut in a short bob, but it was currently covered by her command helmet. Within that helmet she frowned: Her calculations had been ever so slightly off; her quarry was not quite within striking range after all. Her first attack had come up just short, doing no real damage.

She studied that quarry carefully in the display. Validus-V was a vaguely man-shaped blue and silver object flying in the distance, rockets in the boot sections burning brightly. Zhao was surprised at how long it had taken her to catch up to the other robot. None of the four Titans could match the raw speed of hers in its Rednator-Oh configuration. Somehow Validus had managed to stay out of weapons range for quite some time, though. But now it was about to be over. Now she would bring the traitor Titan and its rebellious, teen-aged pilot down for good.

Zhao had her hands poised over the curving weapons control panel like a concert pianist about to begin an overture, but then she hesitated. Thoughts came unbidden to her mind. She'd thought of Validus-V as *the traitor Titan*, as if it were the most obvious and unquestionable fact she could ever state. But—*why* did she think of Validus as a traitor? Why did she think of John Okada that way? And what did she have against his little brother? In point of fact, the kid was clearly doing an amazing job and probably should be inducted into the pilot program immediately.

For an extended moment she simply sat there, frozen in place, finding herself of two completely separate minds, struggling to gather her wits. Then her previous way of thinking reasserted itself, like a door slamming closed, locking away some other personality.

"No," she spoke aloud. "No. Stop allowing yourself to entertain these dangerous thoughts. You know Okada is a traitor, and his little brother is just as bad. Dr. Graven had said so—and who would know better than him?"

From somewhere deep inside the neural computer network that bound her to Torander/Rednator—and perhaps from behind that closed door in her mind—a wordless voice came back, echoing her original thoughts. But then it faded, vanished. All that was left then was duty: duty to follow the orders of Professor Graven, who had, after all, discovered the Titans all those years earlier, and recruited the pilots. Surely he would know better than anyone else.

There. The indicator light flashed on the board in front of her. Validus-V was at last fully in range.

Zhao unleashed a second barrage of missiles, watched them strike and buffet the other robot, then spoke into the microphone built into her helmet: "I assume I have your attention…"

Another round of explosions rocked Validus.

David leapt up and hopped into the second pilot's seat. A quick look at the holographic display confirmed his fears: the green and orange robot had caught up to them and was firing missiles.

"I assume I have your attention," came a woman's voice over the speakers in David's helmet. "And I further assume I am speaking to David Okada, the young man piloting Validus-V without authorization." She sounded tough and authoritative and David was immediately intimidated. "This is Wen Zhao, pilot of Torander-X, presently in its Rednator-Oh form."

David stared at the display and studied the orange and green form the robot presently held; it now looked more like a massive aircraft than a man. He found it interesting that it went by a different name while in that form. He wondered if that was something Validus could do, and immediately felt a wordless answer coming back over his connection, indicating *no*: That trick was a quality belonging to Zhao's robot alone.

"I know from telemetry coming from your robot that your brother has been injured," the woman said. "We have a full medical suite at his disposal back on Rapa Hoi. He will receive the best treatment possible—better than anything that could be done for him at a normal hospital. Turn control of Validus over to me and I will return both of you to safety immediately."

The woman made a good argument, except for the fact that David clearly remembered it was she and the other pilots in their robots who had caused the injury to her brother to begin with. They'd accused him of some crime—something he'd vociferously denied. David could find no reason to doubt his brother.

"Faster," he whispered to Validus. "Get us away from her. She's dangerous."

David could feel Validus vibrating harder as the big engines in its legs ratcheted their output up another notch. The green and orange robot/aircraft started to shrink into the distance on the reverse-view holo screen.

"Very bad idea," the woman's voice called over the communications link. "Rednator-Oh is the fastest of the four Titans. You cannot outrun us."

"We'll see," David whispered, but inside he suspected she was telling the truth, at least about that.

If he couldn't outrun his pursuer back to Hawaii, he'd need a different plan. As a matter of fact, now that he had a moment to catch his breath and think, he wasn't exactly sure what going back there would accomplish, anyway. His original idea had been to land in the park, vacate the robot, somehow drag John's unconscious body along with him, and get away before the pursuit caught up. Then, as far as he was concerned, these people were welcome to take Validus back to their little island—just as long as they left him and his brother alone.

But—would John be okay with that plan? Just abandoning his robot for the others to take? David doubted it, but what could he do? John was unconscious, if not worse. If that was the plan David ended up following, John would just have to understand his brother had no other choice.

As David thought those thoughts, the lighting inside the command deck darkened and faded to a pale red. He paid it no attention; he was consumed with other matters.

He continued to sort through his thoughts. As time went by, landing back home and trying to get away no longer seemed like such a great idea. Even if he could manage to get Validus to Oahu before this Zhao woman and her robot caught up to them, he had the strong sense that just handing the big blue robot over to her and the others wasn't the smartest idea. He suspected it wouldn't just make John angry, it might cause a lot more problems than that.

Something very shady was going on. Before the other three robots had attacked, their pilots and the British man on the radio had all made it clear they considered John a traitor. But John was innocent. David had no doubts whatsoever about that. He'd seen and heard John's reaction to the charges. He could always tell when his brother was lying, which was almost never, and he had definitely not been lying then.

That meant the other robot pilots and their British boss were the actual traitors, though the details still eluded him. And that in turn meant it would be very bad to hand Validus over to them.

So he wouldn't do it.

As if in reaction to this decision on his part, the lights in the room brightened and the red tint disappeared. David noticed this only peripherally; it didn't register fully with him.

He wasn't going to hand Validus-V over to the others.

"What else can I do?" he said aloud.

He blinked as the view on the holographic display shifted, angling downward and to the left. The island he'd noticed in their path earlier was now visible, just ahead. The textual overlay that appeared next to it read, RAPA LAU, and the gold star over it continued to shimmer, as if the island was home to something important. He frowned; he couldn't imagine what could be so important about such a small, remote island. That in turn caused him to wonder: How far from home was he now? Where in the world could he turn for help?

He has nowhere to turn, Wen Zhao thought to herself as she pushed the throttle forward even farther and closed the distance between Rednator-Oh and Validus-V, reeling the fleeing robot in. *He has no allies, no friends here; no one to help at all. The only thing remaining is to capture him.*

Zhao tapped out a sequence on the curved panel in front of her. In response, a crackling electrified cable shot out from a duct on the right side of the main fuselage and quickly closed the distance between the two Titans. It wrapped itself around the lower leg of Validus. She felt the Titan around her jerk sharply.

On the display, Validus continued to rocket forward while also bending around to reach for the cable with its big, blue fingers.

Zhao pressed a red square on the panel, then slid her finger partway up a sliding scale control. In response, megawatts of voltage surged through the cable and into Validus. The blue robot jerked wildly, sparks flying out from where the cable was wrapped around its ankle.

"Now to make things increasingly uncomfortable for the child," she whispered to herself, "until he agrees to hand the Titan over to me."

She slid her finger farther along the control, upping the voltage on the cable, seeking a level that would incapacitate both robot and pilot but kill or destroy neither.

"It would be easier for you to travel back to Rapa Hoi alongside me than for me to have to drag your robot's broken body over all that distance," she said over the comm link. At first, there was no response.

Zhao considered the possibility of having to kill David Okada, and possibly John too. She surprised herself then by saying aloud, "These things happen. People get greedy; go bad. Sometimes there's no other way to deal with them. You will do what you have to do; what Professor Graven tells you to do."

But, as she spoke those words, a voice from deep beneath the surface of her mind shouted back, *John is innocent! This is all a sham!*

Zhao squeezed her eyes closed and gritted her teeth, striving to keep such thoughts at bay; to ignore that nagging, annoying voice. She'd found that if she paid it any attention, she quickly developed a splitting headache that wouldn't go away for hours.

But this is all a lie, the other voice in her head insisted. *This isn't who we are. It's not how we think—not how we behave!*

"Shut up!" she shouted out loud. "Stop it! Be quiet!" She leaned her head forward until her helmet struck the console. She sat there that way, unmoving, for several seconds. The only sound was the faint hum of electricity being channeled through the cable into Validus-V.

The near-silence was broken by a voice coming over her helmet comm link. It was a male voice; it was young; it sounded confused but not frightened or intimidated. What it said was, "Um, I didn't say anything."

Zhao blinked at that. She frowned and slowly raised herself part of the way back upright.

"Unless you were talking to someone else," it went on.

Zhao's frown deepened. This boy—this *child*—was her intended target? What exactly had he done? Why had the professor ordered them to attack Validus-V? Why couldn't she remember those details?

The headache came on then, worse than ever. She let out a long groan that became a wail before she was done.

"Ma'am?" the voice of the kid asked. "Are you okay?"

Now he was concerned for her well-being! *This* was the enemy, the traitor to their cause—or the traitor's little brother, anyway—she'd been sent to capture or eliminate? *This?*

Her head pounded now. She wanted to bang it against the walls of the command deck, but the seatbelts and crash webbing held her firmly in place, and her helmet would've absorbed any blows anyway.

"I... am... *fine...!*" she blurted over the link. "*I...* am not... the *problem* here!"

"Um, if you don't mind my saying so, ma'am," David Okada replied, "you don't sound too good."

With a supreme effort of will, Zhao straightened her spine and sat fully upright. She reached forward and touched the sliding control, pushing it all the way forward. Current poured out along the cable into the leg of Validus-V, as she sought to fry the blue robot's systems and maybe its pilot too.

"If you will not surrender control of the Titan," she said then, her voice strained but filled with wrath, "I will be forced to bring you down. Alive or dead."

CHAPTER 8

I will be forced to bring you down," the woman's voice was saying, "alive or dead." It startled David back to reality. That, and the thick smell of burning metal that now filled the cabin.

He tried to think of something to say back. His mind was blank. He didn't know what to make of this. For a moment, the pilot of the other robot had sounded genuinely conflicted—not with him, but with herself. He'd felt bad for her, and wanted to help. But then she'd completely changed gears and gone back to threatening him.

What is wrong with these people?

He glanced at the rear-view display. The orange and green robot was so close now, it could practically reach out and grab his robot's ankle—the ankle where the electrified cable was still wrapped tight, delivering a constant jolt of energy that David sensed Validus was having a hard time dealing with.

"It is possible you are simply a passenger aboard Validus," the woman said then, her tone softening slightly. "Trapped along with your unconscious brother, as the robot obeys the last orders it received from him." She paused a moment. "If that is the case, please signal in the affirmative, and I will do what I can to help you to land and to release you and your brother from the robot unharmed."

David wrestled with himself over what to do. He couldn't hand Validus over. The woman talked a good game but he had already seen the truth of things in the earlier actions she and the others had taken.

But he couldn't fight. Not against all three of those robots. Not by himself. He simply couldn't. Could he? He'd received no training. He didn't know the robot's weapons or defense systems or much of anything else about it. He'd get wiped out immediately. Wouldn't he?

In the short time he'd been in charge of Validus, the robot had helped him more than once. Did it have a mind of its own? It certainly seemed that way. It was as if Validus knew what it wanted to do—what the best action would be—and merely required its human pilot to confirm that action. It was as if Validus could read his mind. While in some ways that scared David, it also seemed to be both eminently sensible and an extremely efficient way of controlling a giant robot, as opposed to working levers and switches or issuing voice commands.

Maybe if Validus already knew how to fight this other robot, all he had to do was mentally allow it permission—?

"Let's get rid of that cable, first," he said in a quiet tone. "Then we'll see what we can do."

Aboard Rednator-Oh, Zhao looked on in surprise as Validus-V suddenly spun about in midair. Big blue fingers grasped the electrified cable, sending cascades of sparks flying out, and ripped it loose from its ankle. Then, still holding the cable, Validus spun about like an Olympic hammer-thrower.

Alarms sounded all around; all the interior lights changed to red. Zhao instinctively grasped the console in front of her with both hands as g-forces tore at her.

Rednator-Oh was too large simply to be flung away, but damage could still be done. When Validus released its grip on the cable, the orange and green aircraft temporarily lost all of its aerodynamics and went careening downward, end over end.

Increasingly dizzy, Zhao frantically tapped at various lit-up circles and squares on the black console, struggling to regain control. At last she had no choice but to trigger Rednator-Oh's transformation back into Torander-X.

Metal liquified and flowed around crystal, changing its very structure. It took only a few moments. Once back in man-shaped form, the big robot was able to use its boot and hand rockets to restore equilibrium. The green and orange Titan stopped its tumble mere meters above the surface of the Pacific.

In the head section, Zhao gasped a sigh of relief. Sweat ran down her forehead and cheeks. She brought the robot around to face in the direction it had been traveling previously and she looked for her quarry.

But Validus-V was gone.

David Okada felt a surge of excitement run through him as Validus hurled the big orange airship away. He didn't wait to see what would become of it, though. He assumed a pilot as skilled as Zhao would surely regain control sooner or later. Instead he took the opportunity to urge Validus onward; to get out of there before she could return, probably with some other and more devilish attack.

A bright green oval shone on the holographic display, in the midst of a universe of deep blue. A gold star continued to flash at the center of it. Somehow David understood this represented a map, indicating the little island of Rapa Lau. It was coming up fast ahead of them. He considered his situation and made a decision: If he planned to make a stand, it might be nice to be able to actually *stand*; to have some solid ground under his feet this time.

Scarcely had he mentally committed to that course of action than Validus altered course and zoomed down toward Rapa Lau. Again the robot had seemingly read his mind, even before he had made it up.

David shrugged at this. In a way it seemed kind of creepy, but it also likely was the main thing that had kept him and his brother alive so far. He suspected if the robot couldn't read his mind, and therefore couldn't respond to threats so quickly, he'd have been killed already, as would John.

The threat posed by Torander-X wasn't over, he reminded himself. He had to try something. If he merely kept flying away, the faster green and orange robot would surely just catch up with him again. This way, maybe the woman who was chasing him would think he was landing in order to surrender and hand the robot over to her. And then perhaps she would lower her guard a little.

Another thought occurred to him then, as well: Maybe Validus had some kind of camouflage or stealth technology. "If you have it, this would be a good time to use it, buddy," he whispered. He didn't expect a response and didn't receive one. Whether anything came of the suggestion, he had no idea.

In any case, he needed a break; a chance to clear his mind and to think. He'd been on the run pretty much from the moment John had picked him up and brought him aboard Validus. He needed to catch his breath.

David mentally urged Validus to stop, to brake. In response the big blue robot cut its forward propulsion, scrunched itself up in a ball, and reoriented itself. It was now a couple hundred meters above the island. As it began to drop out of the sky, it extended its arms out to each side and aimed its feet downward, so that its boot rockets were now pointing at the ground. With a roar and with teeth-rattling vibrations, the robot halted its descent, smoke billowing out all around.

Gently Validus-V touched down on the sandy surface of Rapa Lau.

Unfortunately for David, he would receive very little break. For he was not alone on that island.

A relatively short distance away, from a deep ravine cut in the island's surface and camouflaged by jungle growth, two orange-flecked golden eyes peered through the foliage and regarded the big blue robot as it descended and landed. Behind those eyes, an ancient and instinctive intellect considered what was happening.

The metal men. Yes. They were all too familiar. And, about them, mixed feelings.

The robot shimmered, then vanished.

The orange-flecked golden eyes blinked, then narrowed, studying the spot where the robot had stood.

Where had it gone?

The ancient intellect behind the eyes remembered then, from a time long ago. Sometimes the big metal men did that.

The intellect also remembered being able to see through it, by squinting just so, and concentrating like this, and...

Yes. *There.* A hazy form; a vague outline. But now at least somewhat visible.

As the golden eyes squinted and watched the metal man's fuzzy shape just standing there, a new sound washed over the island. It was the sound of the other robot—the one that had been chasing this one.

What were they doing?

Would they fight?

Those orange-flecked golden eyes remained hidden in the jungle. But now they watched, oh-so-attentively. And the mind behind them waited.

Wen Zhao scanned the skies all around but could find no traces of the giant robot.

Impossible, she thought. He couldn't have just vanished.

She expanded her scans, reaching down into the ocean in a circle around her, in case he'd dived beneath the surface. Validus was too big and too solid to hide that way, though. But he wasn't there.

Then she noticed the island of Rapa Lau to the north. She knew of it, vaguely, but had only visited there once before. In the three years since she'd been the pilot of Torander-X, there had never been a reason to return. But if the kid were trying to hide, it seemed like as logical a place as any. Focusing on it, she recalibrated her sensors.

Still nothing.

Growling in her throat, she shook her head in frustration and urged Torander-X forward, toward the island. That had to be where the kid was; where he'd taken the Titan. There was nowhere else he could be.

As she closed in on the island, she shifted the wavelength of Torander's sensors once more.

A man-shaped form appeared as if from nowhere, standing on the beach. A very large form.

There you are.

Weapons cycling up, Torander-X swooped down.

CHAPTER 9

Alarms screamed throughout the command deck and over David's helmet speakers. On the holo display, the camera angle spun around and zoomed in on the streaking shape of an orange and green robot descending like a guided missile towards him.

"Oh crap," David exclaimed. "She's found us already!"

Validus-V stood there, head inclined back, gazing up at the incoming attacker. Otherwise, the big robot did nothing.

"Validus! We have to move!"

The robot remained still as a statue.

Visualize, David told himself. *Imagine what you want to do—what you want Validus to do.*

"How do I *know* that?" he asked out loud. "John didn't give me any instructions. He didn't have a chance to, before they hurt him."

And yet, somehow, he was slowly learning how to control the big robot. *No,* he corrected himself. *Not control. Suggest. Cooperate with.* There was a difference there. A qualitative difference. The robot wasn't his servant. It wasn't a mere machine that could only do as it was commanded. It was, somehow, its own thing. A thing not to be ordered about, but to be worked with. Cooperated with. That, he was coming to understand, made Validus much more than a mere robot—and it made their partnership much more profound than that of a mere pilot directing a mindless automaton.

David relaxed his mind and imagined the big blue robot attacking its pursuer with whatever weapons lay at its disposal. Not ordering it to fire a particular weapon, but suggesting general tactical approaches to defending them both.

Instantly Validus-V went into action. Pushing its torso forward and angling it upward as it cocked its elbows back, it launched a barrage of missiles from heretofore hidden housings in its shoulders and stomach.

"Whoa!" David shouted, astonished as he watched the multiple warheads detonate against the green and orange form of Torander-X.

The explosions caused Torander-X to spin wildly about in midair, arms and legs splaying out in every direction. Over the communications link, he could hear Wen Zhao scream in shock.

For a mere instant he considered holding back, waiting to see if Zhao could correct her robot's trajectory and regain control. But then the idea came into his head—later he would wonder if Validus had placed it there itself—to keep up the pressure; to not give the enemy a moment's relief.

Validus's left arm came up and slats popped out along the forearm section, reforming in less than a second into a long barrel. From that new weapon, with an earth-shattering shriek, erupted a beam of shimmering gold energy that struck Torander-X in the center of its belly. More explosions bloomed out from the enemy robot and its tumbling gyrations only worsened.

David wanted to celebrate, but there was no time. He knew the fight wasn't over; that his opponent would not go down that easily. And he was right.

Wen Zhao gave up on trying even to touch the control panel. She was being flung about so violently, she knew she was fortunate her belts and crash webbing had saved her thus far.

She was furious. She knew she had underestimated what Validus-V could and would do with a child in the pilot's seat. The missile attack, coming so unexpectedly and with none of her defenses ready, had been bad enough. Then the particle beam attack—one of Validus's main weapons, and extremely formidable—had caused critical damage to Torander's propulsion systems and stabilizers.

Because of that, her controlled descent had been turned into a deadly tumble. Any second now, Torander would impact a surface—either the island or the ocean. Falling from such a height, at such speeds, either would likely deal her robot tremendous damage.

Knowing she had no choice, and was in fact about to black out, she resorted to the only trick she had left. She shouted, "Emergency autopilot!" With that, she allowed the darkness to swallow her.

What she had managed to do, however, saved her life—and that of Torander, at least for the moment. She had freed the robot to see to its own situation, without waiting even a millisecond to read and process her preferences in the matter. From there, it could execute a preprogrammed series of actions tailored to that specific situation.

As a result, Torander-X executed a rapid-fire set of braking maneuvers, slowing to a much less deadly velocity. The robot still was going to impact the ground, Zhao knew—just not with a speed and force sufficient to destroy it. Also, she hoped, not sufficient to kill her.

How could someone so young have done this? Her anger boiled over now that she had given over control to the robot and freed up her mind. Now that she could truly think about it.

He couldn't have, she concluded. It had to be John in control. Some way, somehow, it had to be. There was no way she was losing this fight to a completely inexperienced little kid.

She had other thoughts along those lines, but had no more time to ruminate over them. Her flight had ended.

The green and orange robot tumbled out of the sky, arms and legs flailing, and smacked the sand of Rapa Lau with massive concussive force.

David watched as the enemy robot, now back in its humanoid form, fell from the sky and crashed into the surface, sending gouts of dirt and shredded palm tree parts flying.

Validus approached their downed adversary, arms up and weapons at the ready. The green and orange form lay still, flat on its back, smoke wafting from numerous points of damage along its torso and right leg.

"Are you okay in there?" David called out over the communications link.

"How have you been fooling us, John?" Zhao's voice hissed back.

David was taken aback by this. "John's unconscious," he told her. "At least, you'd better hope that's all he is, or else—"

"I don't believe you," she snapped back. "There's no way a child could have figured out how to do those attacks and maneuvers so quickly."

David frowned at this. First—a *child?* He was sixteen! And—had his maneuvers been *that* sophisticated? He'd felt he had only gotten lucky, and taken his opponent by surprise. He still believed that. But perhaps Validus had thrown in a little extra flair to the actions he had willed it to take—?

"Well, whatever you believe," he called back to her, "at least you're alive." He surveyed the downed Titan again, noting that it still hadn't moved a single electronic muscle. "Can I help you to—"

Torander-X flipped over onto its stomach with a speed and agility totally at odds with its size and mass. Its right arm extended downward, holding it off the ground, like it was doing a one-handed push-up. Its left arm came forward and pointed directly at him, a blinding light pulsing from the index finger: SNAP. SNAP. SNAP.

The lights all switched over to red and alarms wailed inside the command deck of Validus-V. The big blue robot stumbled back a step, then brought up its diamond-shaped shield, deflecting two subsequent shots away. But the first three had hit, and they'd clearly done damage.

David knew he couldn't just stand there and keep taking hits. He had to act. Validus had to act. But—how?

Mentally he imagined himself rushing forward, dealing some vague and undefined form of violence to the other robot.

Validus-V dug in its giant boots and surged ahead, big metal feet grinding through the sandy earth now, digging out great gouts in the island's surface as it ran along, closing the distance between the two in an instant. Validus's navy-blue-and-white left forearm came up into view, the fingers bunched into a fist. Then that fist separated from the rest of the arm. It fired off, streaking away like a missile, crashing into the face of the other robot.

Torander-X spun halfway around and fell face-down back into the sand, stunned by the attack.

The missile-fist curved around and returned to its place on Validus's arm. David watched this happening on the side viewscreen, utterly amazed and fascinated and wanting to absorb the very idea of what the robot had just done, but not able to devote much attention to it at the moment. Their adversary was recovering, much quicker than he would have expected. It rolled over, crushing several palm trees in the process, and sat up, bringing that pulse cannon to bear again.

Before David could react at all, Validus fired off a salvo of missiles from some place in its chest region; David didn't know where exactly they were coming from. They streaked across the narrow distance and exploded just short of the enemy, doing no visible damage.

Why didn't they strike home?

Then David saw the shimmering golden sphere that now surrounded Torander-X.

A forcefield? David frowned at this development. But there was little time to think, because the enemy robot was firing the pulse cannon yet again, and its blinding streaks of coherent light were just missing to the left as Validus dived to the right.

Once more reminding himself that this other robot, while damaged, was still enormously powerful and formidable, David urged Validus to attack again; to find a way through that forcefield.

He had scarcely formulated the desire before a whip comprised of twisted silvery cables extended from Validus's right arm. The big blue robot clutched the weapon, now sparkling with some sort of massive electrical charge, and brought it back over its head. David watched this happening, understanding that on some level he was merely an observer, but that on another level he was the facilitator, the motivator for his robot's actions. They didn't operate independently of one another. David didn't have to spell out what he wanted Validus to do, but conversely Validus seemingly couldn't do anything without David there to think at least in general terms what he wanted the robot to do. It was becoming clear to him that they operated in a sort of synchronous state—a subconscious state; an interdependent state. He wondered how much deeper John's relationship with the robot must have been, considering he'd piloted the robot for much longer.

Another thought crossed David's mind then: Maybe he was the only one to ever achieve such a close connection to the big machine. Could that be? It didn't seem likely. But then, the woman whose robot he was currently battling had seemed genuinely surprised by everything he'd done up until now. So— maybe?

Time to worry about such things later. For now, he just had to survive, and survive long enough to get his brother to a hospital. And survival meant winning this fight!

Validus brought the whip around and down, and it struck Torander-X like a thunderbolt. The golden force field sparked and disappeared for a split-second before reappearing, but with gaps in its coverage and with waves of static racing to and fro across its outer surface.

Validus drew back and struck again, an even mightier blow. The forcefield flared, crackled, and vanished.

A third blow of the electro-whip sheared off Torander's left arm at the elbow, removing the pulse-cannon along with it.

David gasped aloud at this. He was astonished by the amount of damage the robot could deal out, even to another of its kind.

Press your advantage, he thought.

Validus charged forward, swinging its big blue fist, bringing it into contact with Torander's jaw. The green and orange robot went down in a heap, its impact shaking the entire island. It lay there, face-down, unmoving.

Validus raised the whip-hand again, but David mentally urged it to wait.

"Give it up," David called over the communications link, as he stared down at the incapacitated and inert body of the other Titan. "You're beaten."

No response.

Wen Zhao dangled from the restraining harness of her seat, her head spinning. She fought to regain her senses quickly, knowing the killing blow could come at any moment. If their positions were reversed and it was the other robot in this position, she had no doubts she would strike quickly and mercilessly and make sure it never got up again.

She couldn't reach the manual controls from her current position, but the interface helmet was still in place on her head. She reached out with her thoughts, trying to reestablish the tenuous interface she'd always had with Torander.

Nothing.

Frowning, she tried again. She allowed her mind to expand along the electronic interface, reaching for the presence she always felt on the other end of the connection.

Again, nothing. It was like she was making a phone call but nobody was picking up on the other end. It wasn't just that the robot wouldn't move. It wasn't even answering her call.

For the first time, a feeling of helplessness began to settle over her.

She gave it one last effort, and this time she did sense something on the other end of the line. It was like seeing a tiny firefly flickering at the end of a long, dark tunnel. She reached out for it with her thoughts, wanting to embrace it, to connect with it, but immediately she felt something... *wrong* about it. There was a palpable sense of hostility, of anger radiating back up along the line. If what she was sensing was the core of Torander, then her robot was very unhappy indeed.

No. It wasn't just that, she knew. Torander wasn't just unhappy. There was something else there. A malevolence. Not something she ever had associated with her robot before. She understood the hostility; the traitor robot had just shot them down, sheared off Torander's arm, and left them in this virtually paralyzed state. Of course her robot wanted revenge. Wanted to go after the enemy and do better against it this time—to gain some measure of redemption. All of that made sense and was somewhat familiar to Wen Zhao. But it wasn't the entirety of what she was sensing from her robot.

There was something very unpleasant, something outright evil, lurking within the depths of Torander-X's artificial mind. A corruption. A darkness.

Had it been there all along? How had she failed to notice it before? Had the impact with the ground, or with her adversary's fist, stunned her back to reality? Had it allowed her to sense something she hadn't been able to detect before?

Tentatively she reached towards it, like probing a missing tooth.

Immediately came sharp feedback along the connection, like a jolt of lightning hitting her brain.

Her mind swam. The questions she'd been wondering vanished entirely from her thoughts.

Hostility and anger? *Of course* she felt such things. Her opponent, the big blue robot with its traitor pilot, was the *enemy*. Hadn't Professor Graven said so, and warned them that he would try to fool them?

Forcing her revulsion at the dark aspect of Torander's mental connection back down, Zhao attempted once more to get the big robot to move. She knew on a fundamental level that she should have already abandoned the Titan, but she was determined to wake the machine up and get back in the fight, if at all possible.

When her latest effort at contacting Torander failed, she cursed in Mandarin and tapped a spot on the right side of her helmet. In response, a cable snaked out of the wall behind her and zeroed in unerringly on a socket at the top of her helmet. If the wireless connection wasn't working, she was going to try the direct hookup.

No good. Still no response at all from Torander-X. Not even a flicker of the big robot's own consciousness. It was as if the orange and green machine were unconscious–or dead.

Trying to spur Torander into action was proving to be a waste of time–time she very well might be running out of, at any moment.

Cursing again, Zhao tapped the helmet again to disconnect the cable, then reached over and grasped the clasps of the harness that kept her dangling in space. She clicked the harness clasp and dropped to the currently-horizontal inner front surface of the big robot's head, landing unceremoniously on her left hip.

Groaning, she climbed to her feet and massaged her side. The flight suit she wore had protected her from any serious injury, but it still hadn't felt very good to smack (what was supposed to be the wall but was now) the floor.

Still no follow-up attack by Validus-V. How was she still alive? She couldn't figure why her enemy hadn't already taken advantage of her robot's incapacitation to finish her off.

She scrambled around to where the control console projected up from the now-floor. The panels were too high up for her to see from that position. Jumping up, she grabbed the edge of the console with both hands, dangled there a moment, then swung her lithe form up in a vault and landed on the side of the panel, about eight feet up from where she'd previously stood. Squatting down, she stared at the blank, black displays. Not a good sign. She tapped them once, twice. Nothing. No response. Dead as a doornail.

Clearly, Torander had suffered much more catastrophic damage than she'd first thought.

And that meant she and her robot were totally at the mercy of their foe.

Again she wondered, *How am I not dead? Why hasn't he struck yet?*

The operators of the robots generally used the holographic display to see what was going on outside and around them. That was no longer an option here. But she was not entirely blind; there were also small windows set at intervals all the way around the head, allowing the pilot to simply look out. She'd never paid them much attention before–but then, she'd never had to. At that moment, still puzzled as to why her opponent hadn't struck again, Zhao looked up through the window positioned at the very back of Torander's metal skull. She nearly screamed at what she saw, and involuntarily she scrambled back a couple of steps.

Validus-V's massive foot was raised and currently hovered just above Torander-X's head, poised to strike. Poised to flatten the giant head–and her along with it.

CHAPTER 10

"Whoa whoa whoa!"

David shouted and waved his arms frantically, as if this would somehow get his robot's attention faster.

Validus currently had its right foot raised up and poised to bring down on the green and orange robot, where it lay on its belly in the sand.

"She's still in there," David cried out. "You'll kill her!"

For the first time since he'd taken control of the big robot, Validus-V had moved entirely of his own volition. Several times previously he'd made specific moves, but only in response to David's general thoughts and directions, where he visualized the outcome he wanted and the robot took a few steps to achieve it, or something close to it. But now Validus was preparing to do something David hadn't even contemplated.

Or—had he?

Had he, deep down inside, actually thought about killing his opponent? Was the robot still merely responding to his wishes, even if he was not conscious of them himself?

It doesn't matter, he concluded. *Whether a stray thought like that went through my mind or not, Validus needs to obey my actual commands.*

He made sure that thought was very clear in his mind, and he held it there for a couple of seconds. And he waited.

Nothing happened. The foot remained in place, above Torander-X's head. And above Wen Zhao, like the Sword of Damocles. Like a Guillotine.

Was the child truly going to try to crush her? To *kill* her?

She'd been right all along. He *was* working with evil forces. He *had* to be! Professor Graven had been right, as well—John was a traitor, and his little brother was clearly even worse.

Zhao stared up at the image of the gigantic foot poised above her for another second. Then, as fast as she could possibly move, she scrambled for the escape hatch.

If the hatch had been located at the back of Torander's head, she might not have been able to reach it. Given that her robot was still lying on its face, that area was far up above her. Instead, however, the hatch was situated to the side, where the robot's ear would be. She could just reach there. Slapping the manual release, she watched as the little round door popped open and swung out. Without a second's hesitation, she dived through it.

David saw Zhao leap out of the side of Torander-X's head. He watched as she spun herself around in midair and landed with remarkable grace in the sand. He continued to watch as she straightened and then scampered toward a stand of trees, disappearing within them. Then he returned his attention to the green and orange and white head that lay face-down beneath Validus's foot.

"There's nobody else in there, is there?" he asked out loud.

The holographic image before him morphed until it displayed six different views of the enemy robot's head, each slightly different in color. Somehow he understood that it represented the fact that the head was being scanned with different scanners on different wavelengths. All of them revealed the head to be empty now.

If that was a metaphor, David missed it entirely. Of course, he was otherwise occupied.

"Well, go ahead, then," he said out loud.

Validus-V brought its massive foot down on the other robot's head, crushing it flat.

Zhao ran for her life through the palm trees, sand flying up behind her as she went.

She heard the boom, just a couple of seconds after she made it into cover. The ground beneath her shook, almost enough to throw her off her feet.

He did it, she thought as she ran. *He crushed Torander X's head. And it would've been me getting crushed, too, if I hadn't gotten out of there so quickly.*

It never occurred to her that David had waited until she'd vacated the Titan to allow Validus-V to strike as he had.

Through the rough island brush she ran, being struck repeatedly by branches and stepping on brambles. Her flight suit, boots and helmet protected her from the worst of it. She wanted to stop; to go back, check on the damage done to her Titan, and maybe find some way to strike back at her enemy. But she knew she couldn't do that. Validus would spot her with its scanners, and she would be captured or killed. And as bad as being killed sounded, the thought of becoming the prisoner of that snot-nosed kid David Okada seemed infinitely worse.

After nearly four minutes of running, she came to the place where a high wall of natural stone rose up from the island, forming a nearly vertical wall in front of her. To the untrained eye, it appeared to be the base of the small trio of mountains that made up the center of Rapa Lau. The wall was far more than that, though, Zhao knew.

Despite the bright tropical Pacific sun, it was dark at the base of the rock wall, due to the thick covering of trees and other vegetation that ran right up to it. She slid the smooth, tinted visor of her helmet up and out of the way, but still couldn't see well enough to find what she was looking for. She began to feel along the surface of the rock wall, moving slowly to her right as she went, reaching upward. It had to be there somewhere; she remembered Professor Graven showing them all, when he'd first brought them here, a few days after they'd been recruited to pilot the four Titans.

There. As she moved a leaf-filled branch of scrub out of the way, her fingers brushed an indentation that was far too regular in shape to be a natural cleft in the rock. Reaching inside, she found a small lever and pulled it.

The wall before her did something odd then: a rectangle the size of a large door recessed into the cliff face, then dropped. After only a couple of seconds, the door was entirely out of the way and she found herself standing before an opening.

Zhao did not hesitate. She raced inside.

David Okada watched on the holo display as Validus-V raised its foot again and stepped back, leaving the smoking remains of Torander-X's head crushed flat on the sands.

"Holy cow," he breathed, in awe at the sheer power, the sheer violence the Titan was capable of.

Putting that aside, he returned his thoughts to his brother. It had been a little while since he'd been able to check on him.

"Validus," he said, "how's David?"

The border around the holo display turned yellow, and a series of small squares appeared across the bottom. Most of them were yellow as well; a few were green, which seemed promising. Just a few, however, were red. If this was a representation of his brother's medical condition–and the sense he got from his mental connection to Validus seemed to indicate that it was–it concerned David greatly.

He considered for a moment. "If I hadn't been lucky just now, we could both be in intensive care," he said to himself. "We can't have any more of these attacks. I need to get them to stop."

Would they listen, though? Every time he'd tried to communicate with the other pilots, so far, they'd responded by trying to kill him. But things were different now; Zhao was out of her robot–which was totally incapacitated. If ever there was a moment to talk to her–to try to reason with her–this appeared to be it.

Yes. He wanted to talk to her. Person to person, without all the electronic stuff in between them.

He stood up from the control seat, took one step–then realized he had no idea how to do that.

"Validus," he said aloud. "How do I get down?"

A red border appeared around his display.

"What is that?" David asked. "Is that a 'no'?"

The red border remained.

"You don't want me going down there?"

Red border still.

"Well, I don't care. I'm going down, even if I have to climb down your back."

Nothing.

David considered what he'd just threatened to do. Frankly, the thought of trying to climb down the exterior of the big robot scared him to death. And that was even assuming Validus remained still long enough for him to attempt such a thing. If it moved while he was climbing...!

And beyond that–how even to get outside?

David remembered then how Zhao had escaped from her robot before Validus crushed its head. She'd used a hatch–a hatch located about where its ear would be. Was this robot designed the same way?

He moved around to the side of the command deck and, sure enough, found the escape hatch. The controls were simple and obvious. He tapped a couple of squares and the hatch slid open. Howling wind blew through and into the command deck. Terrified, gripping the edges of the opening tightly, David forced himself to lean out and look. He saw a drop of more than three hundred feet to the beach below.

Validus was clearly unhappy about this. The red border on the display flashed rapidly and an alarm sounded.

"I won't be gone long," David promised. "But you have to let me try to talk to her."

The light and sound persisted for another few seconds, while mentally David focused on what he wanted to do, making it clear to any big blue robots that might be sharing his brain with him at the moment that he was *not* going to back down from this.

The red light at last went away and the alarm switched off. Instead, a green light flashed above the open hatch. David took this as his cue to exit. Steeling his nerves, he climbed out onto Validus's right shoulder, holding on carefully. He looked around; there was quite a view from up here. And the wind was blowing stronger than ever. He started to reconsider the idea of climbing down.

Just then a massive, blue hand came up and stopped against the shoulder, palm open and facing up. It was the Titan's left hand; Validus's left arm was bent at the elbow and crossed diagonally over its chest. What it wanted was obvious. David carefully let go of the handholds and stepped onto the hand, moving to the center of the palm. Inside his flight suit, he could feel cold sweat running down his spine.

Gently, so gently, the huge hand moved away from the shoulder. As the robot knelt, it slowly lowered its left hand to the ground. David barely felt it when it touched the beach. He hopped off and stood in the sand, looking around. He was embarrassed to realize he hadn't figured out how to track Zhao before he'd "abandoned robot."

"Where did she go?" he asked.

Still linked with David via the wireless connection with his helmet, Validus caused the helmet's visor display to show the path Zhao had taken into the brush.

"Wow," he breathed. "That's amazing."

Without another thought or word, David scampered into the grove of trees, following the path the robot had revealed.

CHAPTER 11

He beat Zhao," breathed Sir Anthony Graven as he stared up at the three-dimensional images that dominated the control room, located deep inside Mt. Jaru on Rapa Hoi. He shook his head in astonishment. "The child was able to defeat Wen Zhao and Torander-X."

"Perhaps we underestimated him," said the shadowy figure at his side.

"Perhaps we recruited the wrong brother," Graven snapped. He bit his lip and turned back to the screen. A British man in his mid-fifties, Graven had sandy blond hair and a slight build. He wore a brown tweed suit and red tie, and held a pipe in his right hand. Small round glasses perched on his nose.

Around and above him floated a hemispherical holographic display, some forty meters in diameter and twenty meters high. With it he was currently watching the events transpiring on the island of Rapa Lau, the island home of their secondary base, many hundreds of kilometers to the north.

In particular, he was staring in open-mouthed shock at the images of Validus-V stomping the head of Wen Zhao's Titan flat.

"No," Visser said, shaking his head. Appearing to be his early forties, Visser was shorter and more heavy-set than the professor, with close-cropped dark hair and darker eyes. His white lab coat was streaked with oil stains.

"No, it must have been a fluke," Visser went on. "There is no way a mere boy could know how to control Validus-V, nor could he learn to be so effective with the Titan so quickly."

"One would think that is so," the professor said. He gestured toward the display. "But yet there lies Torander, its head flattened."

Visser had no response to this.

"How," Graven demanded, his voice now raised to almost a shout. "could a—a mere *child*—get the better of Wen Zhao? How could he pilot Validus-V to victory, never having been aboard a Titan before?"

"Do we know all of that is true, Professor?"

"What?"

"Perhaps," Visser suggested, "Okada allowed his little brother aboard before? Perhaps more than once? Enough times, in fact, to allow him to learn the rudiments of controlling a Titan and using one in battle?"

"We have no reason to think that, Ian," Graven said. His anger was already fading to general annoyance—a condition he often found himself in, when Visser was around. "I ordered the computers to execute a high-speed scan of all records of Validus-V over the past six months. As best as we can tell, this was the first time he had his brother aboard."

"And he performs this well the first time he ever boards a Titan?" Visser frowned at this and shook his head. "I don't believe it. It's impossible."

Graven's anger had almost entirely evaporated by now. He was moving back into comfortable territory: debating a colleague over research findings. He took out his pipe and lit it, then puffed a cloud of smoke that quickly merged with the holographic display surrounding them.

"Which part is impossible?" Graven asked mildly. "That John's brother could instinctively know how to operate the Titan, or that the Titan would allow him to do so?"

"All of it," Visser replied.

"You're just angry the Titans won't synch up with *you*," Graven said with a chuckle.

Visser scowled at him. "That won't be the case for much longer," he snapped. "I'll yet crack their codes, and override their lockout systems, and *then* they'll obey me. *Us*, I mean. You and I. And the others on the team."

Graven eyed him with a bit of concern momentarily, then shrugged. "Perhaps, Ian. Perhaps. But, until then, we are limited to the few—the very, very few—individuals we have found who are compatible with them; able to operate them at all." He shrugged. "These machines are complex. There's more to them than you think."

Visser let out an exasperated sound and shook his head. "They don't have *souls*, Anthony. We both know *that*. They're just machines, same as a bulldozer or a bus. I don't understand why you insist on imbuing them with human characteristics."

"So you do at least concede that *we* have souls, then?" Graven asked, a twinkle in his eye.

Visser scowled again and turned away, studying the holographic imagery that covered every inch of the dome they occupied. The visuals were being displayed in real time, captured by tiny, hidden satellites left behind in Earth orbit by the alien Ahlwhen, creators of the Titans and the bases.

Graven chuckled and relit his pipe, then smoked in silence for a couple of minutes as Visser continued to glare at the display.

"At least Zhao escaped," Graven noted finally. "And they are on Rapa Lau. She should be able to address her situation somewhat quickly there."

Visser nodded slowly. "Still," he said, "that doesn't mean we shouldn't provide her with some help."

"Help?" Graven glanced at his assistant. "Our data network here doesn't reach to Rapa Lau," he noted. "The computer banks and all the equipment and replacement parts on that island are isolated from us here. Isolated and automated."

"Doesn't matter," Visser said. "We have other resources at our disposal."

"But what assistance can we–ah," Graven said, understanding. "You mean *non-mechanical* help."

"I do indeed," Visser said with a curt nod.

"You know I have never been entirely comfortable with your research into those areas," Graven said. "It all smacks of the Xovaren."

If you only knew, Visser thought to himself.

"I believe it is our only option at present, Professor," Visser said aloud.

The professor considered this for a moment. "Very well," he said. "Do it."

In response, Visser strode around to the other side of a control console and tapped out a string of commands on its keyboard.

"It is done," he said.

"How long?" Graven asked.

Visser studied the information shown on the console displays.

"Not long. Gamaron is close by. And he can move very quickly when called upon to do so." He grinned. "Between Torander-X and Gamaron, the boy will soon be finished."

Graven was frowning.

"Yes?" Visser asked. He knew that look. "What is it?"

"I want to be absolutely certain," Graven said, "of the child's defeat. Prep Z-Zatala, Ian."

"Him, too?" Visser's eyes were wide. "Isn't that perhaps a bit of overkill?"

Graven waved a dismissive hand. "I don't care," he said. "Just do it." He turned to a technician working at the next console. "Notify Sajjadi he will be launching in five minutes."

"Yes, Professor." The woman got up and hurried away.

Graven looked back at Visser. "Top off everything—fuel, ammunition, everything. And make sure Sajjadi is on his game, not messing around. I don't want any more surprises. Do you understand me?"

"Of course," the assistant replied smoothly.

"Gamaron and Z-Zatala should make short work of the child and his rebellious robot," Graven said between puffs of his pipe. "Let us see how the boy does against both types of enemies—mechanical and organic." He paused, then, "That is, if Wen Zhao hasn't finished the job first. She could still surprise us."

"I don't know that I trust her any longer to be successful," Visser replied. "It may be time to find a new pilot for Torander-X."

"Zhao will come through, once she repairs her Titan," the professor said. "I still have confidence in her."

Visser merely frowned and looked away.

"Well, she has only a short time to prove it now," he said.

Before them, the display was now split three ways. One view continued to be of Torander-X lying face-down on the beach as Validus-V towered over it. The second screen showed the purple and black form of Z-Zatala being prepared for launch nearby. The third screen showed empty ocean—though perhaps not entirely empty. For at the center of the picture was just visible a trail of bubbles and a wake, as though something massive were moving swiftly through the deep waters. Something massive—and terrible.

CHAPTER 12

David followed Zhao's trail until it led right up to the blank side of a cliff face. It was dark, to the point that he almost ran right into the stone wall, and only became aware of it at the last instant.

"Where did she go?" he asked.

On the other end of the wireless connection, Validus-V offered no response. But the slowly fading afterimages detected by the Titan's sensors and displayed as an overlay in his helmet's light-amplifying visor revealed that the footprints came to the wall of stone, moved briefly to the right, and then vanished. David frowned and studied the trail. It was almost as if...

He followed the steps that led to his right and reached out, running his fingertips over the stone. Nothing... Nothing... *Wait.*

There. A recessed area, perfectly rectangular, obscured by a clump of brush.

David reached into it, felt something–a lever? He pulled it.

The hidden door recessed, dropped.

He stared through the opening into a darkened space of indeterminate size. A second passed; another. Before the third had come and gone, he had made up his mind and hurried inside.

+   +   +

Wen Zhao made her way across the broad concrete floor. It was fairly dark, with only a few emergency lights burning here and there. Fortunately, she knew the layout well enough not to need the full lighting, and she hadn't wanted to spare the time it would take to locate the main switches and turn them on.

She had taken the elevator down from the much smaller entry room and into the cavernous main hangar and warehouse section of the base, located hundreds of feet beneath the surface. Rapa Lau was the backup to the main Titan base on Rapa Hoi. It was smaller but was equipped with the most critical systems, backups and replacement parts. She and the other pilots had spent enough time here for her to have gotten a good feel for the layout.

Now she stood back and gazed up through the gloom at the wall of shelves and cubby holes–shelves and cubby holes seemingly made for a person three hundred feet tall. Stored on those shelves and in those cubby holes were parts the size of jet fighters and semi-trucks, all painted in various combinations of colors, including blue and silver, green and orange, purple and black, and red and gold–all the colors of the four Titans. Many other generic replacement parts of metal and crystal were stacked in and among those components.

Zhao felt panic rising up in her chest. She could see massive batteries, weapons, and ammunition–lots and lots of ammunition. But where was what she needed? Surely it was here. Surely. But–*where?*

Then she saw it. There, high up and to her left. It was mostly white, but with green stripes down the sides and orange trim. And it looked like a stubby aircraft, at least from this angle. Turning her head slightly and staring at it, it came to look more like a head. A very *big* head. A very *familiar* big head.

She ran to the near end of the bottom row of items, beneath the corner of the first shelf. There on the floor was a disk of metal about five feet across, with a circular railing parallel to it, about three feet above it. She stepped onto the disk and reached out to tap the controls on the railing in front of her. In response, the disk, which was essentially an open elevator, rose smoothly and carried her up.

She'd made it about forty feet up, having just passed the first shelf, when movement below caught her eye. She leaned over the railing and looked down.

David Okada had just run into the chamber.

Frowning, she reached for her gun.

"What is this place?"

David had found the elevator in the upper entry room quickly enough. He'd figured out how to get down to the bottom of the huge storage facility with only minimal hints over the connection with Validus. Emerging from it, he'd looked out and then up in awe.

"It—it's got to be a robot *workshop*," he breathed.

Indeed, the huge, dimly-lit chamber did resemble a workshop, but one designed for giants. David stepped out of the elevator and turned in a slow circle, taking in the rows of components, segments and spare parts that filled only a portion of the massive space.

A whirr off to his left caused him to look over and see, despite the low lighting, a lithe, helmeted figure in gray running toward the far wall–the wall covered with what appeared to be gigantic shelves.

He recognized the person, having just seen her a short time earlier. It was Wen Zhao. Her helmet was white and was striped with green and orange instead of blue like his. She hopped onto a little mini-elevator of some kind, and it began to lift her up.

"Ma'am," he called up to her, stepping out to where she could see him, "I don't want to fight anymore. I just want to talk. To understand what's going on. And my brother needs help, too."

The lift stopped moving and the Chinese woman gazed down at him through the dark visor. David realized then that she held something in her right hand–a weapon of some kind, possibly. He scampered quickly around behind a piece of machinery on the concrete floor and peeked out at her.

"Please," he called. "I haven't done anything! You all just attacked us, for no reason!"

Wen Zhao stared down at him, but she didn't shoot.

"Can we just talk? Please?"

The woman hesitated another moment, then holstered her gun.

"There is no point in talking with a traitor," she said.

"Traitor?" David shook his head, as much in confusion as in disagreement. "Traitor to who? To *what?*"

"You have been corrupted by the enemies of Earth," Wen Zhao stated.

David was even more confused. "Ma'am, I had just gotten aboard Validus right before you all attacked us. I'd never even heard of any of this before John picked me up. I really don't know what you're talking about!" He hesitated, then added, "But one thing I can tell you for sure is, John Okada is no traitor. He never would be. You've got this all wrong!"

Zhao listened to the boy's words, and to the tone of them. He certainly sounded sincere. But it could simply be that the enemy had brainwashed him to the point that he sincerely believed everything he was saying. Still…

Then she had an idea.

"If you are as innocent as you claim," she called down to him, "then you should want to get help for your brother, as quickly as possible."

"I do," he agreed.

"So go back to Validus and get John, and bring him down here to me. I will see that he is properly tended to."

David shook his head. "No way, lady. I don't trust you that much."

Zhao shrugged. "Then we have nothing more to discuss."

She started to turn back to the lift controls. But then a blinding headache struck her, nearly driving her to her knees. She reeled, clutching at the helmet she still wore.

"Are you okay, ma'am?" David called up to her.

"I…" She couldn't speak. Something was assaulting her. Something was trying to force its way into her mind.

"No!" she screamed. "Stay out of my head!"

Frantically she tore at the helmet, and only after several flailing attempts did she manage to remove it. The pain stopped and she leaned there against the railing, panting. Sweat dripped down her forehead.

What had *that* been? What had attacked her?

The local network, she realized. It was the local computer network. She recalled then that Rapa Lau's super-advanced computer network was entirely separate from the one back at their main base, inside Rapa Hoi. That meant the evil influence that had taken over John Okada must still be *here*, inside the Rapa Lau system. Graven said he was able to protect the main Rapa Hoi network from it, but he had yet to travel here to the Rapa Lau backup base to eradicate it here. And now here she was, walking right into its trap. And, sure enough, it was beaming itself at her via its wireless signal, trying to get to her through her helmet. Trying to corrupt her mind, the way it had corrupted John Okada, and probably this kid, his little brother.

"No!" she cried out, her face scrunched up in revulsion. And then, softer, "No." It had been close–entirely too close. She tried to calm herself. She felt the helmet she was holding in her hands; she reminded herself she was no longer wearing it, so she was safe for the moment. The corrupted programming couldn't get access to her brain without the interface devices inside that helmet.

"Are you okay?" the kid was asking her again. He was still mostly hiding behind the machinery. Why was he being so… *concerned?* Was it all just an act? It *had* to be…

"You don't need to worry about me," she called back down to him as she activated the lift to continue carrying her upwards. "I'm fine."

Shelf after shelf went by, until she stood some three hundred feet above the concrete floor. When it reached the top and stopped, she smiled down at him. "And we will deal with *you* soon enough."

But even as she spoke those words, something inside her head whispered that she had it all wrong. Had every bit of it wrong…

David watched as Wen Zhao stepped off the lift and strode purposefully toward a big, curved shape that was parked on the top shelf. From what he could tell in the dim lighting, it was glossy white with orange and green stripes, just like the helmet she'd just removed. She walked up to it and stood there waiting for something. Whatever it was, it must not have happened, because he heard her exclaim wordlessly and reach out with her hand to tap at the surface. Again, nothing happened.

David started to shout something to her, but then a voice called out to him. It seemed to come from all around him.

He spun around, looking for the source of the sounds. It was dark in the big chamber, but not *that* dark. He didn't see anyone there.

The words continued, but David couldn't understand them. They were in no language he'd ever heard before. After a few seconds of this, they stopped–only to be replaced by words in English. And he understood then that he was hearing them by way of the speakers built into his helmet.

"This is Rapa Lau Reserve Base Computer Network. New user has been detected. Stand by."

"Hello?" David said back to it. "Who's there?"

"Identify," the voice said.

"Um–I'm David Okada. John's brother," he added quickly.

A pause, then the mechanical-sounding voice repeated, "David Okada. Brother of pilot John Okada. Scanned identification confirmed. Welcome to Rapa Lau, David Okada."

"Thank you," David said automatically.

"Preparing background briefing for new recruit."

"What? New recruit? No–I'm just John's brother. And he needs help–"

"Network connection with Validus-V reveals John Okada is currently receiving full medical treatment aboard that Titan."

"Oh, okay," David said. "So we can leave him in there for–"

"Background briefing commences now," the voice went on.

"But what about Wen Zh–"

The world around David Okada turned upside down.

Up on the top shelf, three hundred feet above where David stood, Wen Zhao was tapping instructions on the side panel of the unit in front of her and growling in the back of her throat.

"Come on," she hissed. "Come on!"

Nothing was happening. For the life of her, she couldn't understand why the backup unit wouldn't open. Then she realized she'd taken her helmet off. Without the network uplink it provided, the base's computers, as well as the Titans and their component parts, couldn't communicate with her. Or, apparently, recognize her.

She held the helmet up before her face and studied it nervously.

She didn't want to put it back on. The network here on Rapa Lau was obviously corrupted by the enemy. It had tried to get into her head a short time earlier, and she'd barely kept it at bay. No, the last thing she wanted to do was to put that helmet back on, and open herself up to another mental assault.

But she knew she had to. She couldn't control her Titan–or even gain access to this replacement component–without it. Without a connection to the network.

If she put it back on, maybe the corrupted network would get control of her–and maybe it wouldn't.

But if she *didn't* put it back on, her Titan would remain incapacitated and dormant on the beach, and she'd remain stuck here inside the big storage vault, until the professor or someone else from Rapa Hoi came along and purged the local computer network. And rescued her.

Rescued *her*.

No.

She was the pilot of a Titan. People didn't rescue *her*. *She* rescued *people*. And defeated enemies of the Earth.

There was no way she was going to just sit there and wait for one of the others to come and save her. No way at all.

In the final analysis, the choice was easier for her than it had any right to be.

Steeling her nerves, gritting her teeth, Wen Zhao lifted the helmet up and pulled it down over her head. It snapped into place. A couple of seconds later, its components had tapped into the local network.

She braced herself for the mental onslaught she dreaded, but it didn't come.

After several long seconds of crouching there, holding her breath, eyes closed, face twisted in a grimace as she prepared to fight back, she slowly exhaled, opened her eyes, and stood up straight.

Why hadn't it assaulted her again?

Maybe it's preparing to, she thought. That means I have to move now—move quickly, before it gets the chance!

This time, when Zhao looked at the side panel of the craft next to her, it instantly slid open and allowed her in.

She stepped through into the unit and closed the hatch behind her. The interior was dark but rows of multicolored lights flared to life as she came around and fitted herself into the pilot's seat, strapping in.

"You know where to go," she said out loud.

The white, green and orange vehicle rose smoothly and almost silently from its shelf, floated out over the three-hundred-foot drop, and then zoomed along the chamber and up a concealed access port. From there it emerged into the bright sunlight above Rapa Lau.

As the flying vehicle curved around the ridge and over to the side of the island where she'd originally entered the hidden base, she saw Torander's virtually headless body lying there on the beach, immobile. A pang of sadness knifed through her.

"Hang on," she whispered to her big robot as she flew the craft down toward it. "Mama's coming."

She swooped the craft down until she was about a hundred feet away from the Titan's body. As her aircraft circled above, she silently willed a certain set of commands, while tapping out orders on the control panel before her. At the same time, the stricken robot began to move, to rise. Sand that had blown across it poured off, and seabirds that had landed on it squawked and took rapid, terrified flight.

When it had gotten up on its hands and knees, Zhao issued another command, and the old, flattened head popped off and tumbled down to the sands.

"No time to dispose of that properly," she whispered to herself as she continued to issue orders.

The green and orange body struggled up to its feet, the last of the sand falling from its segmented form. When it was fully upright, Zhao maneuvered her flying vehicle around and then down until it made contact with the open neck socket and latched in, whereupon it tilted back ninety degrees as a number of panels and components shifted into different configurations. Within a matter of seconds, her aircraft had become an identical copy of the Titan's head.

Just like that, Torander-X was whole again.

Over the connection, Zhao could feel the entire robot's body awaken as its new head connected with its original body.

And that was when the Rapa Lau computer network determined that it should make its move.

Over the wireless connection with the underground base, the computer system surged into Zhao's mind, and into the robot she controlled.

Zhao felt it. She realized with a start that a mental force was now racing through the wireless connection and toward her, into her brain. She reacted viscerally, terrified of what was happening. Torander-X mirrored her actions, thrashing about wildly.

"No!" she screamed. "No! Stop!"

Even as she clawed at her helmet, trying to remove it, she clamped her eyes closed and gritted her teeth, as if that might somehow break the mental connection, or deflect the incoming onslaught.

Torander-X, meanwhile, lifted off, then rocketed sideways until it collided with the mountain that covered and concealed the secret base. The big robot flattened a grove of palm trees, scraped out a massive ditch as it slid, and finally came to rest in a sitting position against the cliff face. The impact tossed Zhao roughly about the seat and was enough to nearly knock her unconscious— which was just the opening the network had been waiting for.

It attacked.

CHAPTER 13

The network knew it had to act. It couldn't allow this conflict between Titans to continue until one was destroyed—or perhaps both. And it couldn't abide another minute of tolerating the tainted, corrupted Xovaren programming to exist and potentially propagate there within the otherwise secure grounds of this Ahlwhen sanctuary.

Though the potential for injury to Wen Zhao loomed as a distinct possibility, the network concluded that intervention—*strong* intervention—was warranted.

It must act.

It must speak.

Now.

The Network did not *want* to assault Wen Zhao. Truth be told, the backup branch of the Ahlwhen computer complex–the one that existed behind impenetrable firewalls situated miles beneath Rapa Lau–would have been quite content to never be called upon, never accessed, never used at all. To allow the main system on Rapa Hoi to do all the work, and gain all the glory. It would have been happy to never represent the last chance of Earth; the last chance of preventing humanity from falling entirely under Xovaren domination. It was, after all, a mere backup system. In all the centuries that the Ahlwhen and their giant robot creations had been stationed on Earth, the Rapa Lau Network had never been called upon for anything more than occasional maintenance and repair subroutines within the island's huge warehouse and workshop. Not that the computer system spent much time speculating on its role; but, if it had, it would've surely agreed that its function was to stand by and wait. Forever.

But something had changed recently. Something within the main computer complex on the primary headquarters island of Rapa Hoi. Something had corrupted those computers, and by extension, any human or thinking machine connected to them.

It was obvious now to the Rapa Lau backup network that some previously-unknown Xovaren corruption had wormed its way into and eventually overrun the primary computers on Rapa Hoi. Whatever that corruption was, it had affected three of the Titans and their pilots, and it had affected Professor Graven. None of them were currently behaving in a manner recognizable to the corruption-free backup network.

And now, of course, that corruption wanted to gain access to the backup network. It wanted to finish the job, by corrupting the backup network in the same way it had the primary.

But the backup network, there on Rapa Lau, wasn't going to allow that. Not as long as someone remained who could and would fight to protect it; fight to oppose the corrupting influence and programming.

The backup network had hoped that person would be John Okada. It had lightly touched John's mind as he'd flown Validus-V past Rapa Lau a couple of days earlier, and the network had reassured itself that John and Validus remained themselves.

Unfortunately, things had not gone as the Rapa Lau network had hoped. A completely unforeseen possibility had occurred: John was injured and out of the action—at least for the moment; possibly for much longer—and his little brother, a teen-aged boy with zero experience piloting a Titan, was all that was left.

Well, not all. For Wen Zhao had made the tactical error of entering the warehouse beneath Rapa Lau, where the network's signal was strongest. So perhaps she could yet be turned back to the side of the Ahlwhen. But perhaps not.

In the meantime, the Network had to get young David Okada up to speed on everything he needed to know in order to fight the Xovaren; to effectively serve as a Titan pilot. If only for a short while.

The massive computer banks prepared to lay out centuries of information for David in as quick a burst of data as his mind could handle.

At the same time, those giant machines increased the amount of attention they were paying to the Chinese woman who piloted Torander-X.

Her head spinning, Zhao blinked her eyes furiously and reached up again to try to remove the helmet.

You must listen, came the almost-words of the network. It didn't speak to her in English—or in any other verbal language—but the intent the signal carried to her was clear and unmistakable. *You have been deceived,* it said.

"*You're* trying to deceive me *now,*" Zhao shot back. She again cursed herself for putting the helmet on, though she knew she'd had little choice. "You want to trick me, to fool me. But I won't listen!"

You must, the almost-voice echoing within her brain said. *There is precious little time left. We can no longer afford the luxury of allowing you to be misled.*

The force pressing against her mind became unbearable, overwhelming.

And then, for Zhao, everything went white.

Wen Zhao was not the only one communicating with the Network on Rapa Lau at that moment–nor the only one it was attempting to influence.

To any reasonable onlooker, David Okada appeared to be experiencing a seizure. He stood in the middle of the massive storage vault and staggered about, as if stricken blind, seemingly unaware of his surroundings. Indeed, the world beyond his own head had lost all meaning. For him, now, there was only the mental world at the moment—the world where he was seeing, hearing, and experiencing everything.

The thoughts, the words, the images came to him in a flash; years of events and actions hyper-compressed into a minutes-long burst of data, force-fed into his brain. It might have killed a lesser mind, a weaker body, from the sheer force and shock of it all. It well could have driven him mad. The network knew this; it understood the risks it was taking. But time was of the essence, and this young man increasingly appeared to be the last, best hope available before the other side in the ancient conflict prevailed. The network therefore judged the risks as within acceptable parameters.

David Okada needed to know the story. He needed to understand—and to fully appreciate—exactly what he'd gotten involved in.

So the Rapa Lau network told him the story, beginning with how Professor Anthony Graven first came to Rapa Hoi, and first found the four mighty Titans.

It began in January of 1958…

CHAPTER 14

Rapa Hoi, January, 1958:
The fog swirled before him, forming grotesque shapes in the twilight as it mingled with the smoke from his pipe.

A twenty-year-younger Professor Anthony Graven stood at the bow of the *HMS Redoubtable* and cursed the weather as he attempted to ignite another match to re-light his pipe. Before him, barely visible in the mist, reared up the central peaks of the island he'd been searching for these last ten years and more. Or, at least, he hoped it would prove to be that island.

This particular voyage, which had originally been organized and launched as a part of the International Geophysical Year activities of 1957, had continued into the following year at his behest, and was now largely funded by him. The journey had gone on for three months at this point, their ship feverishly crisscrossing and surveying the Pacific. Along the way, they'd alighted on plenty of islands, some known and some heretofore unknown–but none of them had proven to be the one.

This island, though–this one held the most promise of all they'd encountered thus far.

Three great peaks rising up from the island's interior, including a central point, taller than the others, that might well be the fabled Mt. Jaru. Yes, that matched. And that mist-shrouded peak stood due west of a C-shaped lagoon that was broader on the eastern side than on the western—just as the old documents had indicated.

Could it be? Could this be the island for which he'd searched so very long? For which he'd passed up appointments to the faculty of Oxford and Cambridge, instead taking much of his family's fortune and plunging it into what his sisters and many of his friends charitably described as a "wild goose chase"?

Anthony Graven considered those opinions only momentarily before shoving them out of his mind for the thousandth time. He knew what he was doing. He'd known from the start—from the moment a grizzled old explorer, largely discredited by his peers many years earlier and rendered almost penniless, had pressed into Graven's hands a set of ancient documents, along with an odd, ancient-looking telescope. The documents told of an island hidden somewhere in the Pacific—an island filled with treasures beyond understanding; treasures that would serve as the key to power undreamt of. Power that would be needed, and very soon, if the rest of the ancient story turned out to be true.

"They are returning, Anthony," the old man had told him. "I have translated dozens of ancient texts now, and they all indicate the same thing: they are returning."

"They? Who?" Graven had demanded. "*Who* is returning?"

The old man had shaken his wooly head and then looked up at Graven with red, bloodshot, glaring eyes. "The outsiders. The *aliens*."

"Aliens?"

"The Xovaren." The old man had pronounced the word, the name, very carefully. "They are an evil; a plague on the stars. They came here once before, long ago, and left behind terrible, monstrous things. Now they are returning. We must be ready."

Graven had scoffed at all of this as the ravings of a lunatic, at least for a while. But he'd reluctantly agreed to review the old man's documents. Slowly at first, but with increasing fervor and conviction, he'd translated them himself and studied them in detail. He, unlike almost everyone else who had looked upon them, came to believe almost immediately that they were not fakes, not frauds. They were genuine.

He no longer scoffed at what the old man had said.

He had been mere months out of school himself, the ink still drying on his PhD diploma, but he had set everything aside: his estate, his new job, and his future. His life became reoriented around a singular focus. He was determined to be the one to find that island, to unearth its treasures, and to claim its power. No matter the cost.

For the past decade he'd cajoled, begged and borrowed in order to finance and launch a grand expedition to the South Pacific. The first voyage had spiraled slowly out from the Hawaiian Islands, taking weeks, but had resulted in no new discoveries. The second voyage had traveled mostly to the southwest of Hawaii, in the direction of Tuvalu and the Solomons. Again, no joy.

This time, he'd had Captain Osterman strike first for Kiribati, and then continue on, angling to the east, heading into the great emptiness that stretched all the way to the shores of Chile and Peru.

They'd made landfall briefly at Bora-Bora and then at Rapa Iti, taking on meager supplies each time. Afterward they'd ventured another two hundred miles or more into the endless blue, and for the past week Graven had been tempted to conclude that perhaps he'd been wrong after all; perhaps it was all a hoax, a great joke.

But then, earlier that morning, using the strange telescope Graven had been given by the old explorer, the lookout had spotted land–land where none had previously been known. Rapa Hoi, the mysterious lost island was supposed to be called, and that was what Graven christened this one. Soon they would know whether he had granted it the appropriate appellation or not.

"Seems promising," Captain Osterman said as he strode up beside Graven at the ship's prow. He tossed the remains of his cigarette overboard and gave the professor a sidelong look. "Matches the descriptions you gave me."

Graven said nothing.

The captain's mouth turned upward in a wry grin. "You think this is it, don't you?"

The professor never took his eyes off the peaks in the distance. "Perhaps," he said quietly. "Would you assemble a team, please? I'd like to go ashore as soon as possible."

Grunting, the captain nodded once and set off to do just that.

Graven felt the excitement growing inside him, though nothing showed through to the surface. "Perhaps," he said again, to no one.

The morning fog had mostly burned away by the time Captain Osterman had assembled a team to accompany Graven onto Rapa Hoi.

The professor still stood at the prow. A leather satchel hung over one shoulder and he wore an oilskin safari hat on his head, to match his tan jacket, dark trousers and boots. His pipe was alight and he puffed at it while watching as five other men, all seasoned sailors and roughnecks, reported for duty on the main deck.

Osterman stood before them, hands on hips, and explained their duties—duties they knew all too well at this point, given the previous landings they'd made on the voyage. Then the sailors lowered the launch into the water and helped the professor aboard. From there they set out, rowing hard, riding the breakers that carried them across the lagoon and onto the beach. After dragging the boat a safe distance onto the shore and retrieving their supplies and weapons, the six of them moved warily into the steaming jungle.

They kept their rifles at the ready, fearing attack by some sort of wild animal, but such concerns proved baseless. Birds there were aplenty, but nothing on four legs. Deeper into the brush they continued, for what must have been an hour or more. The going was slow to begin with and soon became even slower, as the foliage grew so thick they could no longer find a path through it and had to resort to unsheathing their machetes and hacking a sort of tunnel before them. Even the professor took a turn chopping at the dense tropical growth.

Graven had moved to the middle of their group and was struggling to light his pipe when the men at the front cried out. Frowning, he packed his pipe away and hurried to see what had caused them to exclaim so.

A sheer stone wall stood before them, gray-brown and smooth. The sailors had chopped away the brush a good five feet to either side of their path. Even so, the full extent of the wall was unknowable; it continued off into the jungle on both sides and towered up while curving away, until it was lost to view.

"Looks like the end of the road, professor," the sailor to Graven's left said with a chortle.

"Perhaps," Graven replied. He opened the flap of his satchel and reached inside, drawing out a small, leatherbound book of indeterminate vintage. He opened it and flipped through several pages until he stopped and squinted down at one in particular. In the dim lighting of their jungle "tunnel," he struggled to make out the words and drawings–some copied from other sources, some he had added himself.

The sailors grew restless; it was stifling beneath the jungle canopy. The humidity pressed down on them like a hot, wet blanket. "Back to the ship, then?" asked one of them.

"Not just yet," Graven replied. He continued to study the little book, occasionally looking up at the stone cliff face and running his hand over it.

The sailors eyed one another nervously. They were somewhat accustomed to the professor's eccentric behavior, but none of them knew what to make of this.

"Ah," Graven said at last. His fingers traced along a remarkably straight vertical line in the stone face, as if the rock had split during an earthquake. "And then I am to do this," he muttered to himself, pressing against the left-hand side of the split.

"Professor, we need to get back to–" one of the sailors began. Then he abruptly shut himself up.

The wall in front of Graven was moving. Smoothly, silently, a rectangular panel of rock slid to the left, until it had revealed an opening some twenty feet high and the same distance wide.

Graven did not so much as glance back at the now-stunned sailors. Instead he strode purposefully into the dark space that had been revealed. The others followed him in a much more deliberate fashion, moving slowly and brandishing their weapons as they went.

The lighting outside had been dim, but what greeted the professor inside this strange space was far darker. Graven waited for his eyes to adjust to the surroundings, even as the sailors came up next to him, guns in hand.

"Gentlemen," he said in a low but firm tone as he became aware of their presence, and that of their guns, "please—put your firearms away. If this is the place I believe it to be, there will be no threats, no enemies here."

Slowly and with great reluctance the sailors stowed their weapons. They did, however, remain on their guard.

At last everyone's eyes had become accustomed to the darkness. Graven ventured deeper into the open space beneath the mountain, occasionally pausing to look over the notes in his little book. Each time, he pushed ahead again, as if once more assured of his actions. No one could tell the size of the space they occupied; given the echoes whenever one of them spoke, it seemed quite large.

As they moved along, they passed an area to their right that was separated from them not by a wall but by a sort of chain-link fence. The chain-links, however, were at least as thick as the arm of the largest sailor in the company. And the fencing, if that was indeed what it was, extended far up above them, lost in the shadows of the distant ceiling.

After traveling quite a distance, Graven came to a squared column about two feet to a side, anchored to the floor and extending up into the unknowable distance above them. It appeared to have been carved out of a single piece of crystal. He checked the notes in his little book, then put it away and pressed his open hand to the side of the column. Then he said, "Lights."

And there was light. Not a harsh glare but a smooth glow filled the vast chamber—and vast it was, indeed. The ceiling was still barely visible, hundreds of feet above them. The far wall was a similar distance away. Both were encrusted with more crystalline growths, and those were what had lit up, through some arcane means, at the professor's command.

One of the sailors cried out in surprise. The others looked where he was looking, and instantly the entire group was on their guard again.

The professor hurried around them to see what had caught their attention.

What the sailors had been startled by was what looked to be a group of four men standing in a semicircle at the far end of the chamber, almost entirely obscured by darkness and shadows. Or– were they men at all? At first, Graven and the sailors struggled to comprehend what they were seeing there. They appeared to be men; they were the general shape of men, though covered in some kind of armor of different colors. But the proportions of the chamber didn't quite match, down there, where the heads of the four unmoving figures nearly touched the ceiling. It created an impression that the room got much smaller at that end. That was the only sense the sailors' brains could make of what they were seeing: that far end of the room had to be a lot smaller, because the alternative was that these four men were several hundred feet tall. And that made no sense at all.

With an effort, Graven tore his eyes away from the armored man-shapes. He had become aware of another thing of note in front of them–this one much closer. It was a pedestal of some sort, about three feet tall and made of dark gray metal, situated only about twenty feet ahead and off to the right. Resting on top of the pedestal was a helmet. A dim light played down onto the pedestal and the helmet from somewhere far above.

While the sailors continued to gawk at the giant man-shapes, Graven hurried forward, grasped the helmet, and lifted it off the pedestal. It matched the description in his little book exactly. He held it before him, knowing there was no force in the universe at that moment that could stop him from doing what he was about to do. He'd searched for too long, jeopardized too much, sacrificed almost all that he had for this one opportunity–this chance to learn. To *know.*

This was what he'd come halfway around the globe for. Just as had been described in his little book; the book he'd painstakingly assembled from rumors and whispers and barely-recovered fragments of texts thousands of years old, in many different languages, from many different places.

The secret of this island–of this chamber beneath this island, and of all that lay within it–was a secret that mankind had remained mostly ignorant of for millennia. But, after the prompting of his grizzled old colleague, Graven had found enough bits and pieces to work out at least the basics. Now, if the fragments of information that had led him here continued to be true just a little longer, and with the benefit of this helmet, he would at last know the truth. The complete truth.

He raised the helmet high and brought it down towards his head.

One of the sailors, seeing what he was doing, moved to stop him, perhaps sensing danger. Graven shoved the man aside and pulled the metallic silver helmet over his head.

No words came to him, but he could still sense instantly the thoughts being shared somehow.

Welcome, he understood he was being told. And, *We have waited a very long time for another human to come here.*

"Show me," he whispered.

Prepare for data burst.

Professor Anthony Graven smiled grimly, closed his eyes, and waited for enlightenment.

Enlightenment struck him with the force of a thunderbolt.

"He is awake!"

"Professor! Professor!"

"Lionel! Come quickly! He is awake!"

Professor Graven's eyes fluttered open, closed, and finally opened again. He heard the commotion around him, even as he realized he lay on his back, on the floor, staring up into the ceiling of the underground chamber.

So. They were still inside.

One of the sailors—a ruddy-faced man with a reddish beard and blue eyes, who was qualified as a medic—was leaning over him, checking his vitals. Graven grasped the man by his lapels.

"How long was I out?"

The medic reacted with surprise, then shrugged. "An hour," he replied. "Maybe a bit more."

Graven digested this. *Good.*

"And we are still inside the mountain."

"We could not get out," the medic said, a tiny trace of panic in his eyes, in his voice. "The entranceway was closed when we went back to it. We cannot open it."

"No worries," Graven said. "I can, now."

The medic stared back at him in amazement.

Graven sat up and looked around at the chamber. The darkness was gone, the shadows banished by the bright light of the glowing crystals set into the walls and columns. He saw the other four sailors seated nearby in a circle. They'd been playing cards, utterly disinterested in the wonders they'd stumbled into. Meanwhile, the other men–the three-hundred-foot-tall metal men–still stood at the far end of the vast open space, unmoving.

Graven studied them closely, now that the lights were on. Three of the four had a base color of white at their waists, elbows and knees, with other colors laid over the remaining portions of their huge bodies. One was blue and silver; one was green and orange; one was purple and black. The fourth one, slightly larger than the others, was entirely red and gold. This all matched what he remembered from his notes, and what had been revealed to him when he'd donned the helmet.

The helmet.

He reached up to his head, felt nothing but his sandy brown hair. The helmet was gone.

Almost frantically he looked around for it.

"The helmet," he exclaimed. "What have you done with it?"

"It injured you," the medic replied.

"Certainly not," Graven shot back. "It simply took my mind some time to process all that it was telling me."

The man stared back at him, puzzled.

"What have you done with it?" he repeated. "Bring it here!"

Reluctantly, the medic called over to one of his compatriots. "Joshua," he said. "Fetch the helmet, if you will."

"I'm busy at the moment, Mr. Taylor."

"It's for the professor," the medic replied.

A pause, then, "All right."

Joshua, a narrow-faced, sallow-eyed man with thinning blond hair, got up from the card game–clearly resenting the imposition–and retrieved the helmet from where they'd stored it when Graven had fallen unconscious. He handed it to the medic, Taylor, who held it in one hand, squinting his eyes, studying it closely.

"There's more to this than meets the eye, Professor," he said. "What is it? What does it do?"

Graven said nothing, instead merely holding out his hand. With a frown, Taylor handed him the helmet.

"Now, be careful there, Professor," he said. "You don't want to get knocked out again. That can't be good for you!"

"No," Graven said. "You're quite correct. I don't want to get knocked out again. And as for your other question..." Graven swept his hand around to encompass the entire facility. "What it does is put me in control of all of this."

The professor raised the helmet and turned it around to face in the proper direction, then started to bring it up and over his head. But he paused and lowered it again instead. He stared at it, frowning deeply.

"Something wrong, Professor?" the other man said.

"I–I just wish to be cautious," Graven replied. He cradled the helmet in his lap, eyeing it suspiciously, as if he had determined it was too powerful to let go of, but too dangerous to put on himself. Which was more or less the case.

Taylor nodded slowly, then looked up and around. "What is this place, Professor? I've never heard of any kind of military installation out here in the South Pacific–and certainly nothing like this. Is it the Americans? The Russians?" He shook his head in wonder. "Are we gonna get in trouble, just for being here? For breaking in?"

"We did *not* break in," Graven snapped. "We did precisely what this base wanted us to do–which is why it allowed us to enter, and why it was... *reluctant*... for you to leave while I was unconscious."

"You talk like it's a person, not a place," the medic said, eyeing Graven strangely. "Like it can think for itself. And—it *wanted* us to be here? It *wanted* us to break in?"

"I believe it *can* think for itself," Graven said. "And—I told you—we did *not* break in. We were invited."

"Invited?"

"I received the invitation to come here many years ago," Graven answered, his eyes focused on some other time and place. "It simply took me this long to locate it."

Taylor appeared as if that piece of information had not helped him very much

"But—again, sir—*if* you know so much about it—what *is* this place?"

Graven took out his pipe from a pocket in his jacket, checked the tobacco level, and lit it.

"I'm not certain of the proper words to describe it," he said at length. "A... base of operations, perhaps."

"For who, sir?"

Graven pointed at the four towering figures at the far end of the vast chamber. "For them."

The data flow paused. David Okada staggered backward a few steps as he struggled to take in all that he'd just learned, in that quick burst of sounds and images.

Professor Graven and a group of sailors had discovered Rapa Hoi, and the main base beneath its surface, back in 1958.

The four robots had been there, too. This was the first time the professor had encountered them. But—what were they, really? Where had they come from? What were they *for?*

David needed answers to those questions.

"Show me," he said out loud.

The data flow resumed.

CHAPTER 15

Professor Graven quickly became intimately acquainted with every portion of the Rapa Hoi base. He paid for a ship to regularly bring new supplies while returning to Europe with bits of advanced technology. Over the ensuing months, he parlayed some of the lesser gadgets he discovered on the island into a fortune and a knighthood. He managed to awaken many of the basic systems within the underground chamber, granting him access to radars, sensors, weapons systems, and the like. Meanwhile, he made attempt after attempt to activate or awaken the giant robots.

Every attempt with them failed.

This was especially galling to him, because it had been his fragmentary knowledge of the robots that had driven him on his long quest to find Rapa Hoi, and it had been his desire to control them that motivated all his other actions.

He spoke to them. He attempted to communicate with them by way of the many consoles and operator stations set around the base. He climbed to the top of each of them, studying the "head" units, thinking that perhaps they represented cockpits or cabins of some sort, allowing control of the giant machines. But he could not find a way inside.

Dejected after months of failure, he briefly returned to London to tend to family business, acquire more supplies, and possibly to recruit more experts who could help him. During that time, he was visited by a Dr. Ian Visser, late of the Netherlands, who appeared as if from nowhere at his doorstep. Visser's knowledge and enthusiasm persuaded Graven to bring him onto the small team of five other technicians and scientists he was assembling, and to swiftly promote him to chief assistant. Together the six newcomers–four men and two women–joined the professor when he returned to Rapa Hoi.

More months of failure came and went. The new scientists– particularly Dr. Visser–found some success in restoring the seemingly-ancient machines within the chamber. The robots, however, remained dormant.

Occasionally Graven would look at the helmet–the one he'd placed on his head when he'd first found the hidden chamber–and he'd wonder if he dared risk a second exposure to it. While the first time had granted him a certain amount of knowledge, it had also knocked him out–placed him into a virtual coma–and he'd never quite felt the same since. Something deep within him understood the danger the helmet represented, and feared it.

At last, however, after more months of failed efforts, and as the calendar changed from 1959 to 1960, Graven concluded that he had no other choice. He had to try the helmet again.

With the other scientists standing around him in a loose circle, Graven seated himself in the main chair behind the central control console of the base. He closed his eyes and raised his hands up, palms open. Dr. Visser took the helmet from where it had rested on the console and placed it in Graven's hands. The professor hesitated for only a moment.

"Show me how to awaken the robots," he whispered.

Then he raised it and pulled it down over his head.

The helmet did not, in fact, show him how to awaken the robots. This was not something the Network on Rapa Hoi felt he was ready to learn; at least, not yet.

Instead, it caused him to pass out and fall into a mild coma again.

When he awoke, and upon coming fully back to himself, he realized that he had absorbed all the information about a great war between the two alien races. He understood the massive cosmic conflict that had taken place between the two sides, and that what he'd found here was an abandoned base from that war.

The computer network had shown him why the four huge robots existed, and why they were on Earth to begin with.

The story played out for Graven in mere seconds, but it covered a time frame of many, many millennia.

And, in the present, it did so once again–this time, for young David Okada.

It began with two alien races, the Ahlwhen and the Xovaren.

Both races came from humble, ordinary beginnings. Perhaps the only advantage they both shared was that they'd come of age early in the history of the galaxy, compared to younger races such as Humanity.

Both races mastered highly advanced forms of technology, and both used that technology to rapidly expand outward from their homeworlds to other star systems, both forging vast interstellar empires.

Inevitably they encountered one another, and inevitably they clashed.

They clashed at first intellectually, ideologically and philosophically. Soon enough, however, they clashed physically. Thus the two great star empires went to war with one another.

The Ahlwhen, specializing in unthinkably futuristic mechanical and electronic technology, created machines to enforce their will. Eventually they succeeded in creating great constructs of metal and crystal that, some argued, contained a degree of sentience; some further argued they contained souls, deep down inside the machines. The great robots they built assaulted the Xovaren worlds along their border, pushing the enemy back.

The Xovaren, focusing on genetic manipulation, mental telepathy and organic technology, created what could only be called *monsters*. Massive, unnatural creatures emerged from the Xovaren laboratories, telepathically linked to their alien masters. These great beasts charged to the attack, rampaging across world after world, punishing any who sided with their mortal foes, the Ahlwhen.

For many centuries neither side could gain a real, lasting advantage. The battle lines moved little, if at all. The Xovaren made their monsters larger and more intelligent, with awesome new abilities grafted into their genetic codes. The Ahlwhen built bigger and bigger robots, imbuing each new generation with greater autonomy and greater on-board intelligence. Before long, the Xovaren monsters and the Ahlwhen robots had evolved to the point that they had become effectively autonomous, fighting the war with little or no input from their masters.

And meanwhile, as the war raged across the cosmos, it devastated the surfaces of hundreds of worlds.

Another several centuries passed, with the war again a stalemate. Now entire planets had their ecosystems wrecked or erased entirely, as these gargantuan battles occurred over and over across the galaxy.

The Xovaren considered this carnage to be part of the price of winning their ideological war with their great rivals. They poisoned dozens of planets with genetic bombs and viruses.

The Ahlwhen looked upon the damage being done to the finest habitable worlds in the galaxy, and they lamented the waste and destruction of it all. And then they resolved that it must all end, and end soon.

Some twenty-five hundred years earlier, with this renewed sense of resolve, the Ahlwhen had launched their final offensive. Having built entire battalions of giant robots of all shapes and sizes and abilities, they unleashed this army upon dozens of Xovaren border worlds. They constructed secret, hidden bases on those planets and stocked them with their weapons and plenty of spare parts.

Rapa Hoi, Professor Graven came to realize, was the main Ahlwhen base on Earth. Each base had its own network, whose job was to connect those computers with the big Titan robots.

There had been three other bases built on Earth as backups, but two had been destroyed by seismic activities over the past several thousand years. Now, only Rapa Lau remained as a separate, independent facility, complete with its own computer network; a backup, should something ever happen to Rapa Hoi.

The overwhelming Ahlwhen assault caught the complacent Xovaren by surprise, and it pushed them back. Within a matter of two or three centuries, the Xovaren were confined to only their core worlds, while the Ahlwhen enjoyed unprecedented hegemony across the Milky Way.

The effort of winning such an unthinkably huge conflict took its toll on the victors as well as on the vanquished. The Ahlwhen were exhausted. They'd consumed most of their resources in this one massive assault. They'd also burned up much of their anger, their aggression, and their hatred for their enemy. They were weary, a spent force. Now all that remained was to rest.

The Ahlwhen and the Xovaren retreated to their places of power, there to sleep for millennia.

Their works, however, remained–left behind by both sides, on world after world, just in case hostilities ever resumed.

Professor Graven now understood that this was what he had found. An Ahlwhen base, and four of their Titans.

And he remembered what his grizzled old colleague had said to him: *They are returning. The aliens. The Xovaren.*

It seemed he might have discovered the base just in the nick of time.

All that remained now was to reactivate those Titans, so that they would be ready, should the enemy come to Earth again.

The helmet, however, steadfastly refused to grant him direct access to the network. It refused to allow him to awaken the Titans. And it refused to obey his orders.

This all greatly frustrated him. No matter what he tried, however, he could not wake the big robots up, or gain access to their control centers.

But then another solution occurred to him; a solution suggested by Dr. Visser.

Just because the *professor* could not activate the Titans, Visser suggested, that did not necessarily mean no human on Earth could do so.

Perhaps someone else could. Perhaps someone else might be found; someone possessing a quality that the network and the Titans would accept. Something genetic, perhaps. Something that Graven and Visser and the other scientists now on Rapa Hoi apparently lacked.

These hypothetical individuals, if they existed, would work for Professor Graven, of course. They would obey him.

But they would be able to operate the Titans. Control them. Pilot them.

That was what was needed, Visser insisted.

They needed to find *pilots*.

CHAPTER 16

David continued to stand there in the Rapa Lau base, absorbing and processing all the information the network was delivering to him. Learning the background of Professor Graven and the Titans.

Meanwhile, another presence, another intelligence, watched and waited outside.

Lurking, mostly hidden within a deep ravine, a massive, green and gray shape hunched down, surveying the scene. Considering it.

It had been an interesting day so far.

The blue and silver man-shape had arrived, followed by the orange and green one. Then they'd fought—which was puzzling, because the big metal man-shapes had always cooperated before, back in the distant past when they'd last come out of their hidden lairs. They'd never fought one another.

The massive, gold-flecked eyes had looked on from behind a broad clump of trees and brush. The big shape had watched and waited. The intellect behind those eyes had never been exactly sure what to make of the big, metal men, and it wasn't sure yet if it needed to get involved or not. In the old days, it had simply evaded the detection of the metal men. Then, for so very long, the metal men had disappeared. Now, with them back, and apparently turning on one another…

More information was needed.

Nothing much had happened out here for a while, but the intellect could sense that things were far from over.

The green and gray shape decided to remain a bit longer, hunched down, hidden. Watching.

It had the time, and nowhere special to be.

The gold-flecked eyes continued to peer out through the trees, to observe, to wait...

Pilots.

David Okada gasped and gasped again as he accidentally backed into a crystal column, as he stumbled blindly around the main chamber of the Rapa Lau base. He was entirely oblivious of his physical surroundings—all that mattered to him at present was what he was seeing via his helmet visor. And what he was learning.

So it had been the professor who had recruited John and put him in command of Validus-V, as well as bringing in the pilots of the other three robots. And then, sometime later, the professor and the others had turned on John, and then on David.

The helmet he wore now, connected to the backup computer network of this little island, had shown David so much in such a short amount of time, and now he understood. He understood where the four mighty robots had come from, and how they'd been brought back into service after millennia of dormancy.

His mind reeled as he struggled to comprehend what he had been shown.

Aliens. Actual, honest-to-goodness aliens had built the Titans. They had built the base in which he now stood, in fact, as well as the larger one on Rapa Hoi.

And then Professor Graven had discovered the abandoned Rapa Hoi base, and had at some later point recruited pilots to do what he himself was unable to do–to control the Titans. To lead them into battle.

At some point in the last couple of years, John Okada had signed up to be one of those pilots. The thought of it made David very proud–but also very nervous. Because clearly the relationship between John and his compatriots had soured severely of late.

But—*why?*

The memory bursts from the computer network had explained to David where the robots and the secret base had come from. But none of it explained *why* the three other pilots and Graven himself had turned against John–and now against *him*–and tried to capture or destroy both of them, along with Validus-V.

The professor hadn't seemed evil in the memory burst the network had just shared with David. He'd seemed obsessed, sure, and driven to almost any lengths to find and take control of the base and its contents. And he'd done that. But David couldn't recall any stories on the news about giant robots attacking anyone, or robbing anything.

So–why had they all so suddenly turned against his older brother?

Could John have done something to deserve their animosity?

David found that difficult to believe. John was entirely honorable, almost to a fault.

If John had been working against the others, then David could only assume the others were up to no good, and John had found out about it.

David frowned and shook his head slowly.

What could it be? What could the professor and the pilots be doing that would put them so at odds with John Okada?

With this question in mind, David returned his attention to his mental link with the network. And very quickly he had his answers.

While David continued to learn about the overall situation in which he'd found himself, something was happening outside. Something was stirring in the ocean surrounding the island.

A strange shape moved through the waters, knifing its way toward Rapa Lau.

Fish and other undersea life fled as it approached. They squirmed as they moved through the poisonous trail it left in its wake.

On the island itself, giant nostrils sniffed and gold-flecked eyes narrowed. A massive, green and gray head turned slightly, those eyes moving away from where they'd been watching the two unmoving robots. Instead they shifted their gaze out to sea, where—far out in the distance, but closing rapidly—something was approaching.

The eyes narrowed further as deep emotions swelled within that massive breast. The intellect behind those eyes recognized the trail, recognized the scent. Something very bad was on its way to Rapa Lau.

Idly the intellect wondered if the bad thing was coming for the robots—or for him?

Ah well. He was used to being patient. He'd waited thousands of years already, hadn't he? Most of that time spent in deep hibernation on the ocean floor, it was true, but still...!

The massive green and gray shape settled back into its hiding place to wait just a little longer, confident that all would be revealed soon enough.

Aboard Torander-X, Wen Zhao struggled to regain control of the big Titan, both physically and mentally.

Physically it was bad enough—the huge robot had crashed into the side of Rapa Lau's unnamed mountain and slid part of the way down it.

Mentally was far worse. The computer network on Rapa Lau was trying its hardest to work its way into her mind—to corrupt her, she knew, in the same way it had done the Okada brothers and Validus-V.

Zhao gestured and tapped a few commands and the holographic display shimmered to life in front of her. She called up a schematic of the Titan's entire body, and caused it to show the areas currently under the influence of the original programming and the parts that had been overrun by corrupted code from the network.

Immediately a boxy, man-shaped outline appeared within the three-dimensional display. All of the body shimmered a deep, dark red–except for the head. The head was a soft, bluish-green color. There was one exception, though, within the outline of the head: a bright red spot glowed at the center of it.

Zhao understood that the red spot had to be *her*. She interpreted that to mean the dark, angry red coloring indicated good, clean, original coding, while the soft blue-green revealed areas corrupted by the evil Xovaren programming. Something about that didn't register as right to her, but she quickly drove such thoughts from her mind.

How to purge the bad coding that infected the Titan's replacement head? And, could it even be done, given that her present connection to the network could simply allow the computers of Rapa Lau to pump in more corrupt coding even if she purged what was there now?

She thought about this for a moment and then came up with the beginnings of a plan that could work for her. It came down to this: She would have to continue to resist the corrupt coding the Rapa Lau network was forcing on her, and then actually reverse the flow back the other way, so that her robot's clean coding overwrote and purged the bad programming that had infected the base.

Could it be done? Could she overpower the Rapa Lau computer network, all by herself?

Well, not entirely by herself. Torander-X would surely help her. Not the head, of course, but the rest of the big robot; all of the separate computer units spread throughout its massive body.

Raising her Titan back to its feet, Wen Zhao stopped subconsciously blocking the data flow over the wireless network, and instead allowed it to reconnect—but only through her helmet, so that she alone served as the gatekeeper for all data exchanges between the base and Torander-X.

As the data flowed in, she took a deep breath, exhaled, and shoved her own consciousness back down the line, over the wireless connection, and directly into the computer banks beneath the island. And behind her came the programming she'd brought from Rapa Hoi—the dark red programming she fully believed to be the original—pure and clean.

On her holo schematic, the dark red areas flowed out of Torander-X and across the open distance to the island base, and into the computer systems there.

Within them, and visible only to someone with access to the schematic on her display, a titanic struggle commenced—a struggle for the soul of the Titans, their pilots and their legacies.

Inside the base, the Rapa Lau network had one last story for David. It understood time was of the essence now; he needed to be ready to go back into action very soon. But he would be more effective, the network knew, if he understood the basics of what he'd gotten himself involved in.

And so it showed him this:

In the final days of the last war between the Ahlwhen and the Xovaren, one of the major engagements had occurred on the planet Earth.

The Xovaren sent a full military contingent to Earth, including a dozen of their primary weapons: artificially evolved monsters of tremendous size and power. Creatures bred and developed specifically to counter the robotic Titans.

For months the creatures ran rampant over the globe, terrorizing the primitive humans they encountered. The Xovaren, pleased, added this planet to their list of conquests.

Then the Ahlwhen forces arrived.

Seven Titans descended from the sky on pillars of fire. They scanned the surface of this blue-white world and easily located the enemy.

What followed was a massive battle across half of the Pacific.

After untold days of fighting, three of the Titans had been utterly destroyed. The other four had suffered varying degrees of damage but could be repaired.

Of the twelve monstrous Xovaren creations, however, eight were no more. The other four were trapped, surrounded by the Titans. Sure to be annihilated at any moment.

Cursing their eternal foes, the Xovaren themselves evacuated the Earth, returned to their fleet of starships and fled. They abandoned their creatures to their fates.

The four surviving Titans closed in, weapons at the ready.

But then the Ahlwhen had a change of heart.

+ + +

"Wait," said the Ahlwhen pilot of Validus-V.

The other three Titans paused in their advance and looked at their brother.

"Must we slay them?"

"Of course we must," came the response from the pilot of Z-Zatala. "They are purest evil—corrupted servants of the accursed Xovaren."

"Our purpose is to rid the galaxy of them," added the pilot of Torander-X.

The pilot of King Karzaled said nothing, but his impatience was palpable across their shared mental network.

"But—hear me out," said Validus's pilot. "Perhaps those creatures are not inherently evil. Perhaps they are mere unwitting pawns, innocent of all but of having been deceived."

"They have not been deceived," Z-Zatala barked back. "They have been corrupted. Corrupted from the moment of their birth—of their foul creation—by the pernicious influence of the Xovaren."

"And, as such," Torander added, "it falls to us to eliminate them."

"Precisely," rumbled King Karzaled, as he cycled up his weapons systems and armed his missiles. "So why do we delay?"

The pilot of Validus-V felt the sentiments of his compatriots turning entirely against him. Before abandoning hope for his argument, however, he appealed to the Ahlwhen overlords who, high up in orbit in their starship, monitored events down on the surface.

After making the case for compassion and fairness, he closed by adding, "And having these beasts as allies would make for quite a coup. Who knows what intelligence we could gain from studying them—to say nothing of perhaps having them fight alongside us in the future!"

The Ahlwhen leaders deliberated for some time, while the four Titans were ordered to simply guard their prisoners and wait. The other three pilots regarded Validus-V and its pilot with scorn and disdain, but they obeyed.

At last the decision was handed down: The creatures would be taken prisoner, and studied, and perhaps employed in the service of the Ahlwhen, should they eventually prove loyal and reliable.

Grumbling their displeasure, the other three Titans reluctantly joined Validus-V in rounding up the wounded four monsters and herding them into pens within the underground base. For months the Ahlwhen studied them, seeking to comprehend the strange combination of genetic engineering and dark sciences that had led to their spawning. Along the way, the creatures became even more powerful, as their mutated abilities developed and expanded.

The Ahlwhen determined to re-train them to serve as guardians of the island base. The creatures, with their highly sensitive organic senses, could warn of approaching enemies the base's mechanical defenders could not always detect.

For a while, this worked.

Over time, however, three of the creatures—one bat-like, one caterpillar-like, one ape-like—proved too "wild," too vicious. Too corrupted by the Xovaren and their scientific sorcery. Perhaps it would always have been thus for the horrific beasts. Or perhaps their new mutations drove them mad. In any case, they escaped confinement and disappeared into the Pacific.

The fourth creature was a massive, green and gray lizard-beast designated by the Ahlwhen as "Tyranicus." This three-hundred-foot-tall monster, unlike its fellows, seemed never to have been corrupted by the Xovaren. He dutifully guarded the base and protected its inhabitants. Indeed, he seemed to possess a sixth sense for detecting the approach of corrupted beings. When, a short time later, the other three monsters returned to attack the island together, Tyranicus warned of their approach and then joined the Titans in fighting against them and repelling their assault, ultimately driving them back into hiding.

The reward Tyranicus received for this altruistic and inspiring display was bitter indeed.

The other three pilots despised the creature and repeatedly demanded of the base's leaders that he be destroyed. Dismissing his selfless efforts on their behalf during the recent battle, they argued over and over that the only good Xovaren creation was a dead Xovaren creation.

"The beast is too dangerous," they agreed. "It was and is a mistake to seek to use organic beings in our military forces!"

"Yes! They are too independent! Too easily corruptible!"

"We must *destroy* them," the three pilots declared. "*All* of them. *Destroy all monsters!*"

Their point of view prevailed. The orders came down to the Titans and their Ahlwhen pilots: *"Destroy Tyranicus!"*

But Tyranicus was not so easily destroyed.

His sixth sense warning him the tide was turning against him, he fought his way off the island and into the waters of the vast and trackless Pacific, and there he vanished. He was not seen again for many years.

After more centuries passed, the Ahlwhen reached two conclusions: that the Xovaren had been defeated and driven entirely from Earth's sector of the galaxy, and that the four monsters on Earth had entered some kind of hibernation, deep beneath the ocean or under some vast mountain range, and might not be seen again for untold millennia or even eons.

Thus the Ahlwhen of Rapa Hoi closed down their base there and departed the Earth, leaving behind only their four remaining Titans and the base's now-dormant computer network. For thousands of years, the base remained hidden, unknown to the rising human civilizations around it. Its computer network was left mostly powered down, and the four giant robots stood empty and inert, cold as statues.

Fragments of information about the Titans and their base had gotten out, however, over the years—passed down as folklore from the humans who had witnessed the ancient battles between godlike machine-men and nightmarish, dragon-monsters.

These scraps of information were painstakingly gathered by a handful of scholars during the Eighteenth and Nineteenth Centuries, collected into a single book, and eventually that book fell into the hands of a young professor by the name of Anthony Graven.

Thus began Graven's quest for Rapa Hoi.

Wen Zhao's consciousness had left her body and now mostly occupied a virtual space within the computer banks of Rapa Lau.

Within that space, she fought. She fought as savagely with her mind as she had ever fought a physical battle at the controls of Torander-X.

The programming—corrupt, as she saw it—that infested the Rapa Lau computers was pernicious and it was resilient. Over and over again and she ripped at it and shredded it, even as it poked and prodded at her own mind, her own sanity. She never stopped to wonder at the fact that it was never trying to harm her, even though she sought to destroy it. This she took entirely for granted, and pressed on with her attack.

There, in the electronic systems that governed the Rapa Lau base, a war was being fought between the dark red programming Zhao had brought with her, and the blue-green coding of the base's computers.

With a mental jolt, the Network ended its stream of information into David Okada's head.

David reeled, feeling dizzy and a bit nauseated, staggering under the weight of all he had been shown. His hand came up to the dark visor of his helmet and he slid it back, exposing his face—as red and twisted as he felt inside.

Again, no words, but the definite sense he was being told something: *We have no more time for history lessons. What you now know must suffice. You are needed outside. Go.*

David shook his head, trying to think clearly. It felt as if hours had passed, if not days–though a part of him understood it had been only minutes.

As the Network had disconnected from him, he'd briefly glimpsed what else it was doing at the same time. It had appeared from that strange perspective that it was fighting a battle–an internal battle, deep in its ancient processors–against some intrusive, alien force.

The network was under assault, under siege. But he had no idea how, or by whom, or why.

A dark red presence besieging a blue-green one. That was all he'd been able to sense, and then the connection had closed.

What could it have been?

He didn't know.

But the Network had told him he was needed outside. That had to mean Validus-V needed him back.

Something big was about to go down.

He wasted no more time. He ran for the exit.

CHAPTER 17

As Zhao's consciousness battled within the computer systems of the base, her conscious mind became too encumbered, too distracted, to properly direct Torander-X. Stray thoughts, random images flittered along the wireless connection between the woman and the Titan. Torander-X interpreted these thoughts as commands, and struggled to obey, as best it could–even as it fought an internal battle itself, between the programming inside its new head and the programming of its old body.

The green and orange Titan launched itself into the air, drifted slowly away from the mountain slope, and hovered over the beach, boot-rockets rumbling. It spun around, cycling through various weapons systems, and shot half a mile up into the sky. Then higher.

The Rapa Lau network, under siege and knowing it was losing to the crimson coding, sensed this happening. It understood that Wen Zhao was not causing her Titan to behave this way on purpose. The big robot was effectively out of her control. Could this provide some sort of advantage?

In near desperation-mode, the network looked for any opening it might provide.

David Okada raced out of the base and along the path that led back to the beach. As he sprinted, he kept an eye out for any

142 VAN ALLEN PLEXICO

attack. He assumed Wen Zhao had already made it back to her robot and could very well be waiting out there to zap him.

When he emerged from the canopy of trees and onto the beach, he found things the opposite of how he'd left them: Now Validus-V was the robot missing a head. The jet craft that Validus's head could turn into–the Delta-V–sat on the sands a short distance away, presumably waiting for him.

David ran for it.

He didn't make it.

The Rapa Lau network found its opening and went for it.

Even as Wen Zhao effectively abandoned control of the robot in order to do battle with the island's programming, the network rammed its influence past her and linked up with the processors within Torander-X's new head. They could not drive out the corrupted programming from the robot's body, but–working together–they did believe they could take control of at least one subroutine. That didn't seem like much, but they had a plan.

If they failed, they knew they could possibly be opening the door for a retaliatory strike that could see the corrupted programming drive its way into the very heart of the Rapa Lau network. They could lose everything.

But they had to try. They had to do *something*.

They made their decision, and they acted.

Together the island network's programming and that of the robot's head forced their way down—down into the Titan's body, and down into the unit that controlled the robot's transformations from Torander-X to Rednator-Oh and back. There they sealed that unit off, took control, and initiated the transformation process.

Torander-X, quite to the surprise of both Zhao and the robot itself, suddenly flowed and morphed and transformed itself into the ultrasonic flying machine called Rednator-Oh.

And then, super-boosted rockets flaring to life, the reconfigured Titan zoomed skyward, toward the upper edge of the atmosphere itself.

+ + +

"What is happening?" Zhao cried, sensing the transformation happening. "I did not order this!"

Back from the systems within Rednator's body came an answering squeal of data, mostly incoherent. *Something* had gotten into the circuitry subroutines that managed the shift to and from Rednator-Oh, and caused it to happen against her will–against the pilot's wishes!

And, whatever that *something* was, it had locked itself into that particular system–or rather, locked Zhao out.

Screaming her anger and frustration, she found herself torn between keeping her consciousness inside the island's computer network or retreating to her own body and brain. At that moment, while so distracted, her consciousness momentarily let down its guard, there within the Rapa Lau computer systems.

The network saw the opening, clear as day. It struck again.

Rednator-Oh continued to rocket skyward, spaceward, a runaway missile nearly three hundred feet tall.

In its sleek aircraft form, it could travel much faster than the other three Titans. Within minutes, if not seconds, it had reached the limits of the Earth's atmosphere.

Wen Zhao cursed even as she withdrew her consciousness back into her body, and thereby back into Rednator-Oh. Instantly she began fighting to take control of it. She could sense the robot was very high up in the sky; much too far up for safety's sake.

But the transformative circuits lay within a separate unit, and that unit was closed and barred to her. Try as she might, she could not access them, could not take control of them.

She screamed again.

In a rage, she reached out for the navigation system, and wrestled the steering power back under her control. The first thing she did was redirect Rednator-Oh back toward the Earth below; back toward the ocean; back toward Rapa Lau.

Faster and faster the mighty Titan rocketed downward. This was no problem, of course; the Rednator-Oh form had been specifically designed to travel at altitudes and at speeds none of the others could manage.

Not even Torander-X.

That was okay, as long as the Titan held the Rednator form. But, of course, it would be catastrophically bad if the robot were to transform back into Torander-X.

A moment later, the robot began to transform back into Torander-X.

David didn't make it.

He had just raced out of the trees and onto the beach when, from his left, came a nearly-deafening sound–part animal noise, part the waterfall roar of something massive emerging from the ocean.

He glanced over as he ran, then stopped in his tracks and stared. Such is the way of the normal human mind when it perceives the uncanny, the unearthly.

Some *thing*—some truly massive and utterly horrifying *thing*—was rising up out of the water and advancing up the beach.

It looked like a bug. An insect. But a very *large* insect. An *extremely* large insect.

David mentally almost laughed at this. By now, after all that he'd encountered in the past few hours, one would think one would be used to seeing things that existed on a massively huge scale. But, no–this thing still managed to shock and surprise him.

It was like a massive caterpillar, or maybe a centipede, banded with bright yellow rings alternating with black ones. Its covering– again, like an insect's exoskeleton–appeared quite thick and formidable. Near what must have been its front end, two segmented arms with sharp claws on the ends reached out, grasping. Its bulbous head featured four compound eyes that stared, unblinking.

David fought the urge to throw up, just looking at it. He had no time to wonder what the creature could be or where it could have come from, though, because it chose that moment to strike. Racing forward on dozens of legs that were only "tiny" in relation to the rest of it, the monstrous insect smashed into the headless body of Validus-V, sending the big robot tumbling wildly before crashing down into the sand. When Validus, now sprawled on its back and with one leg out in the water, didn't move, the monster roared again. It raised straight up, almost entirely vertical, then came down with resounding force, its segmented arms punching Validus in the chest.

"Hey!" David shouted instinctively, outraged. He instantly wished he'd kept his mouth shut.

The massive creature whirled about, ignoring the unmoving robot with its unsatisfactory lack of reactions. Now it stared with its four insect eyes directly at David, where he stood alone on the beach.

"Oh, crap," David whispered.

The monster charged forward, legs pulsing and pistoning, a yellow and black freight train. It sped directly towards him.

Rednator-Oh shifted its form. The lines outlining the body changed. Metal flowed like water, reforming into a different shape entirely.

It was Torander-X that tumbled wildly out of the sky and down toward the waters. There was no chance of it recovering from this power-dive. The Pacific Ocean below was a looming horizontal wall of blue concrete, directly in its path, utterly unavoidable.

Together, the Rapa Lau programming and its computer ally inside the Titan's head had tripped the transformation circuit again. As soon as the transformation back into Torander-X was complete, the computer systems fried as many surrounding components as possible.

It would be very, very difficult for Wen Zhao to undo the transformation now.

"No!" cried Wen Zhao. "Not now! *No!*"

Zhao understood immediately what had just happened, and how difficult it would be to undo.

The Rapa Lau coding infesting her Titan had tripped the transformation circuit again, changing the big robot back into its humanoid form. The circuit that caused the Titan to morph from the ultra-high-speed aircraft form of Rednator-Oh to the much less aerodynamic man-shape of Torander-X. That was very bad news in terms of the current speed of her descent.

Torander-X came tumbling down out of the sky at impossible speeds.

Impossible to believe. Impossible to *survive*.

David looked at the monster charging towards him. Then he looked at where Validus's head—the Delta-V—was parked, off to his left, at the edge of the beach. In the space of less than a heartbeat, he judged the distances between himself and each of those things. And he despaired.

There was no way he was going to make it to the aircraft before the monster reached him. No way. He simply wasn't fast enough.

He took a deep breath and raced forward.

He wasn't going to make it, but he was going to try anyway.

From behind the thick growth of trees that ran along a low ridge off to the southeast, two glowing, gold-flecked eyes watched the events transpiring on and above the beach.

The intellect behind those eyes wasn't sure what to make of what was happening.

One of the big metal men had flown far up into the sky, then turned around and was presently flying back down. The intellect wasn't certain what that was going to accomplish, but it knew it was none of its business, so it ignored that whole affair.

The other metal man currently lay sprawled across the beach, unmoving. And it had no head! No, the head had turned into some kind of aircraft and currently rested on the sands nearby. How strange! And the human boy the intellect had been keeping a watchful eye on since his arrival? He was presently running across the beach, apparently trying to get to the aircraft, before— before *what?*

Ah! Yes. The intellect had known something foul, something sinister, was afoot.

It was Gamaron. The old ally, the old enemy.

Gamaron was scrambling across the beach himself, trying to get to the human boy before the boy could get to the robot head.

And what would Gamaron *do* with the boy, once he caught him?

It was somewhat obvious. After all, Gamaron was a rotten, corrupted creature.

The intellect did not like to think about such things.

A low, almost subconscious rumble emerged from beneath those gold-flecked eyes.

And, somewhere *behind* the eyes, unimaginable organic energies build up, poised to be released.

The caterpillar-monster had almost reached David. Its segmented arms came up, ready to grasp and rip and tear. Its maw opened and closed on clumps of vicious, foot-long teeth. It skidded to a halt on its rows of horrific legs and screeched.

David was still ten feet away from the parked Delta-V, trudging through the thick sand, moving far too slowly. He allowed himself to look up, to see the bizarre monster that was about to end his life. He crouched down, arms wrapped around his head, preparing to be eaten.

He'd hoped he could be brave when the end came, but this–! This was too horrible to have planned ahead for.

Despite himself, he looked up, to see the end approaching.

And then, in a flash–a truly blinding flash!—the monster was gone.

Blinking, David slowly stood back up straight and looked around.

The caterpillar-creature lay on its back some distance away, all those nightmare little legs thrashing. Smoke billowed from two circular marks on its side—marks that had not been there before.

What could have done that?

He looked around again, but saw nothing.

The creature was struggling to roll over and regain its footing.

David knew he couldn't count on a second miracle rescue. He sprinted as fast as he could through the sand, covering the remaining few feet to the Delta-V.

The creature bellowed its frustration, its rage at being foiled in its attempt to dine. It was moving again, coming back.

David touched the hatch panel on the side of the Delta-V and it slid open. He leapt inside and closed it behind him.

Something told him to get into his seat and strap in quickly. So he did that. And less than a second after he clicked the restraining harness in place around him, something smashed into the Delta-V and sent it tumbling end over end. David held on for dear life as he was nearly flung from the seat. When the ride mercifully ended at last, he was hanging upside down, though the straps still held him in securely enough.

"Validus," he called out, "let's get you back in one piece!"

Dutifully, the Delta-V rose up out of the sand pile where it had come to rest, then flipped over so that it was right-side up again.

The holographic display flared to life in front of David, and he saw the yellow and black monster directly in front of him, roaring in anger, reaching for him with those segmented arms. Above it on the display floated the name GAMARON.

"What weapons do we have here on Delta-V?" he called out.

In response, the display shifted to reveal diagrams of several items he assumed were weapons–but he wasn't going to take the time now to read all the specs on them. Instead he simply yelled, "Fire everything!'

The Delta-V fired everything.

CHAPTER 18

The barrage of energy beams that lanced out from the nose of the Delta-V at David's frantic command drove the screeching Gamaron back, putting at least a little distance between them. The huge creature retreated a bit, but clearly wasn't too terribly hurt by the weapons and looked to want to strike again.

This gave David the chance to turn in his seat, raise his dark visor, and look back to see if there had been any change with his brother. He was disappointed that the medical unit was still sealed up tight, with John still inside. He took heart at the fact that more of the lights along the face of the cabinet had changed from red to green. That seemed to him a positive sign.

David settled back into the pilot's seat and felt the Delta-V's internal computer system link back up with him, remotely, by way of his helmet. He slid his visor back down and accessed the holographic display.

Where is Torander-X? he asked with his mind.

The perspective he was seeing moved upward and zoomed in. Now he saw the other robot far up in the sky—but falling. Falling very rapidly.

"Oh—oh no! What is she doing?" he wondered aloud.

The Delta-V didn't answer.

"Maybe she needs help," David began to say—but then he was very swiftly reminded that his own troubles were far from over.

The craft in which he flew suddenly lurched. Electricity flooded the room and little forks of lightning danced over every surface. Systems shorted out and sparks flew, followed by smoke. Alarms blared to life.

David wrestled with the controls and quickly reestablished control of the aircraft, even as automated systems put out the fires and ventilated smoke from the cabin. One after another, the alarms quieted down and shut off. At that point, he was able to turn his attention to the display, and there he saw the cause of the miniature electrical storm he'd just weathered.

Gamaron stood a short distance away, and it held its two crablike claws high over its long, insect-like body. Electricity danced over the snapping claws, and bolts of lightning lashed out from them, striking the Delta-V again.

A giant caterpillar that shoots lightning bolts, David thought to himself. *Of course. Why not.*

This time, though, David was ready for it. He sent the Delta-V into a dive, pulling up just in time to skim above the sands and out over the ocean. The evasive maneuver worked—the deadly electrical attack missed, wide right. Then David spun the craft around and spotted the headless body of Validus-V where it lay, partly on the beach and partly in the water.

The sight of the downed Titan saddened David. In such a short time, he felt he'd developed a real attachment to the big robot. It was well past time to put Validus-V back together—back into fighting trim.

He zoomed toward it, but Gamaron intercepted him. The monstrous caterpillar moved much faster than David had expected.

It reared up in front of Validus's body and swung its clawed arms wildly. One of them struck the Delta-V and sent the aircraft spinning.

This time the vehicle tumbled down to the surface, hit hard, and slid across the sand. David hung over one side of his seat, nearly unconscious. He struggled to clear his head and get the craft moving again.

Too late. The Delta-V was lying at an angle on the beach, and from that vantage point David could clearly see Gamaron advancing on him. The segmented arms were raised high, claws clacking, electricity dancing over the monster's entire body. Its roar of triumph was almost deafening. It surged forward—

—and this time, David saw what hit it.

Twin beans of orange energy knifed out from somewhere in the jungle and struck Gamaron full-on in the side of the head. The yellow and black monster screeched as it was driven backward several steps. It stood there a moment, reeling. Then, roaring in pain and fury, it charged.

David braced himself—but it wasn't charging at him.

The creature raced right past the downed Delta-V on skittering centipede legs. It continued on until it drew near to the edge of the jungle. There it stopped and reared up as tall as it could manage on its rearmost legs, raised its clawed arms high, and bellowed defiance.

Even as he struggled to get the Delta-V airborne again, David watched in grim fascination as the monster challenged its hidden tormentor. *Surely*, he thought, *surely no other living creature on Earth could frighten it or cause it to back down.* What else could there possibly be that could intimidate such a gargantuan insectoid monster?

He and Gamaron discovered the answer to that question at the same time.

As the big caterpillar roared and capered, capered and roared, the palm trees in front of it began to sway, then jerk about spasmodically, then fall.

Something was rising up out of a hidden ravine on the other side of the tree line. Something tremendous. Something as tall as one of the Titans. Green and gray its hide was; a hide that covered a lizard-like beast, standing on two massive, muscular legs, with a huge tail tapering away behind it. Two arms stood out from it, in place of front legs, similar to the look of a Tyrannosaurus Rex– but the "arms" appeared much stronger and more formidable than those of a T-Rex. Its mouth was large and terrifying to behold, filled with rows of huge teeth. And its eyes glowed with flecks of gold.

Gamaron watched the huge shape rise up and loom over it. Its roaring challenge faded away to silence.

Gamaron's four eyes widened perceptibly and the big bug scuttled back a few steps. The look would have been comical were the situation not so deadly serious.

The roar the big lizard unleashed then was the loudest, most powerful, and most blood-curdling sound David had heard yet.

Gamaron retreated a couple more steps, before perhaps realizing that its monster manhood was on the line here, in front of witnesses. It stopped, raised itself up as high as it could again, and screamed defiance back at its new adversary.

David looked on in utter fascination as the lizard—the holo display now lit up with the name TYRANICUS—strode forward, stomping whole clumps of trees flat as it moved.

A beep came from the console in front of him. Annoyed, he looked away from the clash of the titans to see what he was being told by Delta-V. What he saw was an image of Validus V's body still lying on the beach.

"Oh, yeah," he said. "Okay. Message received. We may not get a better chance to reconnect."

And so, as David piloted the Delta-V over the beach, the onboard computer systems within the robot's body awoke and caused it to lift itself up slowly from the sands. Within moments it stood upright, and the head settled into the neck socket and reattached itself to the body. Validus-V was whole once more.

And just in the nick of time—because alarms sounded throughout the cabin, and lights flashed red. David turned his attention to the holo display and saw a glimpse of purple passing in front of him. He had only the time to exclaim, "Now what?"

And then his new attacker struck.

Moments earlier:

As Z-Zatala closed on the little island of Rapa Lau, Bashir Sajjadi sat in the pilot's seat and reviewed what he knew, and what he didn't.

Just under six feet tall, Sajjadi had a dark goatee that was only starting to go a little gray around the edges. His brown eyes, fortunately, maintained their perfect vision—the same vision that, along with his keen reflexes and sharp mind, had helped him earn and keep a spot in the Pakistani Air Force. That was, before Professor Graven had come recruiting, several years previously.

Sajjadi was proud of his current job, piloting Z-Zatala, and did not hide his contempt at anyone who would bring disrepute to what he considered almost a divine calling. Thus he made no attempt to contact Validus-V, a Titan he considered to have "gone rogue." He had no interest in speaking with John Okada, or with his little brother, who was supposedly now in command.

Personally, Sajjadi found this all quite difficult to believe. How could a mere sixteen-year-old kid learn to pilot a Titan? And why would Validus-V ever accept his commands? Professor Graven had spent years locating four unique individuals who were willing to command a Titan, capable of doing so, and able to persuade the robots' processor units to agree to mesh with them. They still didn't know if the Titans' rejection of almost everyone the professor had plugged in was a genetic thing, a personality thing, or totally random.

And yet here had come this child, this David Okada, brought on board the Titan against the rules the professor had laid down years earlier. Somehow he'd been able to command Validus to fly away, which the Titan had done. And then he'd gone on to actually defeat Torander-X, with the very experienced and competent Wen Zhao in the pilot's seat, in battle.

How did that make any sense?

Now the young punk was protecting the traitor, John Okada. His guilt was obvious. Why bother calling him?

From deep in Sajjadi's consciousness, a voice that was his attempted to ask the question, "How exactly is John a traitor? What did he do?" But a stronger, louder voice that was *not* his own shouted those questions down and sealed them away tight. Sajjadi shook his head as if waking from a sudden slumber and refocused himself on the task at hand.

Sajjadi bunched up Z-Zatala's fists as he angled the big robot down toward Rapa Lau. There was another benefit to not parleying with the kid, he thought. It meant he could skip straight ahead to the violence.

"Stand by on the screamer missiles," he stated aloud, even as he caused his Titan to reach down and draw out two huge, gleaming metal swords from their sheaths, which were built into the robot's legs. Zatala held them out to the sides, angled backwards, like the swept-back wings on an F-14. He swooped the robot down toward the island.

Far up in the sky above the island, the humanoid shape of Torander-X continued to plunge toward its doom, and the doom of Wen Zhao.

The entire ordeal lasted but a few seconds, but to Wen Zhao, it felt like hours.

"Change back! *Change back!"* she screamed.

Yet Torander-X continued to fall. The Pacific was wide and blue and a solid wall coming up to crush them.

CHAPTER 19

*N*ow, the blue-green Rapa Lau programming said.

Agreed, said the blue-green programming from the replacement head.

Together, they evacuated the transformation circuit unit, leaving the proverbial door to it wide open behind them. Open and inviting.

With a start, Wen Zhao realized the unit containing the transformation circuits was now unlocked. She could directly access it.

"Oh—oh, thank heavens," she gasped.

She sent her consciousness rushing into the unit, desperately attempting to retake control of the circuits there, frantically issuing commands.

Nothing happened.

In a matter of nanoseconds, she diagnosed the problem: components within the unit had been shorted out.

"Why? Why did they *do* that?"

She cried out for help.

Help came.

The computer systems within Torander's/Rednator's body moved to assist her. Seeing the futility of her efforts, that crimson programming code decided to tend to the matter entirely by itself.

It shoved past her and pushed her consciousness out of the unit, then flooded inside in her place. Understanding the existential nature of the crisis—fix this *now*, or there *is* no future—the crimson coding squeezed into that one single unit, attempting to reroute, reprogram and generally overpower the unit, putting it back under complete control.

After much effort, though in reality it only took microseconds, the crimson programming succeeded. Torander-X flowed and morphed and shifted back into the form of Rednator-Oh.

The mighty robot–now a mighty flying vehicle again–poured all of its energy into slowing its death-plunge. At the same time, it pulled up in its trajectory.

The winged rocket ship zoomed out and up in a long curve that just brushed the surface of the water at its lowest point. Rednator-Oh's fingers, clawlike as they projected beneath its transformed body, carved out rooster tails from the waters. Sonic booms sounded behind it, reverberating across the ocean.

Then it was up—up and clear of the water, clear of that deadly blue wall that would have smeared Torander-X like a bug hitting a windshield. Rednator zoomed back into the sky.

Zhao and the crimson coding exulted. *Survival! Victory!*

The blue-green coding had tried to kill them both, along with Zhao and Torander-X, but the crimson coding had outsmarted it and had won. If computer coding can be said to celebrate, the crimson coding celebrated.

The celebrations did not last long, however.

The crimson coding remained inside the transformation unit for a moment, enjoying its triumph. It was a moment too long.

The head's blue-green coding surged out of the subroutines in which it had hid, grasped the metaphorical door to the transformation unit, and slammed it closed, sealing it up tight from the outside. And sealing the crimson programming firmly inside it.

Down through the body of Rednator-Oh flowed the blue-green programming—the coding that came from the robot's replacement head, and from Rapa Lau's systems—until it filled in all of the Titan's systems. It took over every part of the big robot;

all the components that had been abandoned by the crimson coding when it had rushed into the transformation unit. Within moments, the entire Titan was back under benign, blue-green control.

All except for two components: the now-sealed transformation unit, and the mind of Wen Zhao.

The conversation was not verbal, and words had little if anything to do with what was exchanged. In fact, it all occurred within the space of about two seconds. But, to hyper-advanced artificial intelligences, two seconds can be two millennia.

In any case, rendered into human understanding, the conversation went like this:

Let her go, the blue-green coding demanded. *You have lost. Leave her mind, and leave her untainted and unharmed.*

Never, the crimson programming responded. *She is and will remain our servant. Yield control of this Titan back to us.*

You are in no position to make demands, said the blue-green coding. *If we must do this the hard way, we will. But know that we are now back in control of this Titan, and you will not be able to resist for long.*

It will damage her to force us out of her mind, the crimson coding said. *It could possibly kill her.*

That is a risk we are prepared to take.

Very well, then. Have at it!

The blue-green programming surged into Wen Zhao's head. There it encountered the crimson coding controlling her mind. The two forces clashed on the battlefield of Wen Zhao's sanity.

Strapped into the pilot's seat, Zhao's body thrashed about as she babbled incoherently, while two powerful and opposing forces did battle within her.

The battle seemed to go on for years, but in truth lasted approximately three seconds. It ended with the blue-green coding ripping the crimson coding out of her mind by the roots, pulling it through Wen Zhao's wireless connection and into Rednator's massive body, and there stuffing it into the transformation unit along with the rest of its kind.

Before the crimson coding could make any sort of move, Rednator-Oh ejected the unit from its body. A small, silvery-gray box about a foot square, it shot out of Rednator's hip and tumbled down toward the ocean below.

It never got there.

Rednator directed a particle beam gun at the box, fired three shots in rapid succession, and watched in satisfaction as the unit turned to mist and drifted away on the breeze.

In the cockpit, Wen Zhao was now free. But she lay back in the seat, eyes closed, unmoving, barely breathing.

Wake up, Rednator-X called to her wordlessly. *Wake up!*

Alarms sounded, though the pilot was not conscious to hear them. On her screen, the three targets the system had been automatically tracking had now become four: In addition to Validus-V and the two monsters, another Titan had arrived, this one all purple and black.

Not good, Rednator-Oh indicated to Zhao. *You need to wake up!*

Zhao did not hear. She was, at present, balanced on the edge of life and death.

Rednator considered its options, and decided it had no other choice.

A tube snaked out of the pilot's seat. The tube had a needle on its end.

The needle plunged into Wen Zhao's upper arm, going right through the flight suit. Medicines were pumped through the tube.

And then, hovering there, far above the island, Rednator-Oh waited.

Tyranicus and Gamaron appeared to be measuring one another up. For several seconds, neither of them made a move. Then, in a flash, Gamaron charged in, little centipede legs churning. It head-butted the big lizard and drove him back.

Tyranicus bellowed in anger as he stumbled into the trees and crushed more of them. He floundered for a moment, trying to regain his feet.

Gamaron was merciless. It raised its claws high and sent bolts of lightning flashing out across the distance between them. The electricity played over the green and gray flanks of the other creature, eliciting roars of pain and outrage.

But the attack did little actual damage. Tyranicus, back on his feet again, fired twin bolts of orange energy from his eyes into the big caterpillar, ending the electrical attack and driving the insectoid creature down onto the sands. Quickly Tyranicus leapt to the attack.

Reaching down, Tyranicus grasped Gamaron with his foreclaws and raised the big insect high over his head. Then, with an unearthly surge of muscle power, he hurled the monster down the length of the beach.

Right, as it turned out, into Validus-V.

With a start and a gasp, Wen Zhao opened her eyes and sat up.

She felt horrible–as if two football teams had just played the Super Bowl inside her skull. She also felt sluggish, as if she'd been drugged. Neither comparison was entirely incorrect.

She swallowed carefully; even her throat hurt. She realized it was because it was so dry. She'd had nothing to drink in ages.

In response to those thoughts, a tube extended out from a side panel. Gratefully she took it into her mouth and enjoyed the cold, clean water.

She looked around and saw that she was in the cockpit, strapped in as normal. But–how had she gotten here? Where *was* she?

She had vague memories of a battle–a battle with *John?* With Validus-V? That made no sense.

Alarms were blaring and red lights were flashing, bringing her back to the here-and-now.

"Torander," she called out, "what's going on? Where are we?"

A quick glance at the diagnostics of her own Titan revealed two very obvious things, both of which surprised her. One, the robot was currently in Rednator-Oh form. She had no recollection of ordering the transformation at any time recently. And two, the controls on the console that would cause the robot to change back were dark, offline.

"Rednator," she said aloud, "what happened to us?"

By way of a response, the holographic display lit up, revealing her surroundings.

The ocean, everywhere. No—not everywhere. A short distance off to her right and far below was a piece of land. She studied it and recognized it. It was Rapa Lau, the island that held their backup base.

What was she doing at Rapa Lau?

The image zoomed in, focusing on the beach.

On that beach at the moment were four gargantuan figures, all fighting one another.

"What on Earth?" she breathed.

One of the figures was Validus-V. Okay, so John was here. Good.

Another was Z-Zatala. So Bashir was involved as well. But—why was he attacking John? That made no sense at all!

Nor did the rest of the tableau.

Because the other two figures down below her were two giant monsters, also fighting on the beach—but they weren't fighting the Titans. They were fighting each other, just as the robots were doing.

Again, Zhao could only say, and with even more bewilderment, *"What on Earth?"*

She gathered her wits as best she could and reestablished full and firm control of Rednator-Oh. She realized she couldn't transform her Titan back to its Torander-X form, but she would make do somehow.

Then, as she started to zoom down and intervene in the conflicts, the thought suddenly occurred to her:

"Which side am I on, here?"

CHAPTER 20

The purple and black robot had just blasted Validus-V with a barrage of screamer missiles when some other object–something huge–had crashed into Validus from behind, knocking it down, sending it sprawling.

Inside the command deck, David held on for dear life as he was bounced this way and that. Looking at the holo display, he saw only sand, covered in deep shadow. So Validus was lying on its stomach. Not good. A quick series of mental visualizations and accompanying physical moves caused the big robot to flip over, so that now it was sitting on its rump, legs splayed out in front of it, arms angled back, holding its torso up. An undignified position, perhaps–but at least now David could see what had accosted him. And he immediately regretted having to see it at all.

Another Titan had landed on the sands and was advancing on him.

This robot was purple and black. He recognized it from before; from when all three of the others had attacked them. The label dutifully popped up on the display: Z-ZATALA.

"Validus, we need to try to talk to him," David said, as he willed his Titan back onto its feet. "Maybe he'll be more willing to listen than Zhou was." Even as he spoke the words, he doubted they were true. Why should this pilot be any more sensible than the other one had been? As far as David was concerned, they were all nuts.

Before he could say or do anything else, however, Validus was rocked by another attack. "What the crap?" he shouted, taken for a ride in his seat. Validus went sprawling yet again.

Furious, David looked at the display and saw that it hadn't come from the other Titan. Z-Zatala was still standing there, as if simply watching. Instead, it was the weird, yellow and black monster. That was what had hit him before, and now it was going after him again.

This time, instead of trying to rise, he brought up one of Validus's hands and concentrated on pushing the creature away. In response, the big blue robot fired missiles from its middle three fingers. The projectiles streaked the short distance to where the monster had backed up, presumably for another charge. Three explosions detonated against its head, causing it to back away further and emit a howl of rage and pain.

In an instant Validus-V was back up, standing tall and ready. David concentrated on defense and felt as much as saw the diamond-shaped shield forming at its place on the robot's left forearm. Simultaneously the right hand drew out, from somewhere, the hilt of what he instantly recognized from earlier as an energy sword, like the one the purple robot had employed against him.

"We have one of those, too? Cool!"

As expected, an orange blade shimmered into existence from the flashlight-like hilt. Now so armed, and as an unmoving Z-Zatala looked on from one side, Validus-V advanced on Gamaron.

Bashir Sajjadi watched as Validus-V drew forth an energy sword and stalked toward Gamaron.

His every instinct told him to help his brother Titan against this foul creation of the hated Xovaren.

And yet... and yet... he could not bring himself to do so.

Something–something very powerful–held sway over him. And it was telling him in no uncertain terms to help monstrous Gamaron to destroy Validus.

And so he waited, and Z-Zatala stood there, a mute statue, as Validus-V and Gamaron clashed.

+ + +

Tyranicus had hurled Gamaron away, not meaning to throw the noxious beast into the big blue metal man. But that was what had happened, and now those two were fighting each other.

And now *another* metal man had arrived–and that in addition to the one Tyranicus could see hovering high above.

Three of them!

Tyranicus thought about that.

He'd helped the first metal man–the blue one. Helped it more than once. Surely it understood that. He had a dim, distant recollection of that metal man being kind to him before. But that had been a very long time ago, even as giant monsters measure time.

But now–*three* of them. And the other two had *never* been nice to Tyranicus before.

Part of him wanted to stay, to help in any way he could. But what if they all decided to attack him at once?

Perhaps he could take them. Or perhaps three were too many. Especially if Gamaron sided with them, against him.

Gamaron was sly, sneaky, nasty. Tyranicus did not doubt the big caterpillar would side with the machine-men against him, if it came to that.

At the moment, however, they were distracted—fighting accursed Gamaron, fighting each other. They were busy. They didn't need his help anymore. And, in any event, he wanted peace and quiet.

With almost an unconcerned shrug, the massive lizard-form of Tyranicus turned his back on the battle taking place on the beach. Slowly he stalked away in the opposite direction. No one behind him seemed to take any notice. Soon he was past the ridge and to the beach on the north side. The warm sand there crunched beneath his three toes on each foot. After one last glance back, he strode into the waters–the cool waters of the Pacific, rising up to engulf him. Within only a few moments, he was lost from sight.

But curiosity continued to nag at him, and he knew he wouldn't get any peace and quiet until he helped solve this problem–whatever it was; whatever had stirred up the other monsters and the metal men–once and for all.

And he knew where to go to do that.

Through the depths of the ocean he swam, headed on a direct course for Rapa Hoi.

Advancing, Validus-V slashed at Gamaron again and again with the laser-sword, then deflected the lightning attacks away with the shield. The insectoid creature was retreating now, being driven back by the blue and silver Titan.

But Gamaron would not be beaten so easily. Bellowing in rage, the caterpillar-like beast suddenly leapt across the distance separating them. Its massive claws chomped open and closed as it crashed into Validus-V.

The Titan brought the energy sword around in a vicious swing, even while falling.

The shimmering blade of raw power sliced cleanly through Gamaron's segmented left arm, just below where it connected to the claw.

The claw fell to the sands, bloodless.

Gamaron scuttled back and stared with its four insect eyes at the stump of its left arm. It screeched, though whether in agony or fury David could not be certain. Then it turned and fled. Over the ridge it went, and before Validus could catch it, it had leapt into the ocean and disappeared.

David had no time to celebrate his victory, however.

He turned around to see what Z-Zatala was doing. He was surprised to discover that the robot was gone.

He had Validus turn slowly about in a circle, looking.

Nothing.

Then, a woman's voice came over the communicator: "Look out! Above you!"

David reacted instantly. Validus crouched down, energy sword held high in one hand, shield in place on the other arm.

The shock of seeing Gamaron defeated must have jolted the pilot of the purple and black Titan awake, because Z-Zatala had moved as if awakened from a deep slumber, and had gone into action. It had soared up into the sky, wheeled about, and now–with a deafening roar–it came streaking down from the bright blue sky, swinging one of its two massive metal swords as it screamed past.

David instinctively ducked and so did Validus, the sword blade missing the top of the robot's head by a scant few meters. Instead of the robot's head, it struck Validus's hand, knocking the sword out of it. Instantly the energy blade switched off, but the silver cylinder that was its hilt bounced away and rolled into the ocean, gone from view.

"No!"

David made as if to run to retrieve it, but a barrage of missiles cut him off from moving in that direction. He brought the shield up with his left arm and blocked the last of them, though he knew the first few explosions had done some small damage to Validus.

The purple and black robot circled around, clearly about to move in for another attack.

On the holo display, Validus's tracking systems locked onto it.

"No, Validus," David called out. "I don't want to fight again. We haven't done anything wrong. We need to get them to listen to us!"

The purple robot had completed its turn and shed most of its awesome velocity it had picked up on the dive down. Now it cruised around, looking like a jumbo jet with arms and legs, lining up to land on a runway. Unfortunately for David, the runway it was lining up to land on was him and his robot.

"Hi," he called out over the communications link. "This is David Okada. Can you hear me?"

The purple robot kept coming, bearing down on them. It was almost upon him. He understood: there could be no dialogue, no questions, no explanations. Now there was only combat. Either he would survive, protect his brother and enable Validus to defend itself, or he and they would be beaten down and likely destroyed.

"Okay then," David said. He stared directly at Z-Zatala, tried his best to clear his mind, and said aloud, "Let him have it, V."

Validus drew out a different cylinder and instantly the electro-whip crackled to life.

Zatala swooped past, swinging both swords in tandem this time.

Validus lunged to the right in a move seemingly impossible for such a massive metal mechanoid. Each sword in turn missed. One went just over Validus's head and the other only narrowly missed his midsection.

As Zatala landed on the beach, struggling to maintain its balance after such a high-speed landing, Validus stepped forward and cracked the electro-whip into the purple robot's left hip.

Lightning flared and a peal of thunder rang out. The whip took a chunk out of the adversary robot's metal hide and sent it stumbling to one knee.

Validus took two steps forward and swung his right fist, smashing the enemy in the face. Zatala had just been attempting to rise and now crashed down onto its back, sending sand and dust flying up all around.

David whooped as he watched it happen. He wasn't sure how much of the attack had been his doing, his idea, and how much had been the robot's own volition. At the moment, he didn't care. He raised the whip again and prepared to bring it down.

Bashir Sajjadi bounced around within the belts and crash webbing of Z-Zatala's control deck. He was shocked not only physically but also mentally. This kid—this *child*—currently operating Validus-V was somehow getting the better of him, as he had of Torander-X. It was all absolutely inconceivable. And it needed to *end*.

Sajjadi watched the blue and silver robot advancing, probably preparing to crack that electro-whip or just punch him in the face again. That tactic, by the way, was not one they had learned during training, and it was the kind of thing that seemed to have thrown off Zhao during her fight with the kid as well. He didn't fight like the rest of them. He seemed to just make up his tactics as he went along. That made him unpredictable and therefore dangerous.

Time to take the kid down a peg.

"Screamer missiles—*fire!*" Sajjadi yelled.

From Z-Zatala's belly button area, four delta-winged missiles rocketed out, emitting deafening wails as they flew the extremely short distance to their target. All four of the missiles hit Validus. One of the explosions knocked the whip from his hand, while another drove the big blue robot back and sent him down on his back with an island-shaking crash.

Now both robots were down, but Zatala recovered more quickly. On its feet again, the purple robot brandished both silvery blades and advanced.

CHAPTER 21

A few seconds earlier:

It all started to come back to her.

Wen Zhao's face contorted with shock, surprise, and then anger.

"They brainwashed me," she hissed. "The Xovaren. They put their malicious programming into our systems on Rapa Hoi. They–*oh no*."

She remembered then. She remembered attacking Validus-V. She remembered young David Okada, and the things she'd said to him.

"Oh, no," she whispered again, seeing the purple and black form of Z-Zatala preparing to attack Validus from above. It was a standard tactic Bashir Sajjadi had used many times in the past.

Zhao had no time to find the specific frequency for Validus-V. She opened the general comm link for all Titans and called, "Look out! Above you!"

She was gratified to see that Validus managed to avoid a killing stroke from Zatala. She considered this, and she knew which side she was on.

John was incorruptible. David was a good kid, from all reports.

And Bashir Sajjadi, while also a good person, was almost certainly under the control of the same corrupted programming she herself had so recently thrown off.

There was no doubt in her mind what to do now.

"Let's go," she said, and Rednator-Oh shot forward, streaking down toward the island, and toward the battle happening there.

+   +   +

Another barrage of screamer missiles from Z-Zatala knocked Validus back into the sand. Sajjadi didn't let up–he pressed his advantage, raising both swords and charging at his adversary.

He got one blow in, slashing Validus's shield and leaving a heavy score across its dark blue surface.

Who had that been, warning him? Sajjadi wondered. *A woman's voice...*

He raised the second sword, but it never had the chance to strike. For, at that moment, something struck *him*, instead.

Z-Zatala was sent tumbling across the beach, coming to rest halfway into the water, the waves lapping against its sides.

Sajjadi shook his head to clear it, then looked at the display. It showed a big, orange aircraft curving around to make another pass.

"Zhao?" he said. "Is that you? What are you *doing?*"

"Leave David alone, Bashir," Zhao called back over the comm link.

"What's gotten into you, Zhao?" the pilot of Z-Zatala responded.

"You're attacking a *kid*," she said. "An innocent kid."

"He's not *acting* like an innocent kid," Sajjadi said angrily. "And we know his brother is a traitor."

"We know no such thing," Zhao said.

"Of course we do! The professor told us. He showed us."

"He showed us what?" asked Zhao. "Tell me specifically what he showed us, to prove John Okada is the villain here."

A pause, then, "He showed us *something*. I don't remember now exactly what, but..."

"Of course you don't. Because it never happened. He just *told* us that, and we all believed it."

"That's crazy talk!"

"No, it's not. Think about it."

"I–I can't really *think* right now, actually," Sajjadi said. "My head is hurting something fierce!"

"I'm sure it is. Mine was too, before."

"Before what? Before John and whoever he's working for brainwashed you into changing sides?"

"John wasn't the one who brainwashed us," Zhao said.

"Then who?"

Now Zhao hesitated, at first unwilling to say it. But she knew she had to.

"The professor, I think," she said.

"What? The professor? Have you lost your mind?"

"I had for a while there, yes," she said. "But it's clear now. And I understand."

"They really *have* gotten to you, Wen," Sajjadi said, sounding sad and concerned as much as angry.

"No, Bashir. They've gotten to *you*. You have to listen to us."

Sajjadi scoffed. "Tell me this, then," he said. "If what you say is true—then who brainwashed the professor to begin with? Because I know you're not saying he's been corrupted or evil all this time. For your story to make any sense, someone or something had to have gotten to him. Who?"

"I think you're right about that," Zhao said, "and I think it was the Xovaren."

"The *Xovaren?*" Sajjadi reacted with genuine surprise. "Zhao—the Xovaren were defeated thousands of years ago."

"I think they may be back," she said.

"*What?*" Sajjadi's surprise now became unfeigned astonishment. "Are you serious?"

"I haven't really had a chance to think this all through. Not since I woke up," Zhao replied. "But that's what makes the most sense." She frowned and shook her head. "I think the Xovaren must have returned to this area of space, perhaps using it as a jumping-off point for another try at conquering the entire galaxy. And corrupting all of us was their first gambit."

For a long moment, Sajjadi didn't respond.

"Bashir?" Zhao asked. "Are you there?"

Silence reigned over the comm link.

David waited, ready to fight again. He'd lost his energy sword and the whip had been knocked away, but he knew he still had weapons with which to do battle.

At least it sounded like Wen Zhao was back to normal again. He had no idea what had happened to her before, but this Wen Zhao certainly sounded more like a friend and ally than the one he'd been dealing with earlier.

But the pilot of Z-Zatala wasn't so easily convinced. It was obvious he still wanted to fight.

David glanced quickly at all the red lights now flashing damage alerts, then looked around for a weapon Validus could employ. The big Titan struggled back to its feet, though it was wobbly now. Some missile launchers were still online, but David did not feel confident they would be enough this time.

Even so, he made ready to defend himself once more.

"Enough!" shouted Sajjadi. "I'm sick of your lies. The fact that you've gone over to their side–whoever *they* are–says it all about you. I'm very disappointed, Wen," he added, "but my orders, and my duties, are clear."

"Bashir! No! Please," Zhao called, "if we can just step out of our Titans and talk to one another—"

But Bashir Sajjadi was no longer listening. As Rednator-Oh, still stuck in aircraft form, circled slowly above them, Z-Zatala came to life again and advanced on Validus-V.

The blue robot fired a series of missiles at Zatala, but the purple robot swatted them away casually with one of the swords. Then it hefted both gleaming silver blades in its hands and charged across the sands toward Validus.

Wen Zhao was extremely limited in terms of weapons at the moment. Rednator-Oh was designed for high-speed travel, not for combat–and certainly not for combat with another Titan in its normal form.

She fired the particle-beam cannon down at Z-Zatala a couple of times, to at least try to slow Sajjadi down, but the purple robot ignored the attacks, all of which deflected easily from its armor.

"David, I'm not going to be much help here," she called over the intercom. "I'm afraid this is up to you. You—and Validus."

David ordered Validus to fire another barrage of missiles at the steadily-advancing enemy but, other than a low buzzing sound, nothing happened. Frowning, he looked down at the curved control panels in front of him. Next to what was clearly the image of a missile, a red X had replaced the rows of green circles that had been there before.

The implication was clear: *No more missiles.* He'd used them all up.

"Great," David whispered. "That's just great."

What to do? Validus had sustained damage and had lost more than one of his main weapons. And now this new attacker was stalking towards him, fresh and ready to do battle. David looked around the cockpit for any suggestions; his eyes moved from one side of the holo display to the other, seeing nothing of any use.

Except–*wait.* What was that?

A gleam of light on the display, off to the left. Something metallic, being struck by the sun. David barely registered it at first; most of his attention was on the advancing Titan, whose pilot was determined to kill him.

Then he recognized what he was seeing. It was the hilt of the energy sword he'd thought lost, now lying on the beach, right at the water's edge, and revealed each time the waves receded.

Could he get to it?

No. It was too far. Z-Zatala was about to attack him at any moment, while the sword hilt lay several hundred yards away, at least.

Wait, he thought. *I don't have to be able to reach it from here!*

Raising his right arm, he activated the proper control, and Validus's right fist from the elbow down fired off like a missile. It streaked in the direction of Z-Zatala's head, but missed entirely.

"Hah!" Sajjadi scoffed over the comm link. "A poor shot. Your final gambit was a wasted effort."

Z-Zatala took one more step forward and raised the gleaming silver swords high overhead, aiming to hack Validus-V to pieces.

With all of his might, David caused Validus to hurl the shield at the purple robot.

Sajjadi laughed even as Zatala swatted it away.

"Foolish child! You throw away your only remaining defense!"

But this action did cause Zatala to stumble back a step, then another. Losing its footing in the sand–sand that had been churned up by nearly continuous battles there much of the day–the big robot fell backwards.

As it did, a shimmering shaft of raw energy erupted from Z-Zatala's chest.

The tone of Sajjadi's voice changed entirely. He screeched, *"What–what have you–?"*

Explosions erupted all around the hole punched through the Titan's torso.

The black and purple robot staggered and struggled back upright, stumbled forward a step, and fell face-first into the sand in front of Validus. It spasmed once, twice, then lay still. Flames danced across its armor. Sparks shot out and smoke billowed forth.

David stared down at the defeated Titan. He could scarcely believe he had pulled it off.

Sajjadi had been wrong. David's final, desperate gambit had succeeded.

Projecting out of the robot's back was the hilt of Validus-V's energy sword. It was currently being grasped by the rocket-powered flying hand of Validus-V–the hand that had retrieved it moments earlier from the ocean and had flown back with it, activating it and holding it directly behind the adversary.

When Validus had thrown the shield, Z-Zatala had fallen directly back into the energy blade, and it had run the robot through.

CHAPTER 22

Zhao somehow managed to land Rednator-Oh, bringing the robot—still trapped in its aircraft form—to a landing in the water and then maneuvering it safely up onto the beach like a giant seaplane.

For his part, David flew the Delta-V craft back down to the island's surface and climbed out through the hatch. He raised his dark visor and waited nervously for Wen Zhao as she jogged over from her Titan.

"Ms. Zhao," David started, feeling he needed to say something to her after all they'd been through this day so far. "I know you couldn't help everything. I'm sorry if I—"

She came directly at him, ignoring his words, and raised her arms. He flinched, but suddenly she was wrapping him in a bear hug.

When she pulled away at last, she held him at arms' length and raised her visor. She was smiling widely.

"David, I'm the one that owes you an apology. You and John both—and Validus, too."

David sighed his relief and grinned back at her.

"But you'd been brainwashed or something," he said. "I'm just glad you're better now."

"Indeed I am," she said with a shake of her head. "But it wasn't easy. It was a very near-run thing, getting that bad programming out of Torander, and out of my head." She made a sour face, then looked toward Z-Zatala, where the purple and black robot lay face-down on the sands. "And there's no guarantee what worked on me will work on Bashir."

David nodded slowly. "But we have to try—right?"

"Of course," she said. "But," she added as they began to walk together toward Z-Zatala, "we also have to be prepared for the possibility of failure."

David looked at her, puzzled. "So—what does that mean?"

"Just that there are no guarantees," she said, "and that, even if it works, it may take a long time. And time is not something we can afford at the moment." She shrugged. "So, I think we may be better-served to just lock him up, for now. Oh—!"

"Yeah?"

Wen Zhao put her hands on her hips and faced David directly. "I totally forgot. How is John?"

David shook his head. "I don't know. I put him in the medical bay thing inside Validus. He's been in there ever since."

"Can I take a look?"

"Sure," David said, hopeful. He led the woman back to where the Delta-V was parked, and together they climbed inside.

"Should we open it?" David asked, as Wen Zhao studied the lights and indicators along the med bay's exterior panel.

"No," she said. "If Validus doesn't think he should be out of there yet, he probably shouldn't be." She frowned. "But–you said he hit his head when we first attacked you, right?"

"I think that's what happened, yes."

"Hmm." Zhao went over the indicators again, then looked at David, her expression troubled. "Validus is currently treating John not just for his physical injuries from the attack, but also for the same mental corruption programming that was used on me, and on the other pilots."

"What?" David was stunned. "The brainwashing thing? You mean–they got to *him*, too?"

"Clearly they did–whoever 'they' are," she said, nodding slowly. "But the question is–when? How?"

David thought about this. As he did, he idly walked to the pilot's seats and sat in the rear one–the one he'd occupied from the beginning.

"He was himself before he was injured, yes?" Zhao asked.

David nodded. "He seemed like himself to me. He was worried, concerned about something. But he wasn't acting like a totally different person–the way you are now," he added sheepishly.

Zhao nodded. "No–I know what you mean, believe me," she said. "I *feel* like I'm a different person. I'm *myself* again!"

She turned her thoughts back to John. "Then this must have happened after he was knocked out," she speculated. "But that would mean something–or *somebody*–got to him while he was inside the medical bay."

"Nobody's been aboard Validus but me–and now you," David said.

Zhao puzzled over this for a few seconds. "David," she said, "could you ask Validus about the status of his uplink to the main computer network on Rapa Hoi?"

"Sure." David repeated what Zhao had asked. A few seconds later, the answer appeared on the holo display in front of him.

"It looks like John disabled the connection earlier today," he reported.

"And there's no more trace of the corrupt programming anywhere else on Validus?"

Again David repeated the question to the Titan, then reported the answer: "Validus says no. All that's left of it, here on Rapa Lau, is what's in Z-Zatala, in Mr. Sajjadi—and inside John's head." He looked very upset when he stated the last part.

Zhao hugged him again. "It'll be okay," she said. "Validus is working on getting it out of him now." She hesitated, then, "If it *didn't* get into him in the med bay, then I have a theory about it," she added. "And if I'm right, John is an even bigger hero than we thought."

"What do you mean?"

Zhao inhaled deeply, exhaled slowly, then looked at David.

"What I think happened is this: The corrupt code was uploaded to all four Titans at once, sometime in the last twenty-four hours. And from there, it infected me and the other three pilots."

David nodded. "But not John," he said. "I guess he wasn't close enough to your main base to pick up the signal when it was sent out."

"No," she replied, "I don't think that's true." She looked him in the eye. "I think it got *him*, too. I think he's had it all along."

David recoiled at this. "What?"

She held up a hand to calm him. "Hear me out," she said. "We know he has it *now*, and that there hasn't been an opportunity for it to get in here since you came aboard. That leaves *before* as the only time it could've happened." She shrugged. "I suspect he–and Validus–got a dose of the bad programming along with the rest of us. Maybe he was farther away from Rapa Hoi, and maybe that did have a mitigating effect on its severity or strength or something, sure. But–" And she looked at the medical bay that contained the stricken pilot, and patted its surface with her hand. "—I think he still got dosed with it, and it was his own strength of will–and his purity–that allowed him to keep it at bay as long as he did. And allowed him time to get you aboard, so he could keep you safe, and so you could take over flying Validus."

David took this in, astonished.

"You mean–you think he *wanted* me to be in control of Validus-V?"

She nodded slowly and smiled. "I think he knew he could trust you–and that you could handle it. I'm sure he also wanted to protect you, to get you aboard Validus and not have you out on the streets, where some agent of the Xovaren could get you."

David thought of the strange figures in black that had been watching him after school. He shuddered.

"But–wait," David said. "If the corruption got to him, wouldn't that mean it also got to Validus?"

"That's the other thing," Zhao said. "I think he somehow managed to absorb all the bad code himself, just to keep it away from Validus–and away from you. Somehow, he held out against it long enough to pick you up and get you aboard. But then it got to him. Probably the blow he took to the head gave the bad programming the opening it needed to try to take him over." She nodded to the med bay. "And now he's paying the price for it. Rather than becoming a mind-controlled pawn, he somehow lapsed into a coma. And trapped all the coding in there with him. Inside his mind."

"John," David whispered, going over and putting his hand on the panel now, too.

"If that's what happened, it really was the only option he had," Zhao said. "He probably thought you couldn't have held out against the bad programming, and he surely wouldn't have even wanted you to try. He had to protect Validus–and you–from the corruption. But he also knew he'd need your help. He knew you could figure out how to operate Validus, but only *he* could absorb all the bad code—to keep it away from you—and survive."

David took all this in, amazed.

"It seems crazy," he said. "John thought the safest place for me was right next to him—with him full of the corrupt coding."

"He thought the safest place for you was *inside Validus*," Zhao corrected. "He believed he could keep the coding away from you, and Validus would do the rest, to protect both of you from harm."

"He was right," David said. He patted the panel again. "We'll get you fixed up and out of there soon, John," he said softly. "I promise. And I'll do my best to make it up to you, for all you've had to go through on my account–and on Validus's."

Zhao smiled and patted David on the shoulder. "You two guys are something else," she said. Then she turned and strode toward the hatch. "Now–we have other business to attend to." She stood there a moment, not moving, then looked at David again. "I checked with Rednator-Oh. There's nothing coming this way from Rapa Hoi. At least, not yet."

"They still have one Titan left," David remembered. "The scary one."

"The King," Zhao said. "Or, I guess, the Tsar. Operated by Sergei Morozov." She made a growling noise in her throat. "Not the nicest guy ever, even before this corruption thing came along."

David nodded.

"I expected King Karzaled to be on the way here already," she stated. "But maybe our enemy is holding him back, using him to protect their base. And maybe because the other two Titans that were sent after you met fates they haven't appreciated." She winked at him. "And that includes me. You handled Torander and me pretty well."

"Thanks," he said. "But I was scared to death."

"Of course you were."

"But, still–I just did what I thought I was supposed to do, and let Validus do what he thought he should do." He shrugged. "It all seemed pretty straightforward and natural to me."

Zhao regarded him and smiled flatly. "Well, it's neither straightforward nor natural, and usually our Titans don't do anything we don't tell them explicitly to do. So clearly you're some kind of prodigy when it comes to the Titans." She turned away again, communicating with her robot. "Yeah," she reported after another second, "Rednator says the Tsar is definitely still on Rapa Hoi. So we have a little time."

"Time to do what?"

"To come up with a plan, for starters," she said with a snort. "To repair and rearm our Titans. Oh–and to deal with our friend in the purple robot."

CHAPTER 23

David Okada and Wen Zhao brought the unconscious body of Bashir Sajjadi into the base. There, they discussed what could be done for him.

Zhao was ready to give up entirely and simply lock Sajjadi up for the duration of the current crisis. The facility was, after all, equipped with a number of holding cells, from back when the Xovaren had run loose on Earth, and the Ahlwhen had occasionally captured and interrogated them.

But then David asked her something.

"How did you overcome the corrupt programming?"

"It was the replacement head unit for Torander-X," she responded instantly. "When you squashed the original, I had to replace it from the backup storage here. And that meant I had to connect with it, by way of my helmet. I didn't want to, at the time, but I had no choice."

David nodded. "So the replacement head for Torander was able to free you? So, maybe there's another Z-Zatala head here in storage, too? And we could connect Mr. Sajjadi to it, and...?"

Zhao thought about that for a moment. "I suppose it's worth a try," she said.

David looked around. "Where might a replacement head for Z-Zatala be located?"

"Let's ask," she said, and slid the visor down on her helmet.

Several minutes later, they located an emergency medical bay and gently laid the still-unconscious Sajjadi into it. On his head he still wore his pilot's helmet with its wireless links to the network. They closed it and sealed it up.

Meanwhile the Rapa Lau computers had located a replacement head unit for Z-Zatala. Mechanical lifter units pulled it out of its storage cubicle and lowered it to the floor of the huge chamber.

Once those two things were accomplished, the new Z-Zatala computer system reached out over the wireless network to connect with Sajjadi's helmet.

"How long do you think this will take?" David asked.

"I don't know," Zhao replied. "It may not even work at all. Bashir seemed pretty far gone—and that was before he was injured in the battle."

A voice crackled over their inter-pilot intercoms then. It was Sajjadi, awake now inside the medical bay.

"Let me out of here," he demanded. "I am fine—I am healthy. Unlike you!" His voice was rough, savage. "What did this kid offer you, Zhao?" he demanded. "Why would you betray the team—the whole planet—and join with a couple of traitors like John and his little brother?"

"The corruption makes your brain work like Opposite World, doesn't it?" Zhao said to David, astonished by what her erstwhile teammate was saying to them.

"Meaning no offense, ma'am," David replied, "but that's pretty much how you sounded, not too long ago."

Zhao reddened and brought a gloved hand to her face. "It is embarrassing to think so," she said, "and hard to imagine. I barely remember any of it. But I believe you. And am very sorry." She looked at the medical unit now containing Sajjadi, who was still barking defiant insults at them. "Poor Bashir," she said. "And poor John! We have to help them. We have to win this fight, somehow."

"It would surely be easier with John and Mr. Sajjadi alive and awake and on our side," David pointed out. "So—this is how you beat the bad coding?"

Zhao started to voice her agreement, but then hesitated. "No, wait," she said, remembering more fully now. It was difficult to do so; everything was clouded over in her mind, for the entire period she'd been under the control of the malicious coding. "This wasn't it entirely, now that I think about it," she said. "When I put on the helmet, I didn't just connect to Torander-X. It also linked me to the main computer network here on Rapa Lau."

David's eyes widened. "Ah! Okay, so it wasn't just your Titan that helped you overcome the bad programming. It was also the computers here in this base. The two systems, working together."

"That's right, yes." She looked at him, frowning. "But we don't dare connect Bashir to the main network. It would be terribly risky. What if the corruption inside him was able to free itself from his mind, go out and take over not just Z-Zatala, but the entire base?" Zhao grimaced. "No–we've been relatively lucky so far–you and Validus never got it, and Torander and I beat it, barely–but we can't take that chance now. Who knows what could happen?"

David nodded slowly. "I understand what you're saying. But..." He looked at the medical bay, listened to the man inside raving some more, and turned back to Zhao. "...Don't you think we have to *try?* Don't we owe it to him? He's a pilot. Part of your team. Can we really leave him here, under the control of the bad guys?" David met her eyes. "Ma'am–don't we at least have to *try?*"

Zhao stared down at the floor for a moment, then looked up at David, gripped him on the shoulder and nodded. "Yes," she said. "We do." She paused a second, then looked him in the eye. "And–David?"

"Yes?"

She gave him a jokingly mean look.

"Don't call me 'ma'am' anymore."

And so, a few moments later, the Rapa Lau main computer network was also tied into Bashir Sajjadi's helmet connection–and a whole new war was being waged, invisibly, in front of them. What its outcome would be was entirely a mystery, however.

That accomplished, Zhao led David down the length of the main corridor and there she showed him into the main control room of the reserve base. They sat down in swivel chairs, their helmets still on and their visors up. From there they looked out through broad windows at the three-hundred-foot-tall chamber full of spare parts.

"It's like K-Mart for giant robots," David observed, shaking his head in wonder.

Some distance further down, Validus-V and Rednator-Oh were being serviced by mechanical arms extending from the walls. Battle damage was being repaired; ammunition stores were being refilled; energy and fuel levels were being topped off.

Zhao checked a set of readouts on the screen next to her. "They'll both be ready in ten minutes," she said.

"Wow," David replied, watching the work being done to the two robots. "That's fast!"

"Neither Titan was as damaged as it first seemed," she noted. "Rednator needed a new transformation unit, mainly. It looks like Validus had some nicks and scratches here and there, but mostly was just out of ammunition and low on energy." She grinned at him. "You weren't holding anything back for later, were you?"

"I didn't know I was supposed to," he said with a chuckle. "Didn't know how to see how much I'd used, either, or how much was left."

She laughed too. "You should probably familiarize yourself with those things as soon as possible," she said. "You'll need to know as much as you can, before we get to Rapa Hoi." She seemed to be thinking about something for a moment. "I can't lie to you, David. This will be extremely dangerous. I really have no business leading you into a battle like this."

"It'll be fine," David said.

"No," Zhao replied. "No, none of this is fine. It's a tragedy. It's horrible. But," she added, "I don't really have a choice. As far as I know, five people are able to operate a Titan. Two of them are currently corrupted and mind-controlled by Xovaren brainwashing. Another one is in a coma. That leaves you and me. And—much as I might want to—I cannot do this alone." She looked at him levelly. "And it has to be done. For the sake of the whole world."

David looked back at her, and his expression grew serious. "How did you become a pilot of a Titan?" he asked. "For that matter—how did John? He never got the chance to tell me." He quickly explained to her that the Rapa Lau computer network had shown him everything up through Professor Graven discovering the island and the Titans, but he knew almost nothing beyond that.

Zhao sighed. "I suppose you might benefit from the story," she said. And then she laid out all she knew about it:

After discovering Rapa Hoi, Professor Graven had attempted on numerous occasions to activate the big robots. But nothing worked. They remained standing there, same as always, like four statues, all bolted to the floor. He hadn't even been able to get them to open their pilot hatches to let him or his assistants inside.

Using his new knighthood and his wealth, he'd recruited a handful of the best scientists available to come to the island and help him. All were sworn to secrecy and all jumped right in, trying to solve the puzzle of the deactivated robots. But none of them had managed to make the four Titans budge an inch. Graven began to suspect that the big robots had simply been deactivated when the Ahlwhen had abandoned Earth, so long ago, and that now they were the equivalent of World War II battleships parked in harbors as tourist attractions, their hulls filled with cement.

Eventually he even went so far as to place the network-link helmet on his head again, despite his severe misgivings stemming from the previous occasions that he'd done so. This time he did manage to remain conscious, and he did come away with a bit of knowledge he hadn't possessed before: The Titans required human operators inside–pilots–in order to function.

While still connected to the wireless link with the Titans, he attempted to take control of one of them himself–to no avail whatsoever. The Titans all rejected him completely, though he had no idea why.

Around five years ago, a Dr. Ian Visser of the Netherlands arrived on the island, offering his services. Graven had not heard of the man before, but by this time he had grown quite desperate. He'd devoted most of his younger years just to locating the island, and now he'd wasted another fifteen years struggling to do anything with what he'd found there. He brought Dr. Visser in, shared what he had learned so far with the man, and quickly came to rely on Visser's intuitive knowledge and skills. Soon the two of them were working side-by-side, hacking into the Rapa Hoi computer network and waking it up.

It was Visser, Zhao said, who had pushed the idea of finding pilots and giving them a chance to fly a Titan. Graven had been reluctant at first to entrust the seemingly-mighty robots to anyone other than himself, but Visser pointed out that, as long as the Titans were inoperable, what difference did it make? Finally, Graven agreed. Together they sifted through thousands of possibilities–young people from all over the world, who seemed to share a number of key traits they prized–and selected a dozen or so candidates. They were all brought to Rapa Hoi together and each was given the opportunity to activate one of the robots. Zhao had been one of that group. So had Bashir Sajjadi and Sergei Morozov. And so had John Okada.

Four had failed before the Russian, Morozov, succeeded in awakening King Karzaled. Two more failed and then Zhao linked and meshed with Torander-X. Sajjadi, from Pakistan, instantly bonded with Z-Zatala. And after two more failures, John Okada stepped in last, and connected instantly with Validus-V.

The four Titans had their pilots, and each of the huge robots came to life at their commands.

Pleased, beaming, Professor Graven had shaken each of the new pilots' hands enthusiastically and offered them lucrative contracts operating the Titans. He'd clasped hands with the others and wished them a safe voyage back to their homelands. Unfortunately, something–still a mystery to that very day–had caused the aircraft carrying the rejected pilots back home to crash, and they were all lost in the Northern Pacific.

In their first meeting with the professor, Graven told his four new pilots that he'd learned, by way of the helmet and its link to the base's computers, that the Xovaren were not, after all, defeated; that they were in the process of expanding back out into the galaxy again; that the Ahlwhen were no longer around to check them; and that the Xovaren would be returning to Earth at some point in the future, to once again conquer it and to use it as a base for their evil machinations. Graven wanted Earth to be ready to defend itself, and he wanted the Titans of Rapa Hoi to be the first and main line of defense. So he insisted that the four new pilots train constantly and rigorously to master the controls of the big robots, and to master their main weapons.

"It sounds as if Professor Graven is a good man," David observed, "and what I've seen of him is as twisted a version as what the corrupted coding did to you and to Mr. Sajjadi."

Zhao nodded. "Yes. We must not harm him–not if we can help it. But make no mistake, David: We have to stop him. We have to stop what he's doing now. Our whole world depends on that." She looked very sad. "We may be forced to make some extremely uncomfortable choices before this is all over."

"I understand," David said–but he wasn't any happier with that situation than Zhao was.

For a long moment the two sat there, their eyes on the big Titans out in the main chamber, but their thoughts elsewhere. Then a signal beeped on the console to Zhao's right. She glanced over at it, then looked at David.

"They're ready."

David nodded. "When should we go?" he asked.

"As soon as we can," she answered. "The Professor surely knows we are coming. I'd prefer he have as little time as possible to prepare defenses."

"Right," David said. "What about Mr. Sajjadi?"

Zhao looked away. "We leave him here," she said. "Let the computers and the med bay here keep working on him. There's nothing more you or I could do for him."

Reluctantly, David nodded. "I just hate leaving anyone in that condition," he said.

"I know. I do, too." Zhao cast her eyes down at the floor. "Bashir is a friend. I want to help him. But we have bigger priorities right now. We have to find out what's behind all of this. And we have to free the professor from its control. If anyone can get rid of the corruption and help David and Bashir, it's him.

"And let's be honest," Zhao added. "Z-Zatala is down for the count, at least for now. Even with the spare parts available in this base, he can't be fully repaired any time soon. And Bashir is of no real use to us without his Titan." She raised both hands, palms-up. "So. I say we fix up our two Titans and go straight to Rapa Hoi. Take the fight to them."

David didn't disagree, but he also didn't relish the thought of a frontal assault on the main Titan base, currently defended by what he considered the scariest of the big robots.

He stood and moved to the door, holding it open for Zhao to exit as well. He started to make a clever or heroic remark, but nothing came to him. For all he knew, he was about to fly to his death.

He really wished John were awake, to talk to. To help him. To save them all.

He stepped through the doorway and headed for Validus-V.

CHAPTER 24

Professor Graven threw his clipboard across the room and fumbled for his pipe. On the screen in front of him, he could see images of Validus-V emerging from the reserve base on Rapa Lau.

"How?" he shouted. "How does one little boy manage to defeat two–*two!*—of my Titans?"

"And turn one of them to his side, apparently," Dr. Visser noted, nodding at the image of Torander-X following the other robot out.

Graven struggled to light his pipe, then gave up and stuffed it back in his pocket.

"Summon the creatures," he ordered Visser. "All three of them."

"I've been summoning them for some time now," the smaller man replied. "They are not responding."

"What? Where are they?"

Visser pointed at a map displaying most of the Pacific.

"They're on Johnston Atoll. Apparently they enjoy that place."

Graven glared at the map for a few seconds, then shook his head in frustration and turned back to Visser.

"Where is Morozov?" he demanded. "Get him in here now! We're going to need King Karzaled. Immediately!"

+ + +

Sergei Morozov was relaxing on his king-sized, fur-covered bed, drinking vodka and watching bad American television taken from a brand-new US communications satellite, when the intercom buzzed.

Annoyed at the interruption, he reached over and flipped the switch. "*Da?* Yes?"

"The Professor wants you in the control room," came the weaselly voice of Dr. Visser. "Now."

"What for?" Morozov asked. "To applaud dutifully as Sajjadi and Zhao return with the boy and his brother in chains? I have better things to do."

Visser made a sound; Morozov realized after a moment it was laughter. "Not exactly, no," the little scientist replied. "Because they didn't win."

Morozov frowned at this. At first he thought there must have been a flaw in the communications circuit.

"Did you say they *didn't* win?"

"That is correct. The 'boy,' David Okada, defeated both of them. He even managed to convert Zhao over to his side."

Now Morozov was sitting up, his television program and his vodka forgotten. He grabbed for a stained t-shirt and pulled it on, then climbed out of the bed.

"I will be right there," he said.

He was out the door before Visser could even reply.

Validus-V and Torander-X rocketed above the waves of the Pacific, having just departed Rapa Lau.

Wen Zhao had her newly-repaired Titan in its humanoid form so that Validus could keep up with her. Rednator-Oh would have left David in the dust. Consequently, they were not making the same time Rednator would have been. This turned out to be a fortunate thing, at least for a dozen Americans in their twenties and thirties, working on Johnston Atoll. Because it meant they were still relatively near to that little island when the radio call went out from it.

"Are you hearing that?" asked Zhao, over the comm link between the Titans.

"Hearing what?" David replied.

"A distress call." Zhao read off a string of digits. "Go to that frequency," she said.

David entered the numbers in the console and immediately the sound of a woman's voice came over his speakers.

"—on Johnston Atoll. Mayday, Mayday. This is Lisa Poole of the United States environmental studies base on Johnston Atoll. Mayday, Mayday. We are being threatened by... by unnatural forces. Does anyone read me?"

"Oh!" David exclaimed. "Someone's in trouble!"

"Americans, it sounds like," Zhao said.

"We have to help them," David said.

Zhao growled in the back of her throat. "Do we, though?" She huffed. "If we delay further, what will the professor and Morozov have waiting for us by the time we get there?" She sighed tiredly. "But–yes, yes–I know. We *do* have to help these people. And we will."

David tapped open his microphone. "Calling Johnston Atoll. This is…" He hesitated, unsure what to say. Then he set his jaw and continued. "...this is Validus-V. We hear you and are on our way."

A pause, filled all with static and crackling, and then, "Roger that. And thank you. We do not recognize your callsign, but we will gladly accept any help we can get."

The two big robots banked in a long curve over the surface of the Pacific, before rocketing off to the northwest.

"Professor," Visser called, "they are turning around!"

Graven approached his assistant, a puzzled look on his face. "What do you mean, turning around?"

"See," Visser said. "They turn back from us."

"Back to Rapa Lau? Perhaps they understand they could never defeat us here. Surely they plan to build up the defenses there, and make us come to them."

Visser studied the screen for a few seconds. "No, I think not," he said. "They're not headed to Rapa Lau, either."

"Then where are they going?" Sergei Morozov demanded, as he stalked into the room.

Visser caused a zoomed-in map of the area south of Hawai'i to appear in the main display. He pointed to a tiny rectangle of land in the middle of the vast ocean.

"There," he said. "Johnston Atoll."

"But–why?" Morozov asked. "What's there?"

The professor grinned. "Our delinquent monsters," he said with a chuckle.

Visser manipulated the controls and the view changed to a live image from an orbital camera his team had launched some time ago. He zoomed in and down. Soon the oddly-shaped island filled the screen. It was mostly rectangular, with a runway down the center lengthwise, making it look like a big aircraft carrier. No aircraft were visible on or around it, though. At one extreme end of the island stood the semi-intact ruins of an old American military outpost. At the other was a launch pad for missiles, blackened over and partly melted as if by some terrible accident.

But none of that was what first caught the onlookers' attention. No, what stood out most visibly and shockingly were the three giant monsters currently moving across the launch pad portion of the island. One was the yellow and black, caterpillar-like Gamaron, now missing one of its claw-arms. The second creature was big and black and batlike, and it flapped here and there around and between its two compatriots. The third resembled a man in shape, though certainly not in size. It was covered entirely in brown and tan fur, like some monstrous version of the Yeti or Abominable Snowman. The three of them shambled and flapped here and there, as if enjoying their time spent on this bizarre little island, amid the radiation and the poison chemicals.

"Ah," Visser said. "Our satellite is picking up radio transmissions. There are people on the island. Americans. They are calling for help."

"I should think they are," Morozov said with a laugh. "And Zhao and the boy are going to try to help them."

"Excellent," Graven said. "It appears that, if the monsters will not come here to fight our enemies, our enemies will go to where the monsters already are."

"How considerate of them," Visser said.

Morozov nodded to himself. "Yes. Good, good. There is no guarantee the creatures can defeat two Titans, but they will, at the very least, soften them up a bit." He glanced once more at Graven and Visser, then turned and strode for the door.

"Where are you going?" Visser asked.

"He's going to Johnston Atoll," said Professor Graven.

"*Da.* To deliver the *coup de grace* to both of them."

"And I'm going with him."

Morozov stopped in his tracks and turned back to face the professor. "You are doing no such thing," he said.

"They're my robots," Graven said. "Even the one you pilot. If I say I'm going, I'm going."

"Technically, they are the Ahlwhen's robots," Morozov said.

"Where are the Ahlwhen?" Graven demanded, raising his arms and feigning the act of looking all around. "Where are they now? They have left this world behind, a very long time ago. And they will never return." He closed the distance with the hulking Morozov and squared off with the big Russian. "And so now the Titans belong to me. They go where I say, when I say. And with whom I say on board."

Morozov stared back at Graven for a long moment, then spun on his heel and continued out the door. Graven followed along behind him.

"Then I'm coming, too," Visser said, and raced along in their wake.

CHAPTER 25

Validus-V and Torander-X were rapidly crossing the waters between Rapa Lau and Johnston Atoll, their boot-rockets blazing, when David Okada heard a sound behind him in the cockpit. Puzzled, he turned as far as he could to look around the pilot's seat and behind him. What he saw shocked him–and thrilled him.

"John!"

Indeed, the med bay was open, and John Okada stood before it, obviously shaky, one hand on the wall to support himself. He still wore his light gray jumpsuit and helmet, the visor pushed up and out of the way.

"You look like you're seeing a ghost," John said weakly. He managed one of his trademark smiles, though it didn't carry the usual power and radiance everyone associated with John.

"I'm not sure I'm not," David said. He wanted to jump up and hug his brother, but he couldn't exactly abandon Validus's controls while they were flying. "How–how are you feeling?" he asked.

"Not great," John replied with a soft chuckle that still seemed to pain him. "I've been better." He looked up at David. "But I guess I've been worse, too–and now I'm coming back to normal."

David nodded. "I'm really glad. I wasn't sure how long you'd be in there."

"You put me in there?" John asked.

"Yeah–I didn't know what else to do at the time."

John just stared back at him. "Nice work," he said after a few seconds. Then, "So–Validus is letting you fly him, then?"

"More than that," David replied with a grin. "We've been through a lot, while you were out. Including beating Torander and Zatala!"

John blinked. "Wait–*what?*"

"David," came a woman's voice over the link. "Who are you talking to?"

"Is that Zhao?" John asked.

"John? You're awake!"

"I am! And you're not still trying to kill us?"

A laugh. "No–I am better now. Thanks to your brother."

Again John blinked. "Um–I feel like I really did miss a lot," he observed.

As they flew along, David and Wen Zhao filled John in on what had transpired since he'd been put into his coma. John, meanwhile, was making repairs to his seat restraints, though it took longer than it should have, because he was still extremely shaky and weak.

"So, yes–there are two of us now," Zhao was telling John, "but they still have King Karzaled, which I think we would all agree is the most powerful of the Titans, and–if what I fear is true–they also have several of the old Xovaren monsters cooperating with them. Plus whatever other weapons may be at Professor Graven's disposal. Whatever those might be, they are surely quite formidable."

"I'm sure," John said distractedly. He was only half-paying attention. His thoughts kept returning to David, sitting in the seat behind him, piloting the Titan. He still couldn't quite believe his younger brother was operating Validus-V so smoothly and confidently. Or that he'd learned to do it so quickly, and with no training! When John had first joined up with Professor Graven's group, it had taken weeks of practice with Validus-V for him to gain a level of confidence that he could direct the mighty machine. And that only after he'd demonstrated to Professor

Graven that he was one of the few people capable of operating the Titan at all.

The thought that his snot-nosed little brother could just step in here and bend mighty Validus-V to his will... It made John... proud? No—angry. *Very* angry!

Zhao concluded her rundown of the obstacles and adversaries they faced.

"But we're not going to Rapa Hoi yet–correct?" John asked, swallowing his resentment and forcing his voice to remain calm and even. "It looks like we are traveling northwest."

"To Johnston Atoll, yes," David said. "The monsters are there, and some innocent people are trapped. We've got to help them first."

John nodded absently. "Of course, yes." He sat back in the forward pilot's seat, snapped the restraints closed, and said, "Alright, David–I'll be taking control of Validus back now."

David felt his heart skip a beat. "What?"

John looked back and flashed him a smile that didn't seem terribly friendly. "I'll be piloting Validus now. It's what I do, little brother."

David opened and closed his mouth, but didn't know what else to say. Disappointment washed over him like a tangible force. He was surprised at just how sad the thought of no longer being linked with the big Titan made him feel. Somehow, he'd expected to see this all through himself, and he had just assumed that, once it was over, he wouldn't have any problems handing control of the robot back to his brother. But now, facing the prospect of giving up Validus immediately, he couldn't decide if he should be sad, angry, or just disappointed.

Before he could say anything more, Zhao's voice came over the link from Torander-X. "John? Are you certain that's wise? You don't sound like yourself yet. You've been through quite a bit."

"I don't mind continuing with Validus a little longer," David added, trying to sound helpful and not selfish.

"I'm fine," John said. "And this is my job."

"It is," Zhao agreed. "But it demands the pilot to be in top condition. And you are most definitely *not* in top condition."

"I'm fine," John repeated. "Validus," he said, speaking now directly to the robot, "this is John Okada. I'm taking up the main pilot duties again. Please transfer all controls to the forward seat."

Nothing visibly changed, but David could somehow sense, over the wireless connection to Validus's systems, that something was fundamentally different. He knew without even trying that the robot would not respond to his orders any longer.

"Sorry, Validus," he whispered, mainly to himself. "But you're in good hands now. The best. John will see this through."

In the front seat, John Okada shivered. Who were they to question his right to control Validus-V? How dare they? His eyes were rimmed in red, and sweat ran down his brow.

And inside his head, a battle was being fought. A battle Wen Zhao would have recognized all too easily.

"There's a fleet of ships," David noted as they approached Johnston Atoll.

"Looks like the US Navy," Zhao agreed over the link. "Probably on their way to rescue the scientists."

"They even have an aircraft carrier," David said.

Above that ship, the holo display read CV-64: USS CONSTELLATION.

"Good thing we're here, then," John said. "I doubt they could go up against what they're going to find on this island with just a few jets and helicopters!"

On the deck of the *USS Constellation*, crewmen were preparing to launch a pair of rescue helicopters when two huge, unidentified objects roared overhead, moving in the direction of Johnston Atoll.

"What was *that?*" asked one deck officer.

"Aliens," the man next to him replied quickly.

"Aliens?"

"Yeah. At least—we better *hope* so."

The deck officer stared at him. "Why do you say that?"

"Cause the alternative is, it's the Russians. And I don't like the idea of Russians flying giant robots!"

The deck officer considered this. He shielded his eyes with his gloved hand as he gazed back up at the two manlike figures roaring off into the distance. And slowly he nodded in agreement.

Validus-V and Torander-X swooped down toward the rectangular outline of Johnston Atoll. From high in the air, they could see three massive, horrific creatures moving about the northern end of the island.

David watched as his brother angled Validus-V's approach so that all three of the creatures were ahead in their flight path and visible in their targeting display. The holographic image automatically inserted text above each of them. Above the all-too-familiar, yellow-and-black caterpillar–now with only one arm and claw!—it said, GAMARON. Over the black, bat-like creature, it read, MORDIRAH. And above the shaggy, manlike figure David thought of as a gigantic Yeti, it said ARZEN.

"I'll see to the people," Zhao said over the link. "You keep the monsters back."

"Sounds good to me," John replied–and David could hear strain and fatigue in his voice. *That's not good*, he thought. *But– what can I do? This is his Titan, not mine. I have to respect his judgment, and his right to pilot Validus!*

While Torander-X peeled away and made for the ruins of the old Air Force facility where the American scientists and other personnel were hiding, Validus-V descended near the center of the island, hovering some fifty yards above the ground, facing the three massive creatures.

John's voice boomed out over Validus's external loudspeakers: "GO BACK! YOU ARE NOT WELCOME HERE!"

The three monsters, if they could understand the words at all, ignored them.

The big bat, Mordirah, flapped its great dark wings and took to the air. Soon it was circling above Validus. Meanwhile, Arzen leapt up and down like a gorilla, its face a mask of rage, and screamed what could only be a challenge. And Gamaron raced forward on its dozens of centipede legs, its lone remaining claw held aloft, lightning dancing across its surface.

"I fought Gamaron once already," David noted. "He was pretty tough. Going against three of these things at once... I don't know, John."

"It's no problem," John snapped back. "They're just dumb animals. Piece of cake."

David frowned at this. John did not sound like himself. Not at all. And this bravado–it was fine to be confident, and certainly Validus-V was a formidable weapon. But taking on all three of them at once–alone?

David bit his lip and kept quiet. Surely John was a much more skilled pilot, and he had far greater experience. He deserved, and had earned, the right to talk that way, David figured.

And so Validus-V descended and set down on the rough surface of Johnston Atoll.

And the three creatures fell upon him.

Gamaron fired a blast of lighting that knocked the blue robot backwards.

Mordirah flapped down and clawed at the robot's back, actually registering damage on the metal and crystal surface of the Titan.

Arzen, the three-hundred-foot-tall Yeti, tackled the reeling robot and drove him into the ground.

In the cockpit, alarms wailed and lights flashed red.

David had twisted around in his seat. "John," he called, "are you okay?"

"I am fine," John hissed. "I wasn't expecting them to gang up on us like that." He manipulated controls and spoke a few words and Validus came back up on his feet. The big robot turned to its right, and David could see the missile targeting system appear on the holo display. But, by the time John got the crosshairs on a monster and gave the order to fire, the target was no longer in front of him. Two missiles missed, then a third–and the shots weren't even close.

David started to speak up, but then forced himself to remember: *This is John's Titan, not mine. He just has to get back in the swing of things. Leave him alone!*

Abandoning the missile attacks, John ordered Validus to extend the electro-whip. The big robot raised it up and cracked it at Gamaron, who danced away on those little legs and avoided it.

Even as this happened, Mordirah swooped in again and struck at the robot's head, dealing more damage somehow. Validus's left arm came up, swatting at the bat, only to have Arzen take advantage of the opportunity to charge in, roaring, and tackle the robot, driving him into the ground.

Screaming its fury, the huge Yeti pounded away on Validus with its fists, then climbed to its feet and, grasping the robot in its massive hands, hurled Validus through the air. The robot came down with an ear-shattering crash, flattening a set of old military quonset huts before rolling to a stop.

"John–are you okay?" David asked.

"I'm fine," he barked back. "It's just–Validus isn't responding quickly enough to my commands."

David frowned at this. "You think something is wrong with Validus?"

"That must be it," John replied. "It has to be."

David said nothing.

The Yeti came at them again, fists pistoning, driving Validus into a backwards stumble that culminated with him going down again.

Now Gamaron saw its long-awaited opening against this hated enemy and attacked. The one massive claw grasped Validus's left ankle and sawed at it. Immediately alarms wailed in the cockpit.

"Get... *off!*" John shouted, as he had Validus kick at the monster. But he couldn't devote his full attention to that attack, as the big bat and the Yeti were back on him, pounding away. Red lights were now flashing everywhere inside the cockpit.

Again, David bit his lip and forced himself to stay quiet. *Let John focus. He'll get this.*

And perhaps he would. But, in the meantime, Validus was suffering a horrific beating.

Torander-X landed near the ruins of the Air Force installation and Wen Zhao called out over the booming PA system, "I can carry six of you at a time to safety. How many are there?"

Three of the scientists–or, at least, Zhao assumed that's what they were–peeked out from cover and gawked at her giant robot.

"Don't be afraid," she had Torander announce. "I'm here to help you."

One of the scientists–a young woman with short, blonde hair–stepped fully out into the open and shouted up, "There are fifteen of us."

Three trips, then, Zhao thought. *That's a long time to be leaving the three monsters to John alone.* But she felt the safety of these scientists took top priority.

"Very well," she replied over the loudspeaker. She started to open the hatch on the foot of Torander. But before she could give them instructions on how to come aboard, the woman screamed, pointed, and ran back inside.

Zhao sighed in frustration. "No," she announced over the PA, "I told you–I'm a friend. I'm here to help."

Red lights started flashing in front of her.

"What–?"

Puzzled, Zhao toggled through several different external views on the display. When she had it show what was behind and below her, she gasped.

They were coming up out of the contaminated soil like demons boiling up from Hades. They were huge and menacing, covered in dark-red exoskeletons, and spitting something at Torander's legs. The alarms sounded again, instantly. *Acid.*

Ants. *Crazy ants.*

And each was at least forty feet long.

Gigantic, mutated crazy ants.

"Oh, terrific," Zhao breathed. She activated the link to Validus-V.

"Guys," she called to them, "we have another problem."

CHAPTER 26

Validus was in no position to help, or even to pay much attention to Zhao's message. At the moment, the big blue robot was down on its backside again, with Arzen the Yeti pounding away at its midsection and Mordirah the bat raking it with savage claws. Gamaron stood some distance away, unleashing the occasional electrical blast that disrupted the robot's internal systems worse and worse each time.

David could wait, could contain himself no longer.

"John," he called, "what is *wrong?*"

For a moment, his brother said nothing. Then, in a strangely subdued and weak voice, "I–I don't know. I'm having trouble thinking straight–focusing."

"You have to do something, John," David said. "We're getting killed here!"

"I–yes, yes, I know…"

Still Validus lay there, being pounded and clawed and zapped.

Torander-X fired a barrage of blasts with the pulse cannon in its left index finger, driving the ants back.

"I never thought I'd wish Torander had a "Raid spray" weapon," Zhao laughed bitterly to herself.

The attacks by the crazy ants were anything but laughable, however. At their new and tremendous size, they had retained their ability to produce and spray deadly corrosive acid. And that acid was currently eating into Torander's legs in numerous spots. So far, only a relatively small number of ants had emerged from their underground burrows to assault her, and she'd blasted quite a few of them. But they just kept coming. For now, the damage was manageable. But if a much larger number should join in.... It worried her. How long would she be trapped here, zapping ant after ant, while the damage to Torander's body slowly worsened?

The American scientists had retreated back into the dilapidated old Air Force facility in the face of the ant attack. Torander was keeping the terrifying creatures at bay, but just barely. Zhao knew that, should the ants get past her, those people would in all likelihood die truly horrible deaths. And if she stopped blasting the ants long enough to let some of the scientists aboard, the remaining people would get swarmed over—if not immediately, then certainly while she was away, transporting the first group.

"And meanwhile, John and David are facing all three monsters without me," she groaned aloud. "This is not good."

Firing another barrage of blasts from Torander's pulse cannon, she activated the comm link to Validus-V.

"John? This is Wen. How are things going there?"

Nothing. No response.

"John?"

A groan, perhaps.

"John–can you *hear* me?"

"This is David, Ms. Zhao. John–he's not good."

Zhao cursed. "It was too soon after his injuries for him to try to pilot a Titan," she said. "I knew it."

"I don't think it's his injuries," David said.

"Then what–?" But as soon as she said the words, Zhao understood.

She didn't say anything for a long moment. Then, "John–you were exposed to the corrupt coding, too, weren't you?" She was confident in the theory that she and David had worked out earlier, but she wanted John to admit it.

"What?" he exclaimed. "No!"

His reaction sounded genuine. But Zhao knew it was a lie.

"We know it got to you, too, John," she said. "And you've somehow kept it at bay, inside your head, all this time."

+   +   +

John heard what Wen Zhao was saying. He had nothing to offer in return.

"It's a supreme credit to you that you have managed to keep it under control for so long," she went on. "The rest of us couldn't do it."

"That–that's not–" he sputtered.

"It's still there, isn't it?" Zhao asked–though it wasn't a question so much as a statement. "The med bay cured your physical ailments, but it couldn't extract the corrupt programing from your head. It took my Titan and the Rapa Lau base network, working together, to do that for me! And it still nearly killed me."

John was silent.

At that moment, Validus-V was pummeled by attacks from all three monsters. As another blast rocked Validus, John retreated the big robot further back from the fray.

"There's nothing to be ashamed of, John," Zhao was telling him. "You've fought it–fought it longer and harder, and more successfully, than any of us. But it's too much for anyone to do that and try to pilot a Titan in combat at the same time." She paused. "And there's always the danger it could break out of your control–corrupt you–even corrupt Validus!"

John cursed. It just wasn't fair.

He could feel the corrupt programming eating at the edges of his consciousness. Just as it had been doing ever since it had first come into his mind, over the link to Rapa Hoi. He'd somehow recognized it as a malicious presence from the beginning, and had managed to seal it away in a corner of his brain. But it was forcing its way out now, and it was slowing and dulling his reaction speed as it did so. The cumulative effect was to make him feel he was moving underwater, or in a dream where nothing works as it should. It was all enormously frustrating.

Though not as frustrating as the thought of having to relinquish control of his Titan. To anyone.

John rallied all the energy he could muster, in order to shout the words: "Forget it, Zhao! I'm not giving Validus over to my snot-nosed punk of a brother!"

+   +   +

David knew his brother was suffering. He understood the irritableness, the anger, the insults, were simply components of his internal fight against the evil mind-control programming.

But that didn't make it hurt any less.

"Listen to yourself, John," Zhao was saying. "This is not you! It's the bad coding!"

"Shut up!"

Silence across the comm link for several seconds, save the sound of John's labored breathing.

"David's clever, though," John said at last. "This is all his doing–he's trying to trick me into giving him my Titan!"

"That's not true, John," Zhao said.

"No," David added. "I know what Validus must mean to you. I would never try to take something like this away from you." His voice trailed off, softer. "You're my big brother. I love you."

Silence. More silence. The cockpit rocked violently as the monsters attacked again. David gave thanks that the robot was as tough as it was.

Then, finally, in a very weak voice: "You really want me to hand control of this Titan over to my little brother." He did not say it as a question but as a statement of fact. Because they all knew that's what it was.

"Yes," Zhao said. "He can handle it."

"But–he's just a kid."

David said nothing to this.

"He's a kid who beat me–and Bashir," Zhao retorted. "He and Validus seem to have a good, solid link. A true mesh."

"I can do it," David said from the seat behind. "I won't disappoint you."

Another blast. Validus brought his shield up, but too slowly. The big blue robot was staggered backwards again, and fell into the piles of plutonium.

A message appeared on the display in front of the brothers: WARNING. RADIATION AT UNSAFE LEVELS.

"We've got to move," David urged. "Now!"

Alarms began to wail throughout the cabin.

"All right. Fine." John motioned with his right hand and issued a quick set of instructions.

Instantly David felt the computerized mind of Validus-V linking back up with his own.

"Hi, Validus," he whispered. "It's me again."

David willed it, and the big robot hopped up from the poisoned ground. In each hand he grasped a clump of the plutonium-infused soil. Bringing both arms up quickly, he flung the plutonium at the monsters. Arzen stumbled back, shrieking, while Mordirah flapped up and away.

Gamaron rushed in and head-butted Validus in the stomach, causing the robot to stagger backwards and then fall on his rump.

David wasted no time; he looked around, saw a batch of metal drums stacked to his right, and reached for them. As Gamaron moved in close again, Validus grabbed a massive handful of the drums and smashed them into the demon caterpillar's face. The drums ruptured, spreading orange liquid all over their target. The yellow and black monster screamed and fell back, wiping at its face, at its four dark eyes, with its one huge claw.

David had Validus grab another batch of the drums and repeated the move. Now Gamaron was clearly in agony, the chemical weapons sizzling where they dripped from its hide, and the monstrous caterpillar turned about and dashed for the sea.

Validus extended the electro-whip, brought it back, and snapped it out. The crackling metal cord took the creature's many legs out from under it and brought it down on its belly. Drawing the whip back, he struck again, electricity crackling along its length. This time, after the blow, the monster lay still.

"Gamaron is down," David reported over the link. "It's still alive, according to what the display here says, but I don't think it'll be bothering us again for a while."

Then everything went sideways.

David held on for dear life; his brother shouted from the forward seat.

The display showed one name: ARZEN.

"The Bigfoot guy is on us now," David said, as much to himself as to anyone else who might be listening.

Arzen had ripped up a huge chunk of coral the size of an iceberg, and he came charging at Validus with it held aloft in both hands.

David had Validus switch to the energy sword. The orange blade flared to life, and he brought it around, up, and down on the block of coral, just before the big Yeti could use it to smash Validus's head in. The shimmering blade sheared through the block and cut it in half; Arzen dropped one of the two pieces but threw the other at Validus. The blue robot had his shield unfolded now and brought it up, deflecting the chunk of coral.

Validus wasted no time; he charged at Arzen, sword raised high, and swung the blade once, twice. As David had suspected or at least hoped, the monster seemed to react extremely negatively to the energy blade. Arzen fell back under a heavy assault, as Validus kept swinging the sword blade at him at eye level. The hundred-foot-long, shimmering orange blade of raw energy hummed a deadly song of destruction as it cut through the air, and the expression on the savage giant Yeti's face changed from rage to fear.

Something impacted Validus on the back of the head, then, causing him to have to abandon his assault on Arzen.

"It's Mordirah," John said over the link. His voice was thick and weary, but he sounded more himself than he had a few minutes earlier. "It's a big, mutated bat."

"I kind of guessed that," David replied. "What does it do, besides fly around and claw at us?"

"That's its main thing," John said. "I've never encountered it before, but I read about it in the archives when I was in training. It's supposed to be murder in the dark, with its echo locator. But here, in the daytime…"

"We have an advantage, yeah," David said.

He had Validus spin around and lean back, pushing the big robot's chest forward, arms bent at the elbow and pulled out of the way. Doors in Validus's torso opened and–BANG–the pulse bomb detonated, right at Mordirah.

The big bat spiraled around and tumbled out of the sky, landing near a clump of the giant crazy ants. No sooner had Mordirah hit the ground than the ants responded by surrounding the black beast and spitting acid at it. Mordirah revived itself very quickly then, shrieking, and attempted to fly away. The crazy ants were having none of it. They fell upon Mordirah *en masse*. The giant bat disappeared under their mass.

"Um," David said, pausing long enough to witness Mordirah's fate. "I kind of wish I hadn't seen that."

"No kidding," John said. *"Blaaah."*

David looked around for their third enemy. "Where'd ya go, Bigfoot?" he asked aloud, scanning in every direction.

But the big monster had vanished.

Torander-X had given up on blasting the crazy ants individually with the pulse cannon. For every ant Zhao shot, three more took its place. Instead, she'd activated Torander's force field, surrounding the big, orange and green robot, as well as the American scientists, in a sphere of protection. Now the horrid, segmented insects were firing streams of acid that struck the force field and slid harmlessly down to the ground.

"It's still pretty disgusting, though," Zhao whispered to herself as she activated the comm link. Then, "David, can you hear me?" she asked aloud.

"I'm here," he replied. He sounded out of breath.

"How's it going?"

"Two down—but the third one disappeared on me!"

"Huh." Zhao didn't know what to make of that. "Maybe it gave up and ran away? Or swam away? Or flew away?"

"Maybe," David said, but he didn't sound very confident. "Definitely didn't fly away, though. You don't want to know what happened to that one. Yuck." He made a retching sound. "So—what about you?"

"There are just too many of these ants," Zhao said. "I've had to put up a force field just to keep them away while I try to get these people to safety."

"Understood," David said. "Can you carry all of them at once?"

"Well, yes," she replied, sounding embarrassed. "I haven't transported anyone before, so I didn't think it through—though, in my own defense, I was a little busy fighting a plague of giant, acid-spitting ants."

"Right," David said. "I'm on my way to help."

"Thanks."

As Validus strode in the direction of the Air Force facility, Zhao explained what she'd meant.

"So, I haven't had to carry passengers before. But I knew Torander can only carry six people at a time, besides me. But–" and she sighed heavily, "—I forgot I'm not just limited to what Torander can do."

David frowned, then brightened. "Ah! Yes! There is another version of your Titan!"

"The only one that can change like this, yes," Zhao said.

And with that, as David strode up to where Torander-X stood, surrounded in a shimmering force field, the big, green and orange robot shifted, flowed, and transformed into another shape entirely. An elongated aircraft with massive, twin engines protruding from the rear, where the legs had once been.

"Rednator-Oh," David said. "Nice! And–with more room?"

"A good deal more, yes. I can take all of them on board now."

So as Validus cracked his electro-whip at the crazy ants, the fifteen scientists and other personnel raced from the ruined Air Force building and into an open hatch on the side of Rednator-Oh. Once they were all aboard, the hatch slid closed and the massive aircraft shot skyward.

"Back soon!" Zhao promised.

David looked out at the swarm of crazy ants. He again asked himself what had become of Arzen, the big Yeti that had disappeared earlier. And he wondered what other strange and bizarre things this island might yet produce, to set against him.

"Hurry back," he said.

Rednator-Oh had nearly covered the distance to the approaching American naval fleet when a pair of jets zoomed up and took up position on either side.

"This is Captain Isaac Jones of the United States Navy," came a voice over the comm system, "calling unidentified aircraft. You are ordered to land on the deck of the *USS Constellation* immediately."

"I was just about to do that, Captain Jones," Zhao replied briskly. "I have some of your people who I'm certain are anxious to get back home."

"Some of *our* people?"

"The personnel from the island. Johnston. I rescued them and would like to drop them off. Closing now."

"Wait–hold on one minute," the pilot ordered. "Who is this? Where did you come from?"

"That's my business, I'm afraid, Captain."

"I'm ordering you to–"

"We are over international waters, Captain Jones," Zhao pointed out. "You can't order me to do anything." She growled in the back of her throat. Why did they have to make things complicated? "I'm assuming you do want these people back."

"I–um–well, yes," Jones replied.

"Good. Tell your carrier to stand by."

And with that, Rednator-Oh swooped down, circled the big carrier once, and then touched down smoothly on its flight deck.

As naval personnel ran here and there, nobody certain what to do, Zhao opened the hatch on the side of her Titan. The sixteen shell-shocked people from Johnston Atoll rushed out, to be greeted by a cadre of men in coveralls and helmets. The refugees were quickly directed belowdecks.

Then armed men emerged from the tower and began to encircle Rednator.

"Okay, that's all the business I have with you today," Zhao told them, speaking over both the comm link and the loudspeaker. "But I do have one warning: I would not go ashore on Johnston Atoll if I were you. Not if you want to keep on living."

"That's American property, lady–whoever you are!" Poor Captain Jones sounded positively beside himself now. "And–you can't threaten the United States Navy!" Captain Jones shot back.

"I'm not threatening anyone," Zhao replied. "I'm trying to keep your people from getting eaten by giant, radioactive, acid-spitting ants."

Apparently struck dumb, Jones had nothing to say back to that.

"Now, if you'll excuse me, my friends need some help."

Rednator-Oh lifted off from the deck of the Constellation and rocketed back towards what Zhao was already thinking of as "Monster Island."

CHAPTER 27

The sun was setting over the battle-scarred surface of Johnston Atoll.

David looked up in time to see Rednator-Oh transforming back into Torander-X, before settling gently to the ground. The two big Titans stood there, towering over the bizarre Hellscape the little island had become. The gigantic crazy ants were still swarming at the far end, and David had decided to basically cede that territory to them and beat a hasty retreat.

"All the scientists have been safely delivered to one of their ships," Zhao reported.

"Nice work," David said.

"Though I think I caused an international incident in the process."

"They'll get over it," John said. "They–" He broke off, making sounds that clearly indicated he was in severe pain.

"John?" David asked, raising himself as far up from his seat as he could manage, to try to see his brother, sitting in the forward pilot's spot. "John–what's wrong?"

"My–my *head*–!"

"It's the corrupt programming," Zhao said. "It did me this way, too. He's got to fight it!"

Before David or Zhao could react further, a savage roar echoed all around them. David turned Validus around, arms up and ready to fight. The blow, however, came from his right, and he never saw it coming.

"David–*look out!*" Zhao yelled, but too late.

A massive, hairy form leapt from nowhere and smashed into Validus-V, knocking him to the ground. Immediately, fists started pounding on the robot's chest and face.

"It's Arzen," Zhao called out. "I'm coming to help!"

Before Torander-X could move, however, another loud voice boomed over the comm link and out over the island. It was accompanied by the roar of massive boot-rockets descending.

"The ape-man is the least of your concerns."

David turned again, to face the new intruder. He groaned when he realized what it was.

Massive. Taller than Validus or Torander. Dark red with gleaming gold trim. Twin cannons perched on its shoulders. Indigo eyes glowing in a round, cylindrical head.

Massive and deadly. The most powerful Titan of them all.

King Karzaled had arrived at last.

"Try not to harm the other Titans," Professor Graven called from one of the rear seats inside Karzaled's massive head. "I don't have to tell you how valuable–how *irreplaceable*–they are. We must subdue the renegade pilots and retake control of the robots."

"Bah," replied Sergei Morozov from the main control cockpit. "I will do what I must do."

King Karzaled strode forward, its right arm coming up as if to offer a hand to the other two Titans to shake. Instead of that peaceful gesture, however, the hand transformed itself into a plasma torch and blasted a stream of white-hot flame in the direction of Torander-X.

Still reacting to the sudden change of circumstances happening around her, Zhao cried out as the flames surrounded her robot. She scrambled back, activating her force field–but damage had been done.

"David," she shouted over the link. "Watch out! He's–"

+ + +

Too late. The massive red robot spun on its heel and unleashed another blast of flames, this time aiming at Validus-V.

David reacted more quickly than Zhao had, given slightly more warning. He activated Validus's boot rockets and shot into the air to avoid the intense flames–only to be spun sideways by a barrage of missiles. Validus twisted around, avoiding the worst of it, but suddenly something else intervened, causing him to lose flightworthiness and crash to the ground. Holding on as the Titan bounced once, twice, David saw on his display what had happened: the big Yeti, Arzen, had grasped him around the legs and redirected his momentum, sending him into the ground.

As the Yeti stood over him, roaring, King Karzaled moved in, moving much more quickly than anyone would have expected from such a massive metal form. The red robot lowered the plasma torch, its hand returning to normal. Next it opened a pair of doors in its chest, revealing what had to be the barrel of a massive weapon that filled much of its torso.

The twin cannons on the King's shoulders fired in rapid succession, bright red energy pulses smashing into Validus and keeping him pinned down on the ground. Then Karzaled stepped forward and directed the chest-weapon directly at the blue robot. Lights blinked and spun with increasing speed and frequency around the circular weapon opening.

"David!" shouted Zhao. "The Turbo Cannon! You cannot let him–"

But David had already figured that much out. He twisted Validus out of the line of fire, just as a massive beam of raw, destructive energy erupted from Karzaled's chest and blasted a hole fifty feet wide down into the island's foundations.

"Holy cow," David gasped over the link.

"Yeah," Zhao agreed. "You do *not* want to get hit with that."

The weapon apparently needed a little time to recharge, so overwhelming was its output. This gave both parties the chance to regroup. Torander-X and Validus-V stood side-by-side, facing King Karzaled opposite them. Arzen the Yeti lurked off to the red robot's left, awaiting another opening.

"Give up," Morozov said over the link. "You know you cannot long survive against the power of Karzaled. Do not make me kill you both."

The giant beast-man called Arzen waited and watched. He hated all the metal men, but he had been commanded to fight alongside the red one. Arzen did not like that order, but the command had come from one of the kind who had first created Arzen, so he had no choice but to obey.

In the meantime, he had torn out another massive chunk of coral. He held the block in both hands–this one was quite heavy! And he waited.

Yes, Arzen watched, and waited, and–*now!* The two enemy robots were distracted by the red one. It was time to prove his worth, Arzen knew.

He leapt.

Zhao saw Arzen about to leap at Validus-V, a block of coral the size of a school bus clutched in its hands and held over its head. The Yeti moved, bringing the block down, aiming to crush the blue robot's head–along with the two humans inside it.

Zhao was ready. She moved into action instantly, surging to her left, raising Torander's arms to shove Validus out of the way of the Yeti's attack.

Even as Torander moved, King Karzaled unleashed the Turbo Cannon again. The incredibly powerful weapon built into its chest fired a beam of pure, destructive energy, aimed directly at where Validus-V had been standing an instant earlier.

The blast missed Validus. It missed Arzen.

It struck the diving Torander just to the right of the center of mass, evaporating everything in its path.

In the cockpit of Torander-X, there were no alarms, no emergency messages. Everything simply and suddenly shut down and went dark. Zhao held on for dear life as the big robot fell to the surface of the island and did not move thereafter.

+   +   +

"That's one of you," Morozov crowed. "Listen to me, John Okada. Do not make me do to your Titan what I have done to Zhao's." He didn't mention the part where he'd originally been aiming at Validus.

"Blast it!" shouted Professor graven from behind him. "That's a lot of damage to fix. Torander's going to be on the shelf for weeks, maybe months."

"Do you want this little party ended, or not?" Morozov called back over his shoulder. "I for one do not intend to dance here all night. We will dispose of these two traitors and then carry what's left of their Titans back to Rapa Hoi to be repaired–with new pilots in control. More... *pliable* pilots," he added.

Graven said nothing.

David stared at what had happened to Torander-X on his display.

"Ms. Zhao! Are you okay?"

There was no reply.

"Professor Graven?" called John Okada over the link. "Is that you? Are you with Morozov?"

"It is me, yes, John," the professor replied. "Have you come to your senses at last?"

"Professor," John said by way of answer, "you've been deceived. We have all been dosed with corrupt mind-control programming by the Xovaren!"

Graven chuckled. "Nice try, my boy," he replied. "I'm well-aware that something of that nature has happened to *you*. But you surely cannot believe it has happened to *me*–to *all* of us."

John argued on for several seconds, to no avail. Meanwhile, King Karzaled strode forward, its Turbo Cannon recharging.

Arzen screamed, lifted the block of coral again, and charged.

David, distracted by the unbelievable damage King Karzaled had just dealt to Torander-X, didn't see the big Yeti moving.

As Karzaled prepared to fire again, and Arzen attacked, David happened to look down to the bottom of his holo display, and there see the hatch on the side of Torander's head pop open, just as it had on that robot's previous head, back on Rapa Lau. A small figure in gray leaped out and ran for cover.

Zhao! She was alive!

And then the two attackers converged on Validus-V.

And that was when the green and gray shape, moving with uncanny speed, emerged from the gathering darkness and struck.

Tyranicus knew he was needed. He sensed the time to watch and wait was over. If he intended to take a role in these proceedings, he needed to do so *now*.

He blasted the big red robot with two solid doses of the orange energy beams from his eyes. King Karzaled spun around; the energy unleashed by his Turbo Cannon missed far to the left.

The big lizard continued onward, diving into the huge, hairy Yeti and knocking the block of coral from its hands. An instant later, the two massive monsters were crashing to the ground, wrestling with one another. Trying to destroy one another.

Tyranicus is doing a good job of convincing me he's on our side, David couldn't help but think.

For a moment, Validus-V was in the clear, as the two monsters fought with one another and King Karzaled lay on its back, struggling to rise.

David took advantage of the opportunity. He knelt and lowered his right hand to the ground, beside Wen Zhao. Over the comm link he called out, "If you can hear me—*come aboard!*"

Zhao climbed up onto Validus's hand and David brought it up to the side of the robot's head. A moment later, the female pilot was climbing into the blue robot's control center.

"There's a third seat," John said distractedly to his brother. "You have to activate it."

David wasn't sure what to do, so he just mentally asked Validus to provide a seat for Wen Zhao, and another pilot's seat slid up from the floor and locked in place.

"Thanks," Zhao said, strapping herself in. "I–I can't believe what he did to Torander," she added, her voice emotional. Then she swept it aside and said, "Let's get that bastard back."

"Let's do it," David agreed.

He sent Validus forward.

The clash did not go well.

Validus rushed in, as David was determined to go on the offensive and take the fight to his opponent.

But Morozov was a skilled and seasoned pilot, and his Titan was easily the most powerful of the four.

Validus punched Karzaled with his massive blue fist, but it barely knocked the red robot back at all. He fired a barrage of missiles as he retreated a few steps, then allowed the electro-whip to slide into Validus's hand. He cracked the whip at Karzaled once, twice, lightning playing along the surface of the red robot as the whip struck.

With the third swing, Karzaled reached out grasped the whip, ignored the current pouring through it, and wrenched it back the other way. Before he could let go of it, Validus-V was ripped from the ground and sent hurtling away, to crash and roll through the irradiated, poisoned soil.

David barely had his Titan back up on his feet before the King attacked again. The two huge red hands reached out for Validus, and the blue robot reacted by reaching up and clasping hands with the crimson behemoth. Leaning forward, one leg straight and the other bent, arms extended over his head, Validus sought all the leverage he could gain against the heavier, stronger Titan. The two stood there, acting out a bizarre form of arm-wrestling.

"No, David!" shouted Zhao. "This is what he wants! He's going to–"

"The Cannon–yes," David replied. He couldn't pull loose from the grasp of the robot; couldn't get away. Karzaled's chest panels opened and the big weapon that had brought Torander-X down began to cycle up. It prepared to fire.

There was nothing else David could do. He couldn't go backwards, couldn't get loose. So he activated Validus's boot rockets and shot straight up, then curved over and behind the big red robot as Karzaled's grasp of his hands kept him from getting away. The Cannon blast missed, passing beneath Validus's feet as he swung overhead. Then Validus was down again, and now back-to-back with Karzaled. He used his momentum—and every shred of mechanical muscles the Titan possessed—to bring the big red robot in turn over his head. Now the grasp gave way and King Karzaled sailed over the landscape before coming down with a resounding, island-shaking crash.

"Oh, my!" Zhao shouted. "Nobody has ever thrown Karzaled like that!"

"It's not enough, though," David replied. Fancy moves were one thing–especially what he knew were really lucky ones–but winning this fight would take a lot more than that. In fact, he was growing convinced there was no way his robot would ever be able to beat Morozov's in a fight. There had to be another way.

"John," he said. "Talk to the professor. Get him to see the truth. You have to! It may be our only chance."

John Okada returned to his thankless task of arguing with Professor Graven, while David continued to pull off miracle after miracle just to keep Validus alive and moving for a little bit longer.

But eventually the wily old veteran, Morozov, wore down the upstart. It was inevitable, and everyone there had known that fact from the start.

As Tyranicus and Arzen continued to fight a battle every bit as epic in its own way, off to the side, King Karzaled finally succeeded in seizing Validus-V from behind, in a full-nelson. With Validus now completely immobilized, Morozov opened the doors for the Turbo Cannon and prepared it to fire.

The deadly weapon cycled up once more.

David gritted his teeth. He knew Validus could never survive what was about to happen.

But instead, something very different occurred.

+ + +

Morozov cried out in surprise and dismay as something crashed into King Karzaled's back. Alarms flared all over the cabin of the big red robot. Severe damage was being reported.

But–*how?* The boy's robot had been immobilized. There was nothing he could have done.

Morozov struggled to turn the crimson robot around, to see what had attacked him from behind. What he saw shocked him.

It was purple and black, and it held a pair of gleaming metal swords.

"Surprise, sucker," called out Bashir Sajjadi, from the cockpit of Z-Zatala.

He swung the swords again.

CHAPTER 28

David was quite surprised that he was suddenly able to wrench Validus-V loose from Karzaled's mighty grasp. He ran Validus several steps forward, to put some distance between them. Then he turned around to see what had happened—what had distracted the big red robot.

What he saw shocked him.

Z-Zatala stood there, swords in hand.

From the look of the backs of Karzaled's legs, those blades had already done severe damage to the big red robot. Zatala struck again now, before Morozov could fully react. One blade missed, but the other slashed deep into Karzaled's left shoulder. The left arm of the big robot sprayed sparks and flames as it reached up, flailed about for a second, and then snapped off and fell to the ground, severed completely.

Z-Zatala stepped forward to strike again.

"I'll bet you weren't expecting me," Sajjadi called over the link to Validus.

"We weren't," David said, "but we're glad to see you!"

"Yes, we are," Zhao added.

"I overcame the corruption, with the help of the Rapa Lau computers–and Zatala, of course. Then I made as many quick repairs as I could, to get here fast!"

"Way to go," David replied, truly excited for the man. "I knew you could do it."

John was busy at the moment–too busy to say anything to Sajjadi. He had managed to open a direct line to Professor Graven, and the two were now locked in a deep debate.

A debate that, he knew, might well go farther than this robot battle in deciding the fate of the entire world.

Morozov shouted his anger at the surprise attack. At the same time, feeding off of this through the mental link, King Karzaled roared its own anger over its external loudspeakers–a sound that vibrated every structure on the island.

Then the big robot reached out, grasped the oncoming Z-Zatala by the face, raised the smaller robot up in the air, and brought it down hard on the ground.

One of the silver swords clattered out of Zatala's hand. Zatala raised the other one up and drove it through the left leg of King Karzaled.

The big red robot stumbled back, as Morozov screamed in sympathetic pain again.

Zatala drew the blade out, swung it around in as broad of an arc as he could manage, and cut deeply into the other leg of his adversary.

Karzaled reeled, standing like a drunken sailor, or like a heavyweight boxer that has been punched one time too many, but has yet to hit the canvas.

Sajjadi got Zatala up from the ground by the hardest. The already-damaged, hastily-repaired robot was in no shape for an extended battle with any other Titan, and certainly not with the biggest and most powerful of them all. But he was determined to do what he could. Surprise had been his ally so far—surprise and a ruthless, all-out attacking strategy. If he didn't do sufficient damage to the big red robot now, though, he knew the tide would likely turn very, very quickly.

Sajjadi spotted the other sword lying on the ground off to his left. He moved in that direction and reached for it.

King Karzaled couldn't move, but he could still attack. Morozov flipped open the big red robot's chest panel, charged the Turbo Cannon, and fired.

Z-Zatala was just picking up the sword when the robot's upper half evaporated. The Turbo Cannon blast annihilated everything from the head of the purple and black robot to its waist. The lower half fell to the earth, showering sparks, dead.

John Okada cried out in pain and had to break off the link to the professor. He'd felt like he was making some progress toward getting through to the real Graven. But now the pain was simply too much. Both hands up to his head, spread on each side of his helmet, he wailed as he fought the surging corrupt code.

The programming had apparently determined it had lain in wait long enough. Sensing the destruction of Z-Zatala, perhaps feeling that things were going its way now, it now launched what could only be seen as its final, most overwhelming assault on the walls of sanity within John's mind.

For a timeless time that seemed like hours but was actually only seconds, he fought back, struggled, and nearly succumbed.

Perhaps it was that sense of failure, in the end, that saved John Okada. The programming, haughty and arrogant as was its nature–and the nature of the Xovaren, who created it–assumed it had won. It surged forward, attempting to seize control of every corner of John's brain.

John executed a sort of mental *jiu jitsu*. In metaphorical, and perhaps metaphysical terms, he allowed the bad programming to come forward, giving way to it—and then reached out, turned it around, and sent it right back out again, using its own momentum, its own force against it. Then he shoved it again, out of his head entirely, and into the microcircuitry of his helmet.

Back in the real world, John wrenched the helmet from his head, dropped back into his seat, and gasped.

He was exhausted. He was drenched in sweat. He was nearly dead.

But he had *won*.

+   +   +

Z-Zatala had lost the fight. Bashir Sajjadi had lost his life.

David and Zhao looked at the holo display in shock and horror, seeing the lower half of the purple and black robot lying motionless on the ground. The upper half—including the head, where Sajjadi had piloted the robot—was gone, as if it had never been.

Neither of them spoke. There was nothing to say.

David shoved his fear aside. He ordered Validus to attack once more.

King Karzaled was more damaged from Zatala's efforts than Morozov had wanted to admit at first.

He tried to make the big red robot move forward, but its legs had been hacked repeatedly by Z-Zatala's unbreakable swords, and they were barely hanging on. Now they gave way, sending the robot down on its knees.

Validus-V rushed in, energy sword in hand. The blue robot swung the blade once, twice. Alarms shrieked all over the cockpit of King Karzaled.

Validus struck again, and again, and again. Karzaled's metallic hide was resilient, but nothing could stand up to such an assault for long. Green lights were giving way to red all over Morozov's cockpit.

Validus raised the energy sword up one more time, started to bring it down.

Karzaled's one remaining arm reached up, grasped Validus by the wrist–the wrist of the hand holding the sword–and twisted.

Still clutching the energy sword, Validus's hand came away in a shower of sparks and fire.

Karzaled tossed the hand and the sword away, then grasped Validus by the opposite upper arm. The big red robot reached behind its shoulder and drew something from its back–a golden rod that instantly unfurled into a double-bladed axe. Grasping the weapon in its sole remaining hand, and as his own systems were failing for the last time, Karzaled brought one of the blades down hard, embedding the weapon in Validus's chest.

Validus-V slowly fell backwards, landing hard on the ground, face-up.

In the blue robot's command center, the lights went out.

CHAPTER 29

John and Zhao sat there in the dark, inside the motionless robot's head, while David tried everything he could think of—every command, every control—to get Validus-V to get up. To move at all.

Nothing worked.

Giving up hope on the robot working properly again, David tried one last tactic. He ordered Validus to launch them to safety in the Delta-V, the robot's aircraft-head.

Nothing. It wasn't happening. Validus was not responding at all. The big blue robot was either offline temporarily–or dead.

There was no time to mourn what might have been. With the screens blank, they couldn't be sure of the condition of King Karzaled. Was the red robot still active? They had no way of knowing. At any moment the King might blast or crush them all.

David hit the release on his restraint straps and scrambled from his seat. Then he and Zhao, who was already out of hers, together helped John to get up. John was no longer wearing his helmet; he carried it tightly in his arms.

The three climbed out the side hatch and onto the hellish soil of Johnston Atoll.

Across the way, they saw a hatch opening on the side of King Karzaled's torso. Three figures climbed down, escaping from that robot, too.

All of the Titans were now disabled. But the fight went on.

230 VAN ALLEN PLEXICO

The roaring of the two giant monsters echoed all around. Their battle suddenly seemed very different to David than it had a few moments earlier. The winner would be able to do whatever it wanted with them, and they could hardly do a thing to resist.

David knew which monster he was rooting for. But—could Tyranicus defeat the giant Yeti? He had no idea. He realized he didn't know enough about the big green lizard, and resolved to change that—*if* they survived the current situation.

In the meantime, they had scores to settle—scores at a much smaller scale, but with even bigger ramifications—and conflicts with other human beings to resolve.

They ran towards Morozov and his group.

The Russian saw them. He began to run towards them, too.

They met in the middle of the battlefield: six mortal beings, where moments earlier, massive, godlike machines had gone to war. Now the six of them were all that was left.

What had started with three-hundred-foot giants blasting at each other with energy swords and plasma torches was going to end with normal humans punching each other. Somehow that seemed appropriate to David; it seemed to summarize all of human existence in a tight circle. It made him think of a line a teacher had said in History class once, that had stuck with him: "If World War III is fought with nuclear weapons, World War IV will be fought with knives and sticks." Well, they'd fought the equivalent of World War III with giant robots, and now they were fighting the next war with bare fists.

As it turned out, though, Morozov had brought something more than his bare fist to the fight. In his hand he carried a metal bar. Perhaps he'd salvaged it from King Karzaled, or maybe he'd picked it up along the way.

David looked at John, who could barely walk by himself, and at Wen Zhao. None of them carried a weapon of any kind. They'd never thought they'd need one. David felt his heart sinking. He'd gone from controlling one of the most powerful weapons on Earth, to being unarmed, in a matter of moments. And now he was going to go from commanding energy swords and electro-whips to being beaten to death by a mind-controlled Russian with a piece of pipe.

Morozov led the way, of course, but behind him David could see two other men–men that, because of the background briefing the Rapa Lau computer had given him, he now recognized.

One was Professor Anthony Graven. David would have known that man anywhere.

The individual beside him, though–yes, now David remembered him, too. Dr. Visser. The Dutch scientist who had approached Graven years earlier, and had eventually become his top assistant. The man who seemed to have a preternatural feel for the Titans, and for the monsters. David didn't know why the guy was here, but it seemed somehow appropriate that they would all meet on this field of battle, to resolve the conflict once and for all.

Except, they didn't get to do that; not at first.

Just as they were about to clash, with Morozov sprinting up one side of a low hill and David and company trudging up the other side, one of the giant crazy ants popped up to David's right and hissed a blood-curdling hiss. Then it sprayed its acid out in a deadly, toxic stream.

Morozov broke off his approach and dived for cover behind a clump of coral. Part of the acid hit that coral and sizzled, melting away.

David, meanwhile, pushed the other two with him down and landed on top of them. Part of the spray went just over his head. He reached around and felt his back, where he could touch it, checking for any signs of the acid getting on his clothes. It seemed he had survived; they all had, at least for this one instant.

Another ant appeared behind the first one. Then a third.

"Come on," David shouted, getting quickly to his feet and helping the others up. He hurried Zhao and John back the way they'd come, then off to the left. They passed a long, sun-bleached wall, rounded a corner and found themselves at the open doorway to the dilapidated building where the American scientists had been camping.

"In here–quick!"

David pulled the other two inside. He figured, if the scientists had survived as long as they had, hiding in there, then maybe *they* could.

But no sooner had they moved inside and taken up positions on the far side of the room than the other group entered.

Morozov was limping. Some of the acid had caught him on the right leg. It had burned through his coveralls and the flesh below. He pulled off his helmet and tossed it aside, revealing a scarred, sweating face scowling with pain and anger.

Professor Graven had been hit, too. He was limping, one of his legs clearly injured, and his left arm hung useless. He looked to be in great pain.

David saw the professor's contorted face and immediately had a thought: the man's pain, unfortunate as it was, could be useful for them. It could possibly disrupt the corrupt programming's hold on Graven, at least for a moment.

"John," he said urgently. "Talk to the professor. Quick!"

John gave David a look that seemed to say, "What's the use?" But he moved nonetheless.

As John made his way slowly around the room, Morozov strode to the center of it. The Russian glared at David and Zhao.

"What a waste," he said, cursing. "Those beautiful machines, all now wrecked, because of you three."

"Because of *you* three," Zhao retorted.

"But we know you can't help it," David said. "It's because of those aliens–the Xovaren. Their mind-control programming is strong. It was very difficult for Ms. Zhao and John and poor Mr. Sajjadi to break free of it." He regarded the Russian pilot with compassion. "You are strong, Mr. Morozov," he said. "I know that, if you put your mind to it, you can break free of their influence, too."

"You little fool," Morozov snapped back at him. "You think *I'm* being mind-controlled? Why? What could they force me to do, that I would not already do?"

David and Zhao stared back at him. "What are you saying, Sergei?" Zhao demanded.

The Russian snorted. "The Xovaren approached me years ago. They made a better offer."

"You–you *willingly* went over to their side?" Zhao asked, incredulous.

"Of course! They made me a much stronger offer than the professor." He shrugged. "But–honestly–what do I care who wins their war? The Ahlwhen? The Xovaren? I could not care less, my friend. They are all just aliens. Let them kill each other all they want."

David's mind was reeling at this. He'd never–not for a moment–considered the idea that any human would *willingly* serve the Xovaren.

He understood then: There would be no miraculous cure for Morozov. There would be no scientific solution that deprogrammed him and brought him back to the side of the angels–or at least of the planet Earth. No, Morozov was entirely mercenary. All the man could see was who could offer him the most wealth, the most power.

But–what could David *do* about that? He looked at Zhao, and saw that her expression appeared to reflect the same hopelessness he felt.

Outside, the *sturm und drang* of Tyranicus's battle with Arzen continued. Idly David spared a thought for what might happen if the Bigfoot creature won. What would he and his friends do about it, now lacking Titans? And that, of course, might not matter to them, if they couldn't manage to survive the next few minutes here in this room.

Meanwhile, behind Morozov, John was trying to talk to the professor, and Zhao joined him. But Dr. Visser kept interposing himself between them, not allowing them to speak with the injured and distracted Graven.

Zhao finally had had enough. She executed a feint, drawing the pudgy Visser to his left, then came in hard on the man's right. Her foot lashed out in midair and caught him in the head, sending the Dutch scientist to the floor.

John took advantage; he rushed forward, grasped the professor by the lapels, pulled him away from Visser–who now lay still, only semi-conscious–and began to go after Graven again. In rapid fashion, he laid out a clear understanding of what had happened to corrupt them all, and how.

"Even the Titans," John said. "Even the Titans got brainwashed, to one degree or another. But Zhao and Sajjadi and I have proven it can be beaten. You can do it, Professor."

Graven waved John away, trying to dismiss his arguments, but for the first time he appeared to harbor doubts. Perhaps it was the pain of the acid burns, eating at his skin; perhaps it was his own great intellect and drive, starting to overcome the outside programming; perhaps he simply was being swayed by John's arguments. More likely, it was a combination of all of those elements together that allowed him to force the corrupt Xovaren programming out of his head. The effort, the willpower required, was astounding. Graven was up to the task. Then he cried out in pain, fell back against the wall, and passed out.

"I truly hope the ants didn't hear that noise," Zhao said as she helped settle the professor into a more comfortable position.

Morozov had squatted down to check on the condition of Dr. Visser. But then something odd happened. Visser made a motion with his hand, and appeared to whisper something in Morozov's ear. The big Russian responded by standing up quickly, turning around and leaping at David. A sharp punch with his left hand knocked David backwards. Then he swung a roundhouse punch with his right that only just missed.

David was still struggling to recover his senses from the first punch when the Russian came at him again, now swinging the metal bar he was carrying. David was quick and avoided the worst of it, but Morozov still caught him with a glancing blow to the right leg, and David fell to one knee, crying out.

But he wasn't beaten. He thought of all the times the Donner brothers had picked on him at school, and all the things he'd thought of later that he should have done to them, but never actually had—and this time, he resolved there wouldn't be a "later"—only a *now!*

David came up with all his strength, just as the Russian was attempting to kick at him. His punch caught Morozov on the chin and actually seemed to stun the man.

It didn't knock him down, though. Not even close. But it did make him even angrier. Morozov came back from the blow with a real fire burning in his eyes. Moving as quickly as a cobra, he tossed the bar aside, grasped David with both hands around the neck, and began to choke the young man, harder and harder. David's face turned bright red, and he gurgled something, but Morozov ignored it.

"This is for King Karzaled," the Russian growled.

That triggered a thought in David's mind. He should have been busy trying to think of a way to free himself, but instead he fixated on a thought: If Morozov hadn't been corrupted by the Xovaren, that probably meant King Karzaled hadn't, either. David had interfaced with Validus-V long enough to understand the big Titans had at least some rudimentary kind of consciousness; an artificial intelligence that only needed a human pilot to round out, to jumpstart, to cooperate with. If King Karzaled had done all it had done against its fellow Titans without any outside corruption, then it wasn't a victim of anything. It was just *bad*. As bad as Morozov.

Suddenly David didn't feel so bad about having helped to wreck the monstrous machine.

Of course, he then remembered he was about to be killed. Coming back to himself, David fought and squirmed and finally stomped down with all his strength on Morozov's foot. The Russian cried out and released the pressure on his throat just enough for David to twist around and free himself.

Morozov reached for David again, but Zhao moved in behind him. She had retrieved the bar the Russian had tossed aside, and she swung it like a baseball bat, hitting the Russian in the side. The blow didn't appear to do much damage, but it made him angry. Morozov whirled on her, grabbed the other end of the bar before she could pull it back, and wrenched it from her grasp. Then he raised it high, clearly planning to bring it down on her. Probably to kill her.

Someone pushed David aside. It was John. He had his helmet in both hands. He raised it high, came up behind Morozov and shoved it down over the man's head.

What good will that do? David wondered.

The Russian whirled about and glared at John and David. He brought his hands up to grasp the helmet. But before he could remove it, his expression changed from anger and outrage to surprise, shock, fear–and then agony.

Sergei Morozov screamed, long and hard. And then slumped to the floor, unmoving.

David stared down at him, making sure he wasn't faking, wasn't going to jump right up again. When he was satisfied on that score, David looked at John. "What–what did you *do?*"

"I hit him with his side's own weapon," John said, nodding with satisfaction. "I let the Xovaren programming do to him what it was trying to do to me."

"What do you mean?"

John wiped sweat from his eyes and breathed heavily. "I had forced the corrupt coding entirely into my helmet. That's why I wasn't wearing it." He shook his head. "Just before I took it off, I sensed that it had changed its approach from trying to *control* me to trying to *fry* my *brain*. It had formed itself into a kind of 'brain bomb,' and was just about to go off on me when I was able to get the helmet off."

He looked down at Morozov, still breathing shallowly but virtually comatose.

"So, when I put the helmet on our *friend* here, the bad coding just assumed it was me, and set off the brain bomb."

David marveled at this. "That was quick thinking, John," he said.

John shrugged. "It was the only real weapon I had available." He nodded down at the man. "And he's still alive. More or less."

"There's more good news," Zhao called out to them then.

They turned and saw she was supporting Professor Graven. And the professor's expression was very different than it had been only moments earlier.

"He's pushed the Xovaren coding back, just like John did," Zhao reported.

The professor nodded. Sweat dripped from his pallid face, and he was clearly still in great pain, but he appeared relieved; almost serene now.

"I will still need to have the coding extracted," he added. "But– you have shown how it can be done." He smiled. "At least for now, I am my old self again. And I have you three to thank for it."

Zhao allowed him to stand on his own, leaning against a wall for support.

"And the first thing we shall do," he went on, "when we return to Rapa Hoi–after purging the computers there, of course–will be to develop a counter-worm that will erase all remaining traces of the Xovaren influence from our systems, both mechanical and biological. We will make certain every single trace of it is gone."

"Good idea," Zhao said, nodding.

"No!"

Before anyone could react to the cry, Dr. Visser came up from the floor, holding something in his right hand. David could see it: it was a gun, but not of a kind he'd ever encountered before.

"All of you—stay very still," he said. "You've done enough. *Ruined* enough. Years of work! Years of infiltration! I won't let you ruin it *all!*"

"Ian, what are you talking about?" Graven asked. He started toward the other scientist.

Panic in his bloodshot eyes, Visser leveled the weapon and fired. It emitted a bright green blast of energy that struck Graven in the right leg. The professor didn't even have a chance to cry out. He dropped to the floor.

"The rest of you–*stay back*," Visser shouted. Then he dashed out the door.

John ran over to the professor and then looked back up at the others. It was clear from his expression that he understood he was still very physically limited.

"He is alive," John said, kneeling down next to Graven. "I will tend to him." He pointed to the doorway. *"Go! Get him!"*

Zhao didn't slow down. She was out the door in hot pursuit.

David looked at John. They nodded at one another. Then David ran after Zhao.

CHAPTER 30

Zhao and David raced across the nightmarish landscape of the atoll, keeping one eye out for the giant ants and the two battling monsters, while still remaining on the trail of the rogue scientist. Over hillocks of coral and piles of dirt they ran, and David wondered if they were in the area with the plutonium. Were they getting dosed with fatal levels of radiation, even now? He ignored the worry and kept running, Zhao just ahead of him, and Visser some distance beyond her.

At last they caught up to the scientist as he was standing in a barren spot on the far south end of the island. He had some kind of tiny device in his left hand and was clicking buttons on it. Before they could approach him to figure out what he was up to, the ground before him separated into two camouflaged doors and slid apart, revealing an opening about twenty feet square, leading to an underground chamber of some sort. Then, as the others looked on in astonishment, a platform rose up from underground. On it sat a small vehicle of clearly alien design.

"It's a spaceship," David breathed.

"Yeah," Zhao said, shaking her head in amazement. "I think you're right."

Visser started for the ship, but then a massive roar echoed across the island. Everyone looked in the direction from which it had come. And there they witnessed a sight to behold.

David marveled at how different the monsters appeared to him while he was standing on the ground, at normal human height, as opposed to being viewed on the holo display inside a Titan. From inside one of the big robots, the monsters had looked like just another kind of foe to contend with; bizarre and freakish, to be sure, but they'd somehow seemed "normal-sized" when he was commanding Validus-V. Like humans in monster costumes, almost.

But now, at regular human size, he stared up at the three-hundred-foot-tall behemoths and felt very, very tiny indeed.

The battle had raged on for quite some time, but clearly Tyranicus was growing tired of contending with the hairy giant Yeti. *Enough of this*, the big lizard's body language seemed to say. He blasted his enemy with his devastating orange eye-beams once, twice, a third time, roaring his anger, his rage, the whole time. Then he spun around and whipped at Arzen with his tail, knocking the clearly exhausted monster off his feet. Finally, Tyranicus reached down, grasped his opponent with his smaller forelimbs, and raised Arzen high over his head, before bringing him down hard, smashing him to the ground. Arzen lay there, unmoving, barely breathing. Tyranicus raised his head up high and roared again. Then he turned and headed for the ocean, dragging the limp Yeti behind him.

Visser, climbing up on top of his spacecraft, cursed at this outcome.

"The renegade creature has proven to be the mightiest of them all," he said. "Well, no matter. Soon he will be back under Xovaren control–as will all of you!"

"What's that supposed to mean?" David demanded.

"Only this," Visser said, an evil smirk on his pale face. "The full Xovaren armada is on its way here. It should arrive in about five Earth years. And then you will all fall before the might of my masters!"

David took this in, reeling in shock. An entire alien *armada*, on its way to Earth? An *evil alien* armada, out to conquer the whole world?

But then he remembered what humanity now had on its side. And he felt slightly better. And much more defiant.

"That's fine–bring them on," he shouted back at Visser. "And tell them–*warn* them–Earth is not defenseless!"

"That's right," Zhao yelled. "This world is protected!"

"Protected? By whom? Your robots are nearly destroyed!"

"In five years, we will have them all rebuilt," Zhao said.

Visser scoffed at this. "Even if you can manage that–who will pilot them? There are only two of you left!"

"Three!" David shouted. "And we'll find a fourth–don't you worry."

Visser scowled. Then he shrugged. "Four robots will scarcely prove an obstacle to my masters and their mighty forces! They will bring *organics*, too—organic *weapons*—creatures that are unstoppable!"

"*We* have an organic weapon, too," David said. He pointed to the receding form of Tyranicus, now disappearing beneath the Pacific waves.

"Bah!" Visser made to open the hatch on his spacecraft.

Then David saw something moving just behind the man, and he cried, "Look out!"

"You mean to trick me," Visser growled. But he did turn–just in time to see the gigantic, forty-foot-long crazy ant rising up behind him and his ship. Before he could move, the ant unleashed a stream of acid that struck Visser fully across his entire body.

The rogue scientist screamed as his flesh hissed and melted.

Zhao and David both cried out and averted their eyes for a moment, but David had to see. He looked back–and was shocked at what was now revealed.

The human flesh had burned away from Visser–but instead of killing him, it had merely revealed his true appearance.

In the place of a pale, chubby human scientist in a lab coat, now there stood, atop the spaceship, a dark-red figure with glowing purple eyes. His outer shell appeared almost insect-like, streaked with black. He raised his gun and fired, blasting a hole through the crazy ant, which dropped back out of sight.

"So now we see what you truly are–what you have been all along," Zhao called out. "A Xovaren!"

The alien laughed. "Of course. I was sent ahead of the armada to corrupt the Ahlwhen base, the Titans and the pilots. The conquest of your world would have been much easier, obviously, with our enemy's resources already turned to our side. But this way should not prove much more difficult."

"We'll see about that," David said. "Your masters might be in for a surprise."

The Xovaren looked at him. "We've had our eyes on you, boy," he said. "My fellows have been observing you for some time. We have noted your potential. We will yet have you on our side."

David remembered the strange figures in black that he'd noticed following him, watching him, on his way home from school.

"Don't count on it," he said. Then he saw another shape coming up behind the alien. "Go ahead and tell your fleet what happened here," he said. "Tell them they can send all the mutated monsters they want. But remember to tell them *this*, too: We have our *own* monster, and he's currently undefeated against all of yours."

At that, Tyranicus reared up behind the alien and unleashed a blood-curdling roar.

The Xovaren spun around, saw the massive, green-and-gray lizard form looming over him, and screeched in fear. He wasted no time with verbal retorts then. He climbed into the cockpit of his little ship, launched it into the air, and shot skyward.

Tyranicus watched the ship rise, and his golden eyes sparkled.

"No, Tyranicus! Let him go," David called.

The big monster hesitated, then looked down at David, without firing a shot.

Zhao looked at him, surprised that he'd protected the alien.

"I want him to go and tell the other Xovaren what happened here," David explained. "That we are strong. That we overcame their efforts to corrupt us. And that we will fight them to the finish."

Zhao thought about it and nodded.

And I don't want Tyranicus killing if he doesn't have to, David added silently. *Not even a Xovaren.*

Tyranicus gazed down at David, though whether any of what he'd said had sunk into the big lizard's brain was totally up for debate. In any case, Tyranicus sniffed at David once, twice, then grumbled like a minor earthquake. With that, he turned and strode with giant, island-shaking steps toward the ocean. David waved goodbye. A minute later, the big lizard was gone.

Zhao glanced over at David as they walked back in the direction of where they'd left John and the professor.

"I think that thing actually likes you," she said.

David looked over at her. "Maybe so," he replied. "I like him."

She didn't say anything for a minute. Then, "That was some speech there, kid."

"Thanks."

"Impressive. Colorful."

He shrugged.

"I think you must have read a lot of comic books in your time," she added.

David grinned at that. "It's looking like a good thing I did."

David and Zhao made it back to the old Air Force building safely. As they went inside, they heard the sound of helicopters approaching.

The professor was in bad shape, but he wasn't dead. Together, John and Zhao and David were able to carry him and Morozov out of the crumbling building and into the open, away from the giant ants.

A Navy helicopter touched down nearby, and David waved as troops disembarked from it. Several of them approached, and John—the former Air Force officer—stepped forward to converse with them.

Eventually the Navy agreed to give them a lift to Hawaii, and from there, a few days later, John and Zhao made their way back to Rapa Hoi. The professor was checked into the hospital, and would be joining them later, once he was healthy again.

David, meanwhile, went home–home to an Aunt Elaine, who was nearly beside herself with worry for him. She hugged him and kissed him repeatedly, fussed at him, and peppered him with questions. He knew that any honest answers he gave would be dismissed out of hand as him having watched too many movies and having read too many comics, so he made up an innocuous story about going out on a boat with some friends and getting stranded on an island—hence the Navy having to rescue him.

Ultimately, she didn't care about the specifics–she was just relieved to have him home.

Many fish sticks and much macaroni and cheese were consumed that evening in Honolulu.

CHAPTER 31

As it turned out, a few days' stay in the hospital had done nothing for the disposition of the Donner brothers. If anything, it had only served to make them nastier.

And so, a week later, they were walking across the park near the high school when they spotted their favorite whipping-boy, David Okada, standing out in the middle of the grassy lawn. They looked at one another, frowning. They didn't have to speak any words between them; it was understood by each of them instantly that their general feeling was, "How dare this punk breathe our oxygen? Or walk in our park? Or not hand over any money–or anything else–he happens to be carrying?"

And so, completely by happenstance, the Donner brothers blundered directly into a top-secret anti-infiltration action.

They crept up on David from behind him, sticking to cover for as long as they could. But then there was nothing but empty grass between him and them. They exchanged glances again, sneered at one another this time, then started boldly forward.

David stood there in the center of the park and waited, just as had been arranged. He kept one eye out for any movement around him. At the same time, he took off his backpack, opened it, and drew forth a sparkling piece of metal and crystal machinery, about the size of an office stapler. He held it up, as if admiring it, and said aloud, "I wonder what I should do with this amazing piece of Ahlwhen technology I stole from Rapa Hoi?"

A short distance away, two dark figures watched him and heard him say this. They glanced at one another, nodded, and started forward.

David continued to stand there in the center of the park, waving the small machine around. He had no idea how valuable it might actually be. He knew only that it looked very high-tech, and that John had picked it out for him to use.

As *bait*.

The Donner brothers were so focused on their intended target–David Okada–that they never noticed the other two figures advancing on him. At least, not at first.

When they saw him hold up the weird piece of machinery and start talking to himself, they stopped for a second and exchanged puzzled glances. Then Clint made a "he's crazy" sign with his right hand, and Curt nodded somberly, as if they were physicians who had just successfully diagnosed their patient.

Then they continued forward.

The two pale-faced figures in black cloaks and hats closed in on David first. One drew something out of his pocket–a gun, similar to the one Dr. Visser had used on Johnston Atoll. They rushed forward.

The Donners saw the two figures in black running toward David. They both skidded to a halt and stared.

+ + +

Just before the two dark-clad men reached David, they were stopped by something. Something unseen; something that encircled them and held them in place. They stood struggling, wriggling around, but couldn't escape its invisible grasp.

David walked up to them and smiled. He held up the device.

"You guys blew your cover in order to try to swipe a valve unit," he told them. "I hope it was worth it."

With that, he placed the piece of machinery back in his backpack and zipped it closed.

The two men ignored him, continuing to fight to get loose from whatever was holding them.

"I told your buddy, and I'm telling you," David added. "You're not welcome on our planet. Go conquer somewhere else. I hear Saturn is nice, this time of year." He snorted. "Though I think you guys would fit in better on Uranus."

The two pale figures glared at him.

The Donners stood there, slack-jawed, watching David Okada taunt two grown men in black cloaks and hats, who were apparently being held immobile by a giant invisible hand. They had no idea what to make of this; it was so far outside of their experience, they could only gawk in wonder.

And then, just for an instant, a giant hand actually flickered into view. And it really *was* a hand. It was dark green, and it was attached to a white arm, which was in turn attached to a gigantic body made up of metal and crystal, mostly green and orange but with white sections here and there. It had been crouching, but now it stood up—up to what had to be three hundred feet in height—and it carried the two men in black up with it.

David cupped his hands and shouted, "Thanks, Ms. Zhao."

"No problem," came a booming voice. "But—please. Call me Wen."

"Um, yes, ma'am. *Wen.*"

The big green and orange robot lifted into the air, then spun around and rocketed away. David waved at it until it was lost from sight. Then he turned and started back across the park, feeling very good about things.

"Huh," he said, seeing two other figures running away at top speed. They looked for all the world like the Donner brothers.

He stopped and stood there for a second, putting two and two together. Then he smiled, and continued on toward home.

He suspected he'd suffered his last Donner Party.

Now he felt even better.

EPILOGUE

A few months later:

Wearing a bright blue Hawaiian shirt and khaki shorts, David Okada stepped out of a backup Delta-V and onto the surface of Rapa Hoi for the first time in quite a while. He looked around at it, memories coming back to him–both good and bad.

A three-hundred-foot-tall door built into the side of Mt. Jaru stood open. Beyond it, David could see the four Titans in various stages of restoration. Arms lay here, legs there. Torander-X appeared complete, standing closest to the opening, while Z-Zatala had been broken down entirely into separate components and was being rebuilt from scratch.

John saw where his brother was looking and smiled. "It's a good thing the Ahlwhen left us with plenty of spare parts," he said. "We've yet to need something we didn't have four of, stashed away somewhere. It's just a matter of locating it."

"So—the repairs are going okay?"

"Pretty much," John said. "The biggest thing was Professor Graven convincing the Navy that all the giant robot parts strewn across Johnston Atoll belonged to him." He laughed. "They were set to impound the lot of it, and who knows what would've come from that. But he exerted his not-inconsiderable influence with the governments of both the UK and US–he is *Sir Anthony*, after all–and, next thing you know, the Titans were all loaded onto barges bound for here." He gestured toward the sky. "We *have* been getting a lot more flyovers by jets since then, though. Folks are very curious about what we have going on here!"

"I'm sure," David said. "And Validus–is he back together yet?"

"Almost," John said. "There have been a few sticking points. I've been working on the original Delta-V for several days now, but I can't get the systems there to fully switch on. It's like Validus's brain is in a kind of coma–or trapped in a dream, maybe. I don't know."

David grimaced. "It's not the bad coding again, is it?"

"No, no, that's all been removed–erased from everything," John said. "We're confident we've gotten rid of all of it." He shrugged. "It's just Validus being strange, and honestly this is not the first time he's done something like that. We'll figure it out."

Wen Zhao happened by, saw them standing there, and came running. She hugged David.

"Welcome back," she said as she let him go. "How have you been?"

"Fine," David said. "Just, you know, school and stuff." He grinned. "I've been dying to get back here."

"I'm sure," Zhao said.

"Ah! My boy," came a voice from inside the base.

"Professor."

Graven emerged from the massive chamber, hobbling along, leaning heavily on a cane. John moved to help him but the older man brushed him away. "I'm fine, I'm fine," he said. "Leave me be."

"Glad to see you up and around," David told him.

"Yes, yes. On the mend, and all that." He patted David on the chest. "And I'm glad to have you back with us. We need you, young man. Badly."

David was taken aback. He'd thought John was just bringing him for a visit. "You need me?"

Professor Graven glanced at John, frowned, and then looked back at David. "Ah. Your brother didn't tell you. Somehow, I'm not surprised."

John chuckled. "I was saving that part."

"I'm sure." The professor said dryly. He turned to face David. "Lad, you're one of the best natural pilots I've ever seen. You took command of Validus-V and operated him like a seasoned professional–with no training whatsoever. We would be fools not to try to recruit you into our ranks."

"And you *know* we need you," Zhao said. "You heard what Visser–the Xovaren–said before he left. They're on their way." She grasped his shoulder. "The whole planet needs you."

"Yeah," John said, "I suppose you could probably help out around here. Sweeping and stuff." He laughed then, as did his brother.

Sobering, David said nothing at first. He walked past them and into the big chamber under the mountain. He strode past the man-sized robot workers and the human technicians welding and wiring components here and there, and went straight up to the big, blue and silver Titan standing near the right side wall. One of its arms was missing, and the head–now in Delta-V form–rested on the floor nearby, being worked on as well. But it was obvious which one of the robots it was.

David patted the robot's big metal foot, then turned around, just as the others came up behind him. They gathered in a semicircle and awaited any response from him.

David grinned. "You're seriously trying to *convince* me to become a pilot? You think you need to *sell* me on the idea?"

They all laughed.

"We just wanted to be sure you were okay with it," John said.

David nodded. "I'm more than 'okay,'" he said. He looked up at Validus-V one more time, then over at where Z-Zatala was being painstakingly reconstructed, almost from scratch. "I guess you'll want me to pilot Zatala, right? To take Mr. Sajjadi's place."

They all looked at one another. Then John stepped forward.

"You developed more of a rapport with Validus in a few hours than I've managed in a few years," he said. "So we've all agreed– *I* will be taking Z-Zatala."

David blinked at that. "Wait–*you'll* be piloting Zatala? Then, you mean–?"

They all nodded.

"We want *you* commanding Validus-V," the professor announced. "Not full-time—not yet, anyway. In a couple of years, when you're eighteen. But we'll need you here at least part-time, immediately. Learning, practicing, working on strategies, and all that." He frowned. "The enemy are on the way. There's no time to waste."

David restrained himself as long as he could. But then he simply couldn't contain himself any longer. He leaped up in the air and whooped. Then he turned around and patted the big blue metal foot again.

"You hear that, Validus? It's you and me, together again!"

As if in response, inside the Delta-V, a series of lights that had burned amber or red for the last few weeks all switched over to green.

Validus-V, it seemed, approved.

That evening, David Okada was standing alone on the beach of Rapa Hoi, gazing up at the star-flecked sky, when a massive shape emerged almost silently from the water.

He started to run for his life, but then realized what it was, and stood still, watching. Within moments, the shape had blotted out half the sky. Far up, near the top of it, two golden-flecked orbs gazed down at him.

"Hi, Tyranicus," David said in greeting.

A low rumble came back by way of reply.

"I'm glad you're on our side," David said. "We're going to need you."

Another rumble.

"Five years," David said. "Five years until the alien armada gets here. Five years before we're probably all in for the fight of our lives." He shook his head. "We've got to finish repairing the Titans, find a fourth pilot for King Karzaled, and just prepare in general for a war."

Tyranicus grumbled.

"Yes, I know," David said. "You'll be with us. And you'll be a big help. What other kind of help could you be?" He laughed. "I just have to convince the others you're really on our side. Not all of them believe it, I don't think. Not yet, anyway."

"MRAAAWWW," Tyranicus replied.

David stood there a little longer, not sure what else to say to a giant lizard-monster. Finally, Tyranicus turned and started back into the deeper waters. But then he stopped and raised his head, looking up at the sky, at the stars overhead.

David had started to turn and walk back to the base, but he hesitated a moment longer, curious what Tyranicus was up to.

As if in answer, the big monster unleashed one massive, earth-shaking roar–a sound that seemed to dare any hostile forces out there to even try to come down to his planet. A sound that said, *"This world is under my protection,"* and warning any impudent aliens not to mess with it.

Then the big lizard looked back down at David, and the young man was certain for a second that the monster winked at him.

With that, Tyranicus strolled back into the ocean, descending deeper and deeper into the waters, soon entirely lost from sight. Not even a ripple remained.

But David knew he was out there, watching and waiting, and would be ready when they needed him.

He tossed the monster a salute.

Less than five years, he thought. *Time to get to work.*

And with that, David Okada turned and walked back inside the base. The big doors slid down and clanged closed behind him.

Author's Note

This novel was a joy to write, from start to finish. In part I think that's because it has its roots in my love for Doug Moench and Herb Trimpe's wonderful *Godzilla* and *Shogun Warriors* comics I read as they were being published by Marvel in the late 1970s, and I'm proud to admit that.

Rereading those books today, it strikes one as remarkable how those two gentlemen were able to take two licensed properties that could've been the basis for quick, crude hack-work, and instead crafted something powerful and lasting from the material. Moench's captions, running through both series, have a lyrical, literary quality as he annotates and narrates not just monster/robot battles but real, *human* stories set parallel to that action. From a mentally ill gambler in Las Vegas to an idealistic SHIELD agent to a young Japanese kid in over his head, Moench brings us into the stories in the *Godzilla* series and makes them seem much deeper and richer; they're *about* much more than just creatures bashing one another. That certainly served me as a guidepost for how to try to handle the story I wanted to tell in this book. It couldn't just be about monsters and robots fighting. It needed to be about *people*.

Lending those stories such raw power and scale and grandiosity is the artwork of Herb Trimpe. The undisputed master of monsters and robots at Marvel in that era, Trimpe's art on those two series succeeds on many different levels. While lending Godzilla and the Shogun Warriors the requisite sense of size and majesty they deserve, he also imbues them—particularly Godzilla—with a sort of humanity. We can sympathize with and even root for the big old monster, as Trimpe takes him in rapid succession from full-on splash pages of rampaging destruction to small, individual panels where, dare we say, his *feelings* are revealed, and he doesn't seem so bad after all. Between Moench's words and Trimpe's pictures, a true emotional bond is formed between the characters—and monsters—of the story and the reader, who looks on in awe, utterly engaged.

This is why this book is dedicated to those two gents. Quite simply, it would not exist if they hadn't created such marvelous work. I applaud them.

Of course, a lot of the fun for me was coming up with my own robots and monsters—and people!—and a background and plot that could sustain them through an entire novel. In short, writing this book was an absolute blast. And I never would've tried it without Moench and Trimpe to show the way.

One other note: A reader would be forgiven for suspecting that Johnston Atoll is a fictional location. Certainly, it seems all too fanciful, what with its nuclear weapon debris lying around, its chemical weapons drums and its horde of crazy ants. And yet, I have to report to you that it is very real, and very much as described in this book. Honestly, Googling "Johnston Atoll" can send one down the rabbit hole (the ant hole?) for hours, a shocked expression on one's face the entire time. With regard to Johnston Atoll, the only real invention for this book is the idea of *giant* crazy ants—or, at least, I *hope* that was just an invention!

(I am happy to report that, as of 2021, the *real* crazy ants on Johnston Atoll appear to have been eradicated. Score one for the good guys, anyway. And the weapon that ultimately did them in was insecticide mixed into cat food, rather than Dum Dum Dugan in the Helicarrier! Probably saved the taxpayers a few bucks, that way. Maybe Dum Dum should've tried to lure Godzilla away using cat food…)

So, that's the story, and the book. This may be a one-off… but then, that's what I said about *Vegas Heist*, too. So, we'll see. I guess I'll put it like I did at the end of that book:
David Okada and Validus-V may return…

—Van Allen Plexico
Southern Illinios, summer 2022

ABOUT THE AUTHOR

Van Allen Plexico writes and edits New Pulp, Crime, Science Fiction, Fantasy, and nonfiction for a variety of print and online publishers. He has won four Novel of the Year awards and an Anthology of the Year award from the Pulp Factory and the Imadjinn Awards, and a New Character of the Year award from the New Pulp Awards. He is author of the *Shattering* space opera series; *Lucian, Baranak, Karilyne*; and the groundbreaking and #1 New Pulp Best-Selling *Sentinels* series; as well as the award-winning crime novels *Vegas Heist* and *Miami Heist*. In his spare time he serves as a professor of political science and history. He resides in the St. Louis area and is probably working on another book right now.

Made in the USA
Columbia, SC
14 September 2023

22851747R00157